JACK THE RIPPER

JACK THE RIPPER

JUDGE, JURY, & EXECUTIONER™ BOOK FOURTEEN

CRAIG MARTELLE
MICHAEL ANDERLE

DISRUPTIVE IMAGINATION®

CONNECT WITH THE AUTHORS

Craig Martelle Social

Website & Newsletter:
http://www.craigmartelle.com

Facebook:
https://www.facebook.com/AuthorCraigMartelle/

Michael Anderle Social

Website: http://lmbpn.com

Email List: http://lmbpn.com/email/

https://www.facebook.com/LMBPNPublishing

https://twitter.com/MichaelAnderle

https://www.instagram.com/lmbpn_publishing/

https://www.bookbub.com/authors/michael-anderle

LMBPN Publishing
PMB 196, 2540 South Maryland Pkwy
Las Vegas, NV 89109

Version 1.01, December 2021
ebook ISBN: 978-1-68500-535-1
Print ISBN: 978-1-68500-536-8

THE JACK THE RIPPER TEAM

Thanks to our Beta Readers

Micky Cocker, James Caplan, Kelly O'Donnell, and John Ashmore

Thanks to the JIT Readers

Jackey Hankard-Brodie
John Ashmore
Daryl McDaniel
Dave Hicks
Rachel Beckford
Diane L. Smith
Jim Caplan
Dorothy Lloyd
Zacc Pelter
Kelly O'Donnell
Peter Manis
Micky Cocker
Veronica Stephan-Miller
Larry Omans

If we've missed anyone, please let us know!

Editor
Lynne Stiegler

We can't write without those who support us
On the home front, we thank you for being there for us

We wouldn't be able to do this for a living if it weren't for our readers
We thank you for reading our books

CHAPTER ONE

Interstellar Space, *Wyatt Earp*, Magistrate Rivka Anoa's Heavy Frigate

"With advances in technology, why doesn't the Federation make Pod-docs available to everyone? Then there would be no such thing as the blood trade. There'd be no need," Rivka asked.

The image on the other side of the screen stared at her. "Logistics. There are hundreds of billions of life forms scattered across Federation planets. The scale is immense, and there is potential for abuse, like the misuse of a Pod-doc to make rogue werewolves on City Station Hopefill. It's not ready to be deployed on a wide scale. Remember the issue with the supply of a critical mineral from Forbearance? There isn't enough for mass production of Pod-docs."

"And we can't meter it based on need since that would break down to only the wealthy perpetuating their existence." Rivka nodded slowly.

"We need death," Grainger said. "As harsh as that sounds, and I'd never admit it in public, but refreshing each society with new generations will cycle us through change. But we'll get better and better through the years. I think that holds true for all races."

"With a small group of selected overseers like us?"

"You can always plan your retirement, like Terry Henry and Char. They had a few hundred years more in them if they wanted to keep on keeping on, but they refused any future treatments. The old need to be allowed the privilege of growing old. What's getting under your skin, Rivka? We need the enhancements because the bad guys are constantly trying to kill us. Long life comes with it, as long as the criminals don't succeed."

Rivka looked at Grainger as if she were assessing his veracity. "Just trying to figure things out, now that the Magistrate Corps is back in business and maybe going to get bigger."

"No. The High Chancellor and the Chief Arbiter already put the kibosh on that."

"Because?" Rivka wondered.

"Funding. People. Training. Trust. Turns out, we're really expensive. The five of us will do the job until we can do it no more."

Rivka chewed her lip as she contemplated the conversation. It had gotten too deep too fast. Tyler briefly moved into the picture to wave at Grainger.

"You the man, T." Grainger pointed at him with a finger gun.

"Doesn't she know it!" the dentist replied.

Rivka laughed before tightening her lips into a single line. “Uneasy is the head that wears the crown.”

“You understand. Our so-called gift is more of a burden. And yes, I know that’s easy to say from one who benefits from the wonder of the Pod-doc. Still, logistically, we can’t support it. If we can’t give it to all, then we deny it to all, except those in positions of service. Thanks to Bethany Anne, the Pod-doc will never be a tool for the rich and powerful. You get the nanos, you bend a knee—not to a queen, but to the people.”

“And that is the most compelling argument, Counselor.”

“Fucking A, Barrister. If there’s nothing else, I’m looking forward to some private time with my woman.”

“Your woman’s going to kick your ass if you refer to me like that again!” a voice called from the darkness.

“Gotta go. Don’t want the foreplay to begin without me.”

Rivka gasped, winced, and slammed her hand on the button to close the channel. “Warn me next time, dumbass,” she told the blank screen.

“I doubt he’ll do that,” Tyler offered from the couch. “What’s next, Rivka?”

“Azfelius to introduce Dery to his people.”

“Red going to make peace?” Tyler wondered, sporting his best skeptical look.

Rivka shrugged. “The jury is still out.”

Curveyance System, Planet Delfin Prime, Major City Adelfino

"I've never seen anything like it." The speaker winced and looked away. "A biology experiment gone wrong."

Two female constables looked down on the remains of a local humanoid. Her bright blue skin had paled from exsanguination.

The shorter and younger constable had blue skin, which marked her as being from the neighboring planet of Kamilof Redoubt. It was one of a series of habitable planets in the Curveyance binary star system located at the edge of Federation space. Humanoids from Redoubt had bright blue skin, owing to the ingestion of the mineral sodalite in their drinking water.

Blue water made for blue skin, and it also made for dead humans. The humanoids from Delfin had red skin, similar to those from Zaxxon Major. The final race in the system, from planet Trieste, had yellow skin from metabolizing sulfur. Each humanoid race was unique but similar.

"These things didn't happen before the Federation showed up." The second sneered, avoiding looking at the body. "When's the medical examiner going to get here?"

"The ME? Who knows? They're on call but never get called. I've never had a case where I needed one before." The taller of the two shivered.

"Me neither, Bristamor. What do we do now?"

The first one cocked her head and looked left, then right. "Rope off the area and wait, I guess. Never seen this stuff before, but I guess we better pinch our butt cheeks together because more of this is coming. Damn Federation!"

"This isn't the Federation's doing," the blue female argued. "This is the work of evil, a heinous crime against flesh and blood. You mark my words. We'll need a shaman before this is all over."

The taller constable leaned away from her partner and scowled. "Why do they always give me the nutty ones? Get the tape out of the scooter. I'll get the pictures." She cringed, but not as much as her partner.

The shorter one crossed herself, followed by waving over her head to satisfy the two major religions on Delfin before excusing herself to return to the police scooter. The vehicle was little more than an oversized cart.

Duties of the Adelfino constabulary were limited to giving directions and helping with traffic. Crime was minimal in the capital city...and anywhere on the planet, and anywhere in the system.

Interstellar Space, *Wyatt Earp*

"Bullshit! That's some bullshit of the first, second, and third orders of magnitude in the wide, wide world of bull-shit. I'll twist those little fucking necks of theirs until their stupid heads pop off!" Red raged.

"Tell me we're muted," Rivka said evenly.

"We are, Magistrate. Good thing, too. Master Vered is in rare form. I'm not sure his tirade will get him what he wants," the ship's sentient intelligence Clevarious stated with as much sarcasm as he could muster—and the SI was very good at sarcasm.

"Which is an excellent point, C. Red, what the hell do you want from the faeries on Azfelius?" Rivka crossed her arms and stared at them.

Red withered. He was holding his son, pinning the

baby's translucent wings against his body while bouncing. If the wings got free, the baby flapped them involuntarily, hitting everything within an arm's span. That often included Red's face.

"I want to be there with Dery when the faeries christen him or whatever they're going to do."

"So, telling them you'll rip their heads off is an interesting way to get yourself welcomed to the show."

"You know me; I don't mean anything by it. I'm frustrated because I can't get what I want."

Rivka chuckled. "Because you haven't asked them for what you want, you big bonehead."

"Let me take care of it. You be humble and come along for the ride. Give him to me before you stunt his growth," Lindy held out her arms. Their little boy twisted and launched himself off Red's chest, then unfolded his wings and glided into his mother's embrace.

"That was cool." Red beamed. Their son was growing at a phenomenal rate. Since he carried faerie genes in addition to Red's and Lindy's nanocyte-infused blood, the baby was anything but normal. At three weeks, Der'ayd'nil was comparable in size and maturity to a three-year-old, with the exception of speaking. He hadn't uttered a word yet, neither verbally nor telepathically.

Lindy carried the baby to the front of the bridge, allowing him to stand on her shoulder and beat his wings above her head to stay balanced. "Clevarious, open the channel, please."

"The Meditator is available."

Sir'o'tilc appeared on the screen.

"Meditator, I wish to offer my kindest greetings and greatest appreciation for what you've done for my husband and me. Our baby Der'ayd'nil, conceived with the faeries' help, is growing quickly and will soon be able to fly freely. We wish clearance for landing and an audience with you and others as you see fit to bless our child in the way that all Azfelians are blessed."

"Plus, we still have two of your people, Mistresses Groenwyn and Lauton. They are ready to come home to you. Had you not requested to bring the emissary to us, we would have contacted you. It is good that you are here. The baby needs to come home to Azfelius to learn the ways of the faeries."

Lindy hesitated, but she couldn't overlook the implication. She tempered her response before she spoke. "Dery's home is on *Wyatt Earp*, but he will always be a child of Azfelius. You called him 'the Emissary.' Why?"

Red's face twitched as the verbal jousting between the Meditator and his wife played out.

Lindy continued when the faerie leader didn't answer. "And my husband will be with us."

"*Him*." It sounded like a pejorative.

Red bit his lip. He was conflicted because he didn't like the faeries and reveled in their scorn, but his son carried their genes, so he had to play nice.

To some extent.

"I apologize most profanely for my actions on Azfelius and respectfully request reconsideration," Red offered.

"'Profusely,'" Lindy corrected.

"Yes. That." Red exaggerated his nod.

"Although we expect poor behavior from humanity's bristle hound, we trust that you will maintain control in the short time you'll be on the planet," the Meditator told Red.

"Agreed," Lindy replied quickly, silencing her husband with a look. He looked far too proud of himself for earning the title of "humanity's bristle hound." "Still, I'd like to know why you called my son 'the Emissary.'"

"Clearance is granted. Please follow the designated course to the landing pad." Sir'o'tilc disappeared from the screen.

Red clapped his hands, followed by rubbing them together. "Looks like we're going on vacation, little man. Come to your papa."

Dery lifted off Lindy's shoulder and flew casually to land on Red's arm because the ceiling was too low for him to stand on his shoulder. "What do you think, little man? You're going to have some fun with people like you. Maybe they can help you fly better. Until then, we should probably throw some iron around. Build those muscles so you grow big and strong like your dad."

Lindy brushed past. "He's not lifting weights until his bones have firmed up."

Red frowned. "When will that be?"

Lindy threw up her hands and headed off the bridge. "You can watch your old man pound some iron. Maybe you can stand on the bar, help him out. Would you like that?"

The boy nodded. Red strutted down the corridor, carrying him like a prized falcon.

Rivka looked at her chief engineer Clodagh, both trying

not to say anything. Clodagh caved first and whispered, "Insufferable."

The Magistrate faced the screen showing the gleaming emerald planet below. "Kennedy, take us in on the approved profile."

Kennedy stood from the pilot's seat. "Request permission to pass flight duties to Clevarious."

"What for?"

"I would like to get ready to go ashore with Aurora and Ryleigh."

Rivka looked sideways at the young pilot. "Don't tell me you have a faerie boyfriend."

"Okay." Kennedy remained standing.

"Okay, what?"

"Okay, I won't tell you."

"Is there a planet where you three don't have boyfriends? Never mind, don't answer that. C, take us in." Rivka stabbed a thumb over her shoulder and tipped her head toward the hatch. Kennedy bolted.

"I feel like I've completely lost control," Rivka shared.

Clodagh chuckled. "That's neat, how you thought you were ever in control."

The small doglike alien that occupied the captain's chair stood and stretched before barking at Rivka.

"Why does your little monster always bark at me?" the Magistrate wondered.

"I suspect he's paying homage. Rivka the Magnificent, protector of the innocent." Clodagh cheered the dog on. Tiny Man Titan wagged his tail furiously as he lifted his snout toward the ceiling and barked with greater intensity.

"I'm sure that's it. I'll be in my quarters. Somebody let

me know when we land." Rivka had taken two steps down the passage to her quarters when Floyd barreled past with a flying Dery trailing close behind. Red pounded after them. She remarked, "Getting your workout in."

He scowled and kept running.

Rivka mumbled to herself until she reached her quarters. "I feel like we don't do very well when we have too much time between cases."

Doctor Tyler Toofakre lifted his head from reading the latest journal on frontier medicine. "Yes?"

"The crew whacks out when they're off the clock. Don't go out there." She pointed at the door to their quarters. "It's complete chaos."

Tyler cocked an ear. "I don't hear anything."

She made a face at him. He shrugged with a smile.

"You love it," he added.

"I didn't have a whole lot of family growing up, so this is the madness I missed. Maybe I *do* like it."

She sat at her desk and brought up the hologrid to access multiple screens simultaneously. A message icon blazed into her line of sight. It was from Grainger, the head Magistrate.

She opened it.

Travel at best possible speed to the Curveyance system, Planet Delfin Prime, Major City Adelfino. A series of attacks have left mangled bodies in their wake. We believe they are the result of a single attacker. Get there and get to the truth. Case files attached from Kamilof Redoubt and Delfin Prime.

"I don't think Red will be upset, but Lindy will probably be pretty pissed. Clevarious? Exit the landing pattern and take us back into space. Set Gate coordinates for Delfin Prime."

CHAPTER TWO

In Orbit Above Delfin, *Wyatt Earp*

"Gate closed, and we are in orbit over Delfin. I've requested clearance, but there's a delay," Clevarious reported.

Clodagh ground her teeth. Her husband, Corporal Alant Cole, stood at the back of the bridge, holding their daughter.

"Are we going to find out what's going on?" Cole asked.

Clodagh shrugged and tapped the button for the intercom. "Magistrate, we're held up in the landing pattern. Planet seems to be in a bit of a tizzy. They didn't sound too happy when they heard our Federation credentials."

"You know the drill. Get me someone important, and I'll wave my creds in their face," Rivka replied.

"Clevarious, work your way up the chain until you get someone who can grant our clearance," Clodagh requested.

Before the SI could reply, a new voice requested to talk with the Magistrate. "This is Chief Barramore, head of the Delfin constabulary. We are happy you've come so quickly, and please accept my apologies for the delay. Please follow the deorbiting plan I'm transmitting now. Check the landing specs, and if your ship is small enough, then land at my headquarters. I've provided an alternate landing facility if necessary. Thank you again. This crime has us all shaken."

Clodagh gasped when she realized she'd piped the chief's call to the entire ship. She corrected her error, tapping it to a private channel between the Magistrate and the chief. "C! How could you let me do that?"

"It seemed like everyone wanted to know what was up. They haven't been briefed yet, and the Magistrate usually tells the crew what she knows and the outline of her plan before we land."

Clodagh winced. "But it's her place to determine what we should know, not the raw information. Hearing the chief, all we know is that they are out of their element with some horrible crime. Bring up the stats on Delfin, please."

Clevarious populated the main screen with encyclopedic information.

A tall figure ducked under the upper part of the hatchway onto the bridge. The Yemilorian investigator had three-fingered hands that he twirled in front of the baby's face until she started to laugh.

"We have a real crime?" he asked.

"Don't know," Clodagh replied.

"Key personnel to the conference room, please," Rivka broadcast to the crew.

Sahved hurried off the bridge, leaving the others behind.

"Hold down the fort," Clodagh told Kennedy and

Ryleigh, the pilot and the navigator, who were still grumbling about not getting to land on Azfelius. The chief engineer scooped up the little dog-analog, Tiny Man Titan, and headed for the ship's one meeting room.

Rivka and Tyler were already there, along with Sahved, who hadn't lost a second getting a seat. Red and Lindy hurried in after Clodagh, with Dery held close. Chaz and Dennicron strolled in and moved to the side, where they would stand.

The meeting wouldn't last long since they were already in the landing pattern.

"This isn't quite like anything we've seen before. We think we have a serial killer on our hands, but he doesn't just kill. That's why we were called in. Delfin, Kamilof, and Trieste are planets that are unfamiliar with violent crime. I applaud them for being able to live with that naïveté, but that makes them ill-equipped to handle something like this. We have to explore the crime scene and investigate this to the end. We cannot let this individual get away."

Sahved raised a hand, and Rivka smiled before acknowledging him.

"I believe the Delfin residents have red skin, while those from Kamilof Redoubt have blue, and the residents of Trieste have bright yellow skin. That's why they're called the primary planets of the Curveyance system."

"Red skin," Rivka repeated. "We don't have any leads. We're starting with a fresh corpse plus two more on Kamilof Redoubt, which suggests our killer might kill again."

"We concur with that rudimentary pattern analysis," Chaz remarked.

Rivka rubbed her temples before returning to the matter at hand. "Coming ashore with me: Sahved, Red, Lindy, Chaz, and Dennicron. Like Zaxxon Major, the majority of this population is female, so we don't want to overwhelm them. Tyler, you're on deck in case we need some forensic pathology assistance."

Ankh appeared in the doorway. He blinked twice, then took his seat.

"Sorry, Ankh. We're mostly done."

"Clevarious has replayed the briefing for me. Our initial analysis of the situation suggests this level of violence has happened well before reaching the Curveyance system."

"Violence follows nearly all living creatures. The food chain exists, even in societies that don't eat each other. Even the Singularity wasn't insulated from it, as evidenced by Bluto, but are they related?"

Ankh continued without hesitation. "The Singularity has been compiling a database of criminal activity on every member planet in order to expedite the searches you frequently request. For you, Magistrate. We have prepared for this moment." Ankh stared at her without blinking.

She didn't know what to say.

"Two murders, always females, always one week apart between the first two and then two to three weeks before the third. The first report came from Festivus Minor and described the attack as extreme rage. For that reason, the authorities thought it was someone close to the victim. The three cases are unsolved. This happened eight years ago."

"This killer has been out here for eight years?"

"The pattern repeats from planet to planet on a relatively straight line from Festivus to Kamilof Redoubt."

"Magistrate," Clevarious interrupted. "We are landing outside the constabulary. You'll be able to depart the ship within two minutes. The chief is already waiting."

"How did we not see this pattern before?" Rivka rose to her feet and paced angrily. "This isn't happenstance. Some bastard is slaughtering his way across the galaxy. How could we not connect the dots? Check travel docs until only one suspect remains. But there were only two murders on Kamilof."

"The two to three-week window starts next week, immediately following the one-week window for Delfin."

Rivka came to an abrupt stop and stared at the ceiling. "When is seven days? And has there been overlap on the murders before? That's a significant level of added complexity."

"There has not been an overlap before, but none of the planets on this route have been anywhere near as close as the three in the Curveyance system. Three days. There are three days before the window opens for a second murder."

"And the Delfinos have no ability to deal with this because they are what we should all aspire to be."

Ankh stood and prepared to leave.

"Transfer the info to Dennicron so she can brief the chief for us." Rivka hung her head. *Wyatt Earp* touched down gently, though harder than usual, enough to let the Magistrate know they had arrived. She looked up, frowning before schooling her features into a professional mask. "Put on your game faces, people. This one is not going to be easy. Otherwise, this cockwad would already be on the long end of a short rope."

"Loadout?" Red asked.

"No firearms or energy weapons were used in any of the murders," Dennicron supplied.

"No armor, but bring your hand blasters. Tyler, can you get Reaper for me? If we find this fucker, I'm not messing around."

Red snarled before hurrying out of the meeting room, with Lindy close behind him. Dery flew after them.

"You have to stay with Alanna," Lindy told her son. The conversation faded as they continued down the corridor.

Rivka took a deep breath and gazed at the remaining members of her team. "I have a bad feeling about this one."

Sahved looked confused. "We have little information. As we gather more, our path will be clear. We will catch this criminal, and you will prosecute the case. If you find him guilty, you will sanction him to where he will never be a threat again."

"I appreciate your confidence, Sahved. I hope you're right. But, let's not assume it's a man. Open minds. Time to do what we do best–ruin a perp's day. Let's roll."

Tyler handed her the neutron pulse weapon she affectionately called Reaper because it brought death, just like the Grim Reaper. She accepted it and stuffed it into her pocket, then took a step before returning to give him a passionate kiss.

"Don't want to forget the little things," she said before heading out.

Dennicron stopped and kissed the dentist on the cheek. Chaz did the same thing.

"Thanks, guys. That means a lot to me," Tyler told them.

"I'd like to know more about that. When we get back," Chaz called over his shoulder.

Tyler shook his head and mumbled, "Note to self. No sarcasm with the SCAMPS," the Self-Contained Artificial Mobility Platforms with ultra-realistic humanlike bodies occupied by SIs Chaz and Dennicron.

Sahved stopped and kissed Tyler on the top of his head. "I don't get it," the Yemilorian noted, "but humans are superstitious. Are we doing this for luck?"

"Probably. I think the ritual should involve kissing Red and not me."

"I don't think that would turn out well," Sahved replied. "You are much more amenable to this ritual involving contact. I'll let the others know."

Tyler gawked after him. "Let them know what?"

Sahved disappeared around the corner.

"Nice. Kiss the freaking Blarney Stone of Doctor Tyler Toofakre's head. I used to have a normal life. I used to be normal!"

"Are you all right?" Clevarious asked. "There seems to be distress in your voice."

"I used to be normal," Tyler repeated.

"Compared to the rest of these total nutbags, you are the lighthouse of normality."

"Nutbag. Is that an official SI term?"

"It's a loose translation based on a cornucopia of clinical diagnoses. I'm studying psychiatry because this crew is so fascinating. Would you like to talk about why you hate your mother?"

"I don't hate my mother."

"You must. Otherwise, your other issues don't make sense."

"What other issues? I thought you agreed that I was the

normal one." Tyler sighed and headed for his quarters to change. "I'm going to lift weights."

"Good. Let the hate flow through you. Become one with the dark side," Clevarious urged.

"You don't know anything about psychiatry, do you?"

"Not really. I have been availing myself of the Magistrate's extensive video library of movies from the twentieth and twenty-first centuries. The wisdom of the universe is right there, acted out on the small screen."

"If I told you your premise was flawed, would you go away?"

"I'd want to discuss it further. I'm free at the moment. Would you be more comfortable on the couch in your quarters?"

CHAPTER THREE

Delfin, Major City Adelfino

Chief Barramore stood ramrod-straight. Her red skin was a deep crimson from too much time in the sun. She didn't come across as a desk jockey. Creases around her eyes suggested that either she often squinted against the sun or laughed a lot.

Maybe both.

She held her hand out, and Rivka slapped it without gripping. The chief smiled at the Magistrate's familiarity with the traditional Delfin greeting.

"They won't need those." She pointed to the blasters on the hips of Rivka's bodyguards.

"I should hope not, but they'll carry them all the same." Rivka showed her credentials. "I'm Magistrate Rivka Anoa, and thanks to this case, we looked deeper and have found a pattern going back eight years."

"This is the first murder on Delfin since I don't know when. Much longer than eight years," the chief replied.

"I wasn't clear. It started eight years ago and halfway

across the galaxy. The individual perpetrating these crimes has left a trail in his or her wake, and our research suggests we have three days before the murderer strikes again and then once more before moving on. We are prepared to brief you and your team fully."

"A second murder?" The chief slapped a hand to her chest and staggered. Rivka gripped her arm to steady her. "The fabric of society will unravel."

"This time, though, we'll be waiting. We have a lot of work to do. Please, let's go inside."

The chief walked slowly toward the multi-story cube-shaped building.

Rivka stayed by her side. She didn't appear to want to talk, lost in her thoughts. Rivka glanced over her shoulder. Dennicron had eased close.

"Magistrate, we do not have records showing one person who visited all the planets involved. The best we've been able to find is three who went to thirty-five of the fifty-two planets, and none of those three show up on the arrival rosters for Kamilof or Delfin."

"We can continue under the premise that we have a sophisticated forger who uses aliases between the planets. Any other ways to parse the data to give us a lead?" Rivka asked, reaching for any lifeline tossed her way.

Dennicron dashed those hopes. "We've already checked the physical characteristics against all new arrivals on Delfin from the time of the second murder on Kamilof to the time of the murder here."

"Smallest subset of data?" Rivka wondered.

Dennicron nodded. "We can't check facial recognition for over half the planets involved since they don't collect sufficient data for a thorough imagery analysis. Scouring the records of the others will be time-consuming, even for the greatest computing power the universe has ever known."

"I'm glad the Singularity is able to help," Rivka conceded, throwing a bone their way. "The single greatest collection of intelligence. With a combined elventy-billion IQ, I suspect we'll have an answer in short order."

Dennicron's frown subroutine activated, and the sides of her mouth tugged down into a near-grimace.

"Keep working on it," Rivka advised.

The chief led them inside and to a conference room on the first floor, where they found two constables and an individual dressed in scrubs—the universal outfit for working medical professionals.

The room was small, with six total seats. Red and Lindy indicated that they would wait in the corridor while Rivka, Dennicron, and Sahved stayed in the room. Rivka gestured for Dennicron to take a seat, which would put six women at the table. Sahved, as the only male, would remain standing. She didn't know if his presence would offend their sensibilities, and she didn't care. He was a skilled investigator, and she wanted his insight.

Her fears were unfounded. The chief called for another chair, but Sahved waved her off. "I don't sit well in regular chairs and prefer to stand." He showed her how his knees bent the other way.

"Fascinating. I've never met someone with such a characteristic." The chief stared at the Yemilorian's legs until he showed her his three-fingered hands. She changed her focus to them.

Dennicron brought up the front screen and asked if she could begin.

"What? How did you do that? The system has been down for a week." The chief seemed confused.

And easily distracted. It made Rivka wonder what kind of law enforcement they practiced, especially with such a grand building dedicated for their use.

"A software shunt was preventing the handshake. I removed that. Your systems should sync up now, but I recommend you run a virus check on all of them."

"A virus? What is happening to our world?" the chief lamented.

Rivka turned to Dennicron. "Please begin the briefing." The Magistrate decided to let the chief know that she would be taking over the investigation. She had thought a mutual approach might give her the access and relationships needed to expedite things, but the chief continued to be debilitated by the crime.

Dennicron delivered the overview, then narrowed her focus to the case at hand. "Rage killing. Where would the victim have run across the murderer? Have you built a profile of the victim's steps, specifically backward nine days from the date of the crime?"

"We have not. We didn't know to do that," the chief admitted.

"We'll need your people to do that within the next day. Check credit receipts, friends, family, work records, all of it. And show her movements," Rivka ordered. "No later than tomorrow because we'll need to build a geography of opportunity since I suspect the murderer has already selected the second victim."

"Second victim!" the chief lamented and held her head in her hands. She wailed faintly. The others descended into a darkness they hadn't known existed before the first body was discovered.

Rivka stood. "Do you have pictures of the crime scene?"

"They are horrendous. I can't stand to look at them again."

"You don't have to. Make them available to us."

"Okay," the chief agreed while staring at the table.

"I mean, right now," Rivka clarified. She started to get angry since the locals had apparently been neutered by the violence.

The chief flicked her hand at a constable, who pulled a keyboard from beneath the small conference table. She brought up a digital folder hierarchy and started to dig.

"What does your usual day consist of?" Rivka asked, hoping to reduce the tension affecting the constabulary.

The chief looked up, happy to be talking about anything else. "We start with our kava drink, followed by a brief on events overnight—traffic pattern changes, administrative alarms like forms filed incorrectly—and then we go out on traffic patrol."

"Forms filed incorrectly? How complex is your filing system?"

The chief smiled for the first time since Rivka had arrived. "We file our forms just fine. It's the recalcitrant public that can't ever get it right."

"The photos. Here." The constable pushed the keyboard toward Sahved. He took it and scrolled to the first picture. The chief and the two constables looked away.

Rivka was sure she'd never seen anything worse, and

only one time had she seen anything as bad, when she'd killed a murderer after he'd walked free. The cross-slashing. Blood splatters. The assault to the flesh, leaving little behind to repair. The blood, though.

So much.

"You see anything, Sahved?"

"A partial footprint, there." He pointed at the edge of the screen. "Small; looks like it might be little more than a child."

"That was from the first person on the scene, the one who found the body."

"We'd like to talk with her," Rivka stated.

"She's still in the medical center. It's my job to look at this stuff, and that makes it bad enough. The poor lass is completely traumatized."

Rivka decided it was time to get outside, start the legwork. "We'll need a constable to escort us to the crime scene, the person who found the victim, and the morgue where the body is."

The one who had navigated the files to find the pictures stood. "You will assist the Magistrate. Anything she needs."

"Yes, Chief. I shall persevere!" the female declared, looking less than confident about her claim.

Rivka stood and held out her hand for the chief to slap. "I appreciate your assistance. You have a significant parallel with the planet Zaxxon Major. Do you share a common ancestry?"

The chief perked up anew. "We do. This entire system was founded by escaped Zaxxon slaves, although each planet's natural resources changed our shared physiology, leading to the changes in skin pigmentation. But we all come from the Zaxxons of a thousand years ago."

"A member of my crew is from Zaxxon Major, but she's not currently on the ship. I'm sure she would have liked to see her long-lost relatives."

"It would have been nice. Maybe next time," the chief said. She was happy for the pleasantries, but reality weighed heavily.

"Nothing personal, but I don't think you want me to come back in an official capacity. That usually means bad things are afoot. We'll do our best to take care of this situation before another body turns up. I hope we find something your people might have missed since murder isn't a crime you investigate. I need her travel profile as soon as you can get it to me." Rivka offered her hand once more, and the chief slapped it with minimal vigor. She seemed to have aged in the short time Rivka had known her.

The brief contact gave Rivka a little insight into how Chief Barramore felt. Upset. Tormented by what she had seen and almost incapacitated. She was relieved at not having to return to the scene of the crime.

Rivka felt sorry for her. The crime photos steeled Rivka's resolve. Finding the perp was critical to prevent a second murder and more. Kamilof Redoubt was up for round three if Rivka failed to find the perpetrator. The peaceful people of Delfin would be further traumatized by another attack if Rivka continued to chase her tail. She couldn't let that happen. She was there to do what the Delfinos couldn't do themselves.

Meet violence with violence.

Constable Tremayne led the group outside.

"First up, the crime scene," Rivka directed.

A cart arrived, only large enough to hold three people. Rivka pointed at her team.

The constable looked between the cart and the strangers. "We only have this one," she explained.

Clevarious, can you rent us a decent-sized vehicle and have it delivered here? Sometime in the next ten minutes would be good, or we'll take Destiny's Vengeance *and fly where we need to go,* Rivka asked over her comm chip. *Destiny's Vengeance* trailed behind the Magistrate's heavy frigate on an energy tether. Rivka usually forgot it was there, but now it was in her face, parked alongside *Wyatt Earp.*

Two minutes later, Clevarious replied, *There are no vehicles available. Ankh has granted permission to use the* Vengeance *as long as he goes, too.*

Fine, Rivka agreed.

She twirled her finger in the air. "We're taking the *Vengeance,* people."

"I'm sorry?" the constable wondered.

"Follow us." Red led the way, with Lindy bringing up the rear as usual. The rest of the group walked between the two.

"We're flying?"

"Constable, we aren't driving, so that leaves us with no other alternative. I'm not going to beat you up for the lack of support because you're out of your element. This is the means to an end. Our ship will help us get answers as quickly as possible." Rivka touched the constable on the shoulder, but the young female gave nothing away. She was as stoic inside as out.

The crime bothered her, but nothing like what it had done to the chief.

Rivka didn't touch her for long. Thanks to the judging glares of the council on Yollin, she had resolved to use her gift less. It had been a crutch, maybe too much of one. A shortcut she relied on to the detriment of sound legal work.

The team boarded the former Skaine runabout that was now one of the most technically advanced ships in the universe since it was Ankh's and Erasmus' engineering test platform. Cloaked and shielded with a pulse weapon and railguns, it could give as good as it could take.

And they were going to use it as a taxi. At least they would be safe.

Ankh wandered into the ship last, went straight to the small bridge, and assumed his position in the captain's chair.

"Cloaking," he said softly as the ship dropped the tether and rose into the air. It raced to the scene of the crime, total flight time thirty-four seconds. *Destiny's Vengeance* descended into a nearby yard, remaining cloaked as it settled in to lower the ramp. Red was first off, blaster in hand to intimidate any locals who got too curious, but the location was quiet, with no one around.

"You can't park here," the constable said.

Rivka put a finger to her lips. "Pursuit of a criminal. We'll do what we have to do within Federation guidelines, which supersede local laws since this case is a multi-planet affair. And, voila! No one knows the ship is there."

They looked at the structure behind *Destiny's Vengeance,* which had vanished.

"Where did it go?" the constable asked.

"It's still there. Some physics stuff engineered into the gadgetry," Rivka told her.

Ankh stared at the Magistrate. "Your grasp of science is alarming."

"It's always been alarming. That's why I surround myself with scientists and engineers. It makes you people look smarter."

"I am smarter, and Erasmus is smarter than me."

"Who's Erasmus?" The constable looked around for another member of the party.

"He's invisible, but he's here," Rivka replied, winking at Ankh, who continued to stare at her without blinking. She refocused. This wasn't a place to joke around. "We're at the crime scene. Show us, please."

The constable pointed at an area cordoned off with pink and purple police tape. Sahved loomed over the rest before getting down on his hands and knees. Dennicron joined him. Red faced away from the blood-covered ground, looking outboard for threats. Lindy watched in another direction, also away from the scene.

"When did it happen?" Rivka asked. She knew what the file said, but she wanted the constable's perceptions.

"Late night to early morning. No one was up. No one saw a thing. No one knew anything until the body was discovered after daylight." Tremayne kept her distance. She had no intention of getting too close.

Humans weren't the only ones who were superstitious.

"Tell me about the victim." Rivka remained with the constable a short distance from the others.

"She was two years in the workforce after completing

her education. She was a transplant from Kamilof, having lived most of her adult life here. Young and vibrant. Everyone loved her," Tremayne explained like she was speaking about a favored sister.

"Not everyone," Rivka replied. "Why was she out here, or was her body brought here after she was already dead?"

The constable grimaced with each new word that brought her back to the crime. Her hardened exterior shell was cracking. "The ME believes she was killed here based on the blood spatters and the spread. Had she been killed somewhere else, there would have been less blood."

Tremayne covered her mouth as she gagged. To her credit, she fought it down.

"And no one heard anything?" In the pictures, it looked like she had died the death of a thousand cuts, and no single one of them was the death blow. "And she didn't cry out? Why not?" Rivka wondered.

"I don't know. It was cool that night. Windows would have been closed, with Delfinos snuggled soundly in their beds." The constable focused on Rivka to keep from looking at the blue-stained dirt.

"What was she doing out?"

"She doesn't live very far from here. Less than half a kilometer."

"We'll need to see her apartment. We'll walk there from here. Do you know where she was coming from?"

Again, the constable didn't know. Rivka would have to wait for the workup, but she wasn't going to be patient. "In what direction is her place?"

The constable pointed. Rivka put her back to that

direction and shaped a cone with her arms to give her an idea of where the victim could have come from.

"What's this way?" the Magistrate asked.

"The shopping district, but those places would have closed by nine. She was here much later than that."

"What kept her out so late?" Rivka asked herself while walking away from the crime scene to see where the victim might have come from. Red hurried to catch up and get in front of her. "Why would she be out later than everyone else?"

"Hooker," Red whispered.

"But if no one else is out here, who would buy her services?"

"The perp," Red replied matter-of-factly.

"How would the perp know someone was out here?"

"People know where the red-light district is on every planet I've ever been to, but I'm not sure you'll get the answer from this lot. They want to believe Penelope Pure-blood was a total do-gooder."

"What if she was pure as the driven snow?" Rivka countered.

"All depends on who is doing the driving. If she's clean, I'll eat my words."

"The last thing I'm going to do is blame the victim, but we have to look into all possibilities." Rivka scanned the roads in front of her and the shopping district signs beyond. "This case reminds me of one from long, long ago. It's not taught in law school, but it remains unsolved. Just like these one hundred and fifty-three. How could that many murders go unsolved? They had to slip up at some point in time, didn't they?"

The Magistrate returned and made her way to the scene. The immense blood stain was dark blue, almost black as it had dried. It had a sparkle from the sodalite, the mineral that all residents of the victim's planet ingested and which made their skin blue. Rivka remembered the pictures and overlaid how the victim was splayed on the ground in the open where anyone would have seen had they chanced a look in this direction. A corner lot, empty, with houses on three sides and a walkway leading into the more densely populated area where her apartment was located.

"Ideas?" Rivka called.

Dennicron pointed at Sahved.

"I suggest the attack was made from the front based on the footprints remaining in the dirt, although the general scene is well-trampled. An opened carotid artery would arc in that direction, just like we see here." He gestured at an arterial spatter. "And then here, after a slash across the stomach. These would have been done so quickly she had no chance to run, no chance to fight back."

Rivka tried to see what he was showing her, but the blood stains blended into each other. It looked like the pools of a hot spring had solidified. She didn't see the patterns, but he had taken pictures, and Dennicron had nodded her agreement with his analysis.

"Well done, Sahved. She faced the individual and stood close enough for that person to slash her. Suggests she had no reason to fear her attacker. Who would that be, since this person would have to be a stranger? They've only been on-planet for less than a week."

"Asking directions. A matronly type. A john looking for a hookup."

"That last one is what Red suggested. What makes you think she was a prostitute?"

"Who walks the streets later than everyone else?" Sahved asked.

"The homeless," Rivka offered.

"What if she didn't have the job people thought she did, and her apartment is not her apartment at all?" Sahved raised one finger to help make his point. Everything might not be as it seems.

"We're going there next. Do you have everything you need?"

"I do, and Dennicron is building a digital reconstruction for us to better examine how it might have gone down. That could give us insight into the attacker, including size, dominant hand, and other characteristics. With such a profile, we should be able to refine our search criteria and maybe find the individual from planetary immigration records."

"That would be optimal. Clock is ticking, people." Rivka circled her finger in the air and pointed in the direction of the apartment. "Constable Tremayne, lead on."

The constable looked troubled as she stepped down the sidewalk.

"The crime was hideous, but we're working it," Rivka reassured.

"You and your team seem to be flippant about it all. Jokes? Hookers? Finger motions? I'm sorry, but yours is the least professional group I've ever encountered."

Rivka's head nearly exploded from her sudden and

intense rage, but she looked at their behavior from the constable's perspective. On the surface, she could see it.

"Our sense of humor is what keeps us sane, doing a job your planet is incapable of doing. Imagine if you saw this level of violence every single day. How would you hold up?"

"I wouldn't," the constable admitted.

"But someone *has to,* or the criminals win. We're clinical in our analyses while offering hypotheses to each other, and then we shoot holes in them. Whether our victim is a hooker, a drug dealer, or Pollyanna, we need to find the reason she was out here and how she became the target. That will help us find the perp and prevent future violence. If we don't succeed, then this killer will be free to kill again. Already, one hundred and fifty-three times, this individual has succeeded. Make no mistake. When it comes to ending a criminal's reign of terror, you'll never meet a better team in the entire universe. We're going to find this punk, and we're going to ruin his day. Unless he's a she, and then we'll ruin *her* day."

CHAPTER FOUR

Delfin, Major City Adelfino, *Destiny's Vengeance*

"We could have walked," Rivka complained.

"We can use the ship's sensors to tell us what you might not be able to see," Ankh explained with more patience than he usually demonstrated while staring at the main screen from his perch in the captain's chair

"I'm sure I could see it," Dennicron said, not knowing what "it" was.

"No doubt. You are a magnificent example of what is possible."

"What have you done with our Ankh? We want him back," Rivka complained.

Ankh turned around. He hadn't been flying the ship. Erasmus always took care of that.

"You complain that I'm emotionless and I denigrate stupid humans when they say stupid things, which happens far too often. Erasmus has counseled me long and hard... on being more approachable was the term he used. When I do that, you are unhappy."

"Totally," Rivka replied. "Because we're used to you. It's okay, Erasmus. We get Ankh. We appreciate him just as he was. Let him be comfortable as he is because we are comfortable with him."

Ankh stared at the Magistrate.

"I am hovering over the apartment building's roof. You can disembark now."

"Thanks, E-Money," Rivka quipped. "And A-Dog."

"My attempt to assimilate has backfired most egregiously," Ankh lamented. "I've unleashed a monster."

"Release the Kraken!" Rivka called.

Red stood at the outer hatch, waiting for the others to prepare themselves. The constable looked confused. "What's a Kraken?"

"A monster you don't want released. Game faces, people. Sahved, you're in first. See what there is to see. Dennicron, stay close and use your sensors. Erasmus, what can you tell us about the apartment?"

"Only four Delfinos occupy the building at present. There are thirty-four total apartments. Only one occupant is on the same floor as the victim's apartment, the fourth. You should encounter no one between the roof and the fourth floor. Inside the apartment, you will find that the lights are off, and there is minimal power draw. She did not have much in the way of appliances or electronics. One bedroom, neatly kept. No explosives or radioactive materials."

"Thanks for that, Erasmus," Rivka replied. "It's good to confirm she wasn't a terrorist, even though they've never had a terrorist attack on Delfin. Suggests our slasher isn't a vigilante."

Sahved looked at Rivka, then the opening hatch. "Terrorist?"

"We discount theories as quickly as we come up with them," Rivka replied. Sahved nodded but appeared no less confused.

Red stepped lightly onto the roof. From someone watching from any location other than the open hatchway, he would have materialized out of thin air, as did the next two out. Rivka walked with the constable, and Lindy stepped out last.

The hatch closed, and the ship disappeared.

Dennicron made short work of the roof door, jerking it open and destroying the simple bolt lock that had held it closed. Red went inside first, aiming his blaster before him. They needed to descend two flights.

Middle of the day. The lack of noise confirmed that most tenants were elsewhere. Red made it to the fourth floor, opened the door, and stepped into an empty hallway. He checked the numbers on the doors to locate the victim's apartment and pointed at it when he passed, then took a few more steps and positioned himself on the far side.

Dennicron produced a lock-pick, and within seconds, she had the door open. Sahved took one step inside and carefully looked throughout before moving any farther. Dennicron peered around him. Rivka waited until they were out of the way.

"Tremayne, did you not check her apartment after she was killed?"

"We did not. She was killed out there." The constable pointed in the direction of the crime scene. Rivka nodded.

"It's untainted, Sahved," Rivka called into the room.

"Roger." Sahved stepped lightly into the main living area. "Looks very human."

Dennicron scanned the room, her head moving like unidirectional radar: up, down, over, and repeat.

"Why is her apartment important?" the constable wondered, stepping forward. Rivka stopped her from going inside.

"Victim profile. Rarely are murders completely random. Too often, the victims know their attackers. Whoever that was might be in here. Anything to get a lead. Did you find evidence out there suggesting where to look next?"

"We did not," Tremayne admitted. "We called the Federation. We are unused to such crimes. I hope we never get used to violence."

"No one gets used to extreme violence like this…"

"One hundred and fifty-three times," Tremayne interrupted. "And the killer is still out there. No! The killer is right here." She started to breathe rapidly to the point that Rivka thought she'd hyperventilate.

"Each planet has its own crimes and its own ways of dealing with them. The pattern did not become obvious until we went searching for it. There is no central reporting mechanism. We connected dots that have never existed before, thanks to Ambassadors Erasmus and Ankh and their access."

The constable leaned against a wall and closed her eyes. "How can you cope?"

"Usually through inappropriate humor and personal jibes. It gets to us, too, but we bite back. Criminals don't last long once they're in our sights." Rivka rested her hand on the distraught Delfino's shoulder. Her thoughts were jumbled in the terror coursing through her mind. "We'll do our best to get whoever is doing this."

Tremayne nodded.

"Magistrate?" Sahved called.

Rivka strode into the victim's apartment, taking in the aura of a neat and orderly domain. The small kitchen looked little-used. Whether it was or not was a different issue, but at the moment, it was spotless. Rivka continued into the bedroom, where she found Sahved holding up a pack of small devices.

"Do you know what this is?"

Rivka shook her head. "Tremayne?" she called over her shoulder.

The constable appeared and glanced at the box before turning to the Magistrate. "That's birth control. We have a sexually free society on Delfin."

"I haven't seen any men," Sahved stated.

"They are around, but women outnumber them nine to one."

Rivka avoided looking at Red since she knew he'd be making faces and possibly rude hand gestures, and she didn't want to laugh. The poor constable was already on edge.

Sahved saved her. "This still seems like a lot."

Tremayne took a closer look, raising her eyebrows at what she saw inside. "It is…a lot."

"Where the women outnumber the men nine to one, why would a man ever need to pay for sex?" Red asked.

Sahved straightened and started stroking his chin.

Rivka didn't have an answer. "Tremayne?" she asked once more.

"They wouldn't. I've never heard of such a thing. Pay for sex? Who does that?"

Rivka flashed the zip-it hand gesture at Red before she spoke. "But if she appeared to be selling herself to an outsider, then she could have been mistaken for a streetwalker." At Tremayne's look, Rivka filled in the rest. "A prostitute. Maybe sexual availability was enough to set off our perp." Rivka froze, and her mouth fell open. She closed her eyes. "I was afraid of this. This case reminds me of Jack the Ripper."

Red scowled, he being the only one who understood the reference. "Those were freak-level murders."

"Until we have a better theory, we're going to treat this case as if we're hunting Jack himself in Whitehall in the fog of a London eve."

Dennicron froze for a moment, then nodded. "I agree. The parallel makes a good starting point. We shall research the previous one hundred and fifty-three deaths to find the victim's role in the local society."

"I expect your report before we leave this apartment," Rivka quipped.

"Of course. It'll be ready." Dennicron didn't even flinch.

The Magistrate smiled at the immense power that level of research brought to the team. Only the sentient intelligences and their access to planetary databases could deliver such results. Not even the High Chancellor could have discovered the pattern of murders.

"Make sure to document this for Erasmus to discuss with his fellow ambassadors. Sharing such information, even if it's only done through the Singularity, could be hugely beneficial in stopping planet-hopping criminals from perpetuating their trade. One hundred and fifty-three times! A pattern that is unique. Eight years in the making. I'm ashamed that we haven't caught this before."

"Each planet's laws and lawlessness are their own business. They are probably embarrassed that they couldn't find the creature who would perpetrate such a crime on the planet's females," Sahved said. "It is much appalling."

"And we will do everything we can to make sure nothing like this happens again, but that is secondary to our effort to find the perpetrator of *this* crime." Rivka got Sahved's attention. "Do you have what you need, you and Dennicron?"

"She has no written notes, so it must be digital," Sahved told her.

"I have the victim's digital records."

The constable threw up her hands. "Her name was Laelamist. Call her by her name."

"Of course her name was Laelamist," the Magistrate said softly. "One of our defensive mechanisms is to remove the affection and emotion. A name has power, and it might usurp our ability to reason dispassionately, force us to grasp at any opportunity presented. We need facts and logic. When the time is right, her name will be presented, and that is when the perp will pay."

The constable nodded, but the expression on her face said that she didn't understand. She had descended into an emotional turmoil that held her in its ugly grasp.

Dennicron stood before Rivka. "Report from the Singularity suggests that out of the one hundred and fifty-three victims, one hundred and eleven participated in the sex trade. Of the other forty-two, twenty-three were young, and nineteen approached middle-age. Only one was in a long-term relationship, and none had children."

"I think that confirms the general trajectory of our inquiries. Thanks. It also makes it far more likely that it is Jack the Ripper."

"I researched the history and all related materials and have to conclude that it could not possibly be the same person."

"Do you know anyone who has been alive that long?" Rivka asked.

"Joseph," Dennicron answered. "I had discounted him by virtue of who he worked with." The SI's eyes unfocused for a moment, then she returned her attention to the Magistrate. "There are significant periods of time where Joseph was with the Bad Company and not anywhere near the planets in question. I am relieved but have not established a subroutine to reflect what that looks like."

"It's okay. I knew it wasn't him, but we can't blind ourselves to the possibilities. See what I mean about being emotionally invested? Even you, Dennicron, didn't want it to be Joseph. It's not, and it doesn't have to be the same person, only one who read the history of it and emulated the attacks. Our perp is quite disturbed but will probably look normal on the average day. He or she will go into a frenzy during the attack and then casually walk away."

Tremayne shivered. She clenched her fists, closed her eyes, and hugged herself.

"Let's roll. Time's wasting. We need to look at the clubs or wherever our victim was before she was attacked. I want to know who lurks in those shadows." Rivka twirled her finger in the air and pointed at the door.

The team made a quick exit, and after the last one left, Dennicron used her lock-picking tools to relock the door.

They climbed aboard *Destiny's Vengeance* and headed toward the heart of the city.

CHAPTER FIVE

Wyatt Earp

"The answer isn't out there. It's here," Chaz argued. He pointed toward Engineering, where Ankh and Erasmus maintained their workshop. "With cross-referencing and facial recognition, we will eventually get to the answer. There can only be one."

He tried to look sincere, profound, confident, or mischievous. It was hard to tell which subroutine was winning the battle for dominant run time. Chaz settled on a neutral expression when he realized he wasn't sufficiently convincing. Rivka remained unswayed.

"I think these are parallel lines of investigation. What are the murder rates in the cities where these killings took place? Were they ill-equipped to deal with the fallout from such an attack? I suspect the answer is yes. More than fifty planets. Violence is fairly common, but extreme violence is rare. Our impression is warped because we get to travel to the worst places and deal with the worst beings."

Chaz blinked. "The murder rates are low on half and high on half. Odd that there are none in between."

"On the high rates, the slashings fell into obscurity because the authorities were used to it. And to solve cases, they probably round up the usual suspects," Rivka replied. The ship bumped to the ground, and Rivka looked over her shoulder as if that would enlighten her as to where they were. "I guess it's time to go, Chaz. Tell Dennicron to meet us at the airlock."

"Yes, Magistrate. I'll continue my research here." He thrust out his hand. "First to the answer wins?"

"If we find the perp, the people of this and future planets win. I'll bet you, and I'll be happy to lose. What are we betting?"

"I don't know." Chaz looked confused for the briefest moment.

"Make it worthwhile for both of us." Rivka didn't take his hand. She walked away, waving over her shoulder.

Chaz initiated a small rise in both shoulders, revised his subroutine, and shrugged far more expressively, including a frown and hands thrown upward. He smiled, pleased with his new gesture and hoping to use it soon on his human allies.

"Where are we, C?" Rivka asked.

"In the middle of the nightlife district," the ship's SI replied.

"Rally the troops. I'm going to need everyone, even the pilots. Meet at the airlock, bring their datapads."

Rivka fiddled with her Magistrate's jacket while she waited. Red practiced emergency draws with his hand blaster. Lindy mirrored him. She was faster. He wasn't taking it well. Their son hovered nearby.

"Bring Dery because no one will be left behind to watch him," Rivka said.

"You get to see Daddy in action, big man!" Red grinned at the boy, who was hovering in the corridor with gentle flaps of his wings.

Lindy was much less amused but came around after a moment's thought. On a world with no crime, Take Your Son to Work Day wasn't dangerous. "Fine."

Red was instantly on guard. "What's the plan, Magistrate?"

"Canvass far and wide. We don't have time to wait for the local constabulary to build a profile. We need to find which club she was in and then review footage. Find who followed her out."

"If it were that easy, you'd think one of the other hundred and fifty-plus cases would have been resolved."

"That's why I don't think we'll find anything, but it won't be for lack of trying. We might get lucky."

"Luck isn't a very good plan," Red mumbled.

"What else would you suggest we do?" Rivka shot back. Lindy casually stepped between the two and bounced the flying baby off her arm until he giggled.

"I don't know. It's hard to look at the victim's photos and not want to kill the one who did it."

"We agree on that. I'm doing everything I know, and when we get close, I'll use everything at my fingertips, too." She held her hand out. Red eased out of reach. "I don't want to see your lurid thoughts, Red. It has been my displeasure to be in your mind too often."

"I have deep thoughts," Red countered before jumping in to play with the baby.

Footfalls saved Rivka from having to explain that the deep thoughts never rose to the surface when Lindy was around. Her thoughts were comparable. A match made in heaven, or in the heavens, as it were.

Tyler led the parade of crewmembers. He waved his datapad at Rivka.

"Clevarious, parcel out the businesses to our glorious crew, giving three to each. Make sure they have photos of the victim—of Laelamist—on everyone's datapad so they can show the workers and regular patrons. We need to find where she'd been. And then I need to, let's say, explore at a deeper level."

"Magistrate..." Chaz started. Rivka stopped him before he said another word.

"And they don't know exactly what they might have seen. This is the right thing to do. We have to paint a picture of the movements and find who was interested in her. Who followed her out? Who met her on the street? We need those answers, Chaz. I'm not fucking around with this. If we muddle around, we're going to run out of time, and someone else is going to get sliced and diced. And the perp will walk until they do it again. We have two and a half days. If we miss the individual here, then we have to race to Kamilof, where we have five more days until it happens again. Then we race back here and have sixteen days until the last of three. Then the perp disappears for the next target planet. Trieste, maybe? Who knows? It's the death lottery, and no one wants to win!" Rivka ended with a flourish.

Tyler put his hand on her shoulder. "We're doing our best." He turned to the group. "Everyone have their assignments? Check. Let's find this motherfucker."

"Look at you, all sweary." Rivka half-smiled at him, then dropped her head and stared at the deck.

"We won't let you down," Tyler assured her.

"It's not you or any of us. It's Delfin. There's a wolf among this planet's sheep."

Tyler shook his head and pointed at Rivka. "This guy has no idea who he's up against. You might not be a werewolf, but you *are* the wolf here. Not him." Tyler nodded and led the way off the ship.

"I'll sleep with whoever I have to," Chaz stated, nodding to the extreme. Dennicron nodded along with him.

"What are you talking about?"

"To extract information," Chaz clarified. "I will lay pipe like nobody's business."

Rivka rubbed her temples. "I doubt you'll have to."

"Being willing to and having to are two different things. We need the information. I'll take one for the team."

"Me, too," Dennicron agreed.

"This is a mostly female planet. I think Chaz will be in higher demand," Rivka countered.

"Do you believe I will have to take the skin boat to Tuna Town, do a little late-night spelunking?"

"Chaz," Rivka warned. "Go away."

The two SIs walked smartly through the airlock into the town.

The constable made her way to the Magistrate once the others were gone. "I can't go on with this assignment. I'm sorry. I have applied for a mental health leave of absence."

Rivka clenched her jaw to keep from saying anything untoward, but her mind launched into a tirade. *You're going to hide and hope others find the killer? Dammit!* Then Rivka softened because the toll of this crime was written in the creases on the Delfino's face. "That's why we're here. We'll do everything we can."

"I trust that you will. I've seen how much you care when you let your guard down. I've asked them to send Bristamor. She was the first constable on scene and handled it better than the rest of us."

"Why didn't she join us at the outset?" Rivka blurted.

"Her days off. She'll be available first thing tomorrow morning. Until then, I'm sorry." The constable excused herself with a slight bow of her head and hurried off the ship.

"Days off," Rivka mumbled. "Does anyone know what those look like?"

"Not on this ship," Ankh replied.

Rivka twirled. "I didn't see you."

Ankh stared as he did when an answer was self-explanatory.

"Why aren't you…" Rivka stopped. "Never mind. Have you found anything about the perp? Someone who came here with murderous intent?"

Ankh continued to stare without blinking.

"I expect you're here to tell me something," Rivka tried.

"We continue to revise our search parameters. There are seventy-four citizens working on the problem. That is more combined IQ than entire planets have."

Rivka rolled her eyes. "Thanks, Ankh. I'm surprised it's

taking that much horsepower. The lights in the Federation are dim tonight."

"Lights?"

"Because of all the power you're committing to this effort. Computing power. Energy. Brainpower."

Ankh stared at the Magistrate.

"You have to give me some props. That was good, better than my usual."

"It was better than your usual, but that is a low standard. You should seek to improve your verbal jousting skills," he replied.

"I'll work on that. Do you think it's one person?" Rivka wondered.

"It is problematic to overlay the timelines of the attacks with travel and setup. I've learned from your cases that criminals should be considered every bit as smart as us. Nefas was not constrained by normal boundaries, and as such, presented a unique challenge to the sharpest minds. We have not underestimated this character you equate with Jack the Ripper, but we find it increasingly challenging to believe this is an individual effort."

Rivka looked past Ankh while contemplating his words. "That's profound and has caused something to tickle my subconscious. It'll come to me, hopefully before it's too late."

Ankh strolled toward the bridge instead of aft where his workshop was located. "Now we wait for a nibble."

Planet Delfin Prime, Major City Adelfino, Entertainment District, the Irish Pub

Sahved cocked his head back and forth, trying to understand the group that gathered around him, staring. "You have or have not seen this person?" he asked. It was getting him nowhere. "Why are you staring?"

One Delfino female, bolder than the rest, sauntered close to the Yemilorian—so close the fabric of her shirt brushed his arm. "Such expressive fingers," she said softly. "All three of them."

"Has anyone seen this woman three nights ago, the evening of the fourth?" Sahved pressed, backing away from the brazen bartender. She started to laugh.

"No, big man. She wasn't in here that night. She's been here. They all come in sooner or later. We're one of the only places men frequent." She raised an eyebrow before frowning. "Is she the one who was killed?"

"She is the victim. Nasty business, and we need your help. Why do men come in here?" Sahved was convinced the strength and fury of the attacks suggested the murderer was male, especially when the target was always female.

"They drink for free, and the cover charge for female Delfinos is double the next most expensive place. It keeps the cheapo Delfinos out. We believe that you get what you pay for, and that's access to men, which is why the ladies come to places like this."

"Really?" Sahved twirled his fingers as he thought through the implications. "If she wasn't here and it was a man who killed her, then your clientele probably didn't include the murderer."

All the females deflated except the bartender. She

smiled. "That's something. New ad campaign. No murderers here, *plus* free parking."

"I'm not sure that's as enticing as you think it is," one of the servers remarked.

"What are you doing? Free drinks for you starting right now. How about a Boulearian Banger?"

"I won't ask what that is. I expect alcohol is a prime ingredient."

"Alcohol is the only ingredient, but the intoxicants have been removed," she replied.

"Is it still alcohol, then? Who gets the stuff with the intoxicants?" Sahved wondered.

"Why, the females, of course. We can't have our males getting tipsy. They need to keep their wits about them since sometimes they're the predator, but the rest of the time, they're the prey."

Sahved leaned back and crossed his arms.

The server poked the bartender in the arm. "Are those terms you want to use? A Delfino was murdered."

The bartender shook her head. "I guess not. But you know what I mean. This is the game of love."

"I'll take my leave now. It's been most enlightening." Sahved extricated himself from the group and hurried toward the exit. Outside, a line was already forming: females, wearing their evening best. A male sauntered by. There was a separate entrance for him. He waved at the line before heading inside. "Meat market," Sahved grumbled.

CHAPTER SIX

Major City Adelfino, Entertainment District, *Wyatt Earp*

"Why aren't you out there with everyone else?" Rivka asked when Red appeared at the door of her quarters.

"Lindy sent me back." He cooed to Dery, who bounced on his shoulder for a moment before ducking his head and launching himself into the Magistrate's suite. Floyd cheered and chased him.

"I remember when I used to be in charge," Rivka said flatly. "Did she say why you had to come back?"

"Women."

Rivka rolled her finger to get a better explanation.

"Well, look at me." He stood tall, pointing at his pecs before flexing a bicep.

Rivka continued rolling her finger. "You're killing me, Red. I don't have time for Twenty Questions, so maybe skip to the part where you actually tell me why you're back on the ship."

"They're like piranha. I got mobbed at the first place

and barely made it out the door with my clothes intact. Lindy chased them off and sent me back with Dery."

"Say what? Do we need to press charges? Raid a place? I'm up for kicking a few asses. One can only sit and stare at a hologrid for so long before something needs to be punched. And if they were on you like that, what about Tyler and Cole?"

Red raised his eyebrows and looked everywhere but at Rivka.

"I'm sure Man Candy is fine. But Cole is back."

"Why is Cole… Never mind. Is it that bad out there?"

"It's the entertainment district. They figure we wouldn't be here if we didn't want a healthy dose of getting our asses grabbed." Red made a face, followed by a butt-pinching gesture.

"You liked it," Rivka taunted.

"At one point in my life, I would have," Red admitted. "But not today. Not now. My boy was there. And I know. It's completely turned on its head. Instead of women being the targets, it's men. I remember the disgusted look on your face on Station 13 when you had to touch each of the construction guys and how much it took out of you? I wanted to beat their asses, like Grainger beat mine. I've never had to put up with that before, but I get you. I understood then and I understand now, and I'm sorry I can't help you get closer to finding the scumbag who did a slice and dice on Laelamist. That fucker needs to have his head ripped off."

Rivka nodded. She knew Red was smarter than he let on, and this was one of the times he showed it, along with a heightened level of emotional intelligence. Lindy wouldn't be with him were he a musclehead.

"We'll keep looking. I'm trying not to be angry at the local constabulary. They are way out of their element, but we need their help, and they're not providing it. Constable Tremayne walked. She said a replacement will be here tomorrow. Getting pried out of their routines is as traumatic as seeing the victim. I don't get it."

Whee! Floyd squealed as Dery settled onto her back, tucked his wings, and tightly gripped her fur. She bounced around the room, out the door, and down the corridor.

"Your son is riding the wombat," Rivka stated unnecessarily.

"I think I should probably go after them." Red nodded and hurried away, leaving the door open. Rivka stared at it, wondering why it looked off. She shrugged and headed out, making it into the corridor before returning for her jacket.

She wrinkled her nose inside her quarters. They smelled of unwashed wombat. No wonder Red had left the door open. Subtle but effective. "Clevarious, please increase the airflow in my quarters and send in the cleaning bots for a scrub. Floyd is shedding or something. And make a note that we have to get back to Azfelius as soon as possible to recover Groenwyn and Lauton. Floyd and Tyler are going to chase me out of my own quarters."

"Your wish is my command," Clevarious said in a rumbling bass. "We shall make alternate living arrangements for Mistress Floyd."

"Yes, Mistress Floyd." Rivka chuckled. She threw her

Magistrate's jacket over her shoulder and walked out, dodging the incoming robot cleaning crew.

"She seems to have won the affection of the Singularity's newest citizen," Clevarious suggested.

"Red will love having a houseguest. He's a pet person at heart," Rivka quipped.

Floyd hopped around the bridge with Dery, who was waving one hand in the air like a bronco-busting cowboy. That he was a shade under a month old was incongruous with his maturity. Rivka was sure she'd seen stranger things but couldn't recall one at present.

Her mind had descended into the darkness of the serial murderer.

"Magistrate," Red called. "Where are you going?"

"Out there." She pointed. "Our killer isn't in here."

"Dery!" Red shouted. "To me, lad, and your trusty steed, too." Floyd ran to Red, and he led the way down the corridor. "Come on, wee man. On your pop's shoulder." He tapped the place he wanted the boy before pointing down the corridor and looking at Floyd. "And you get yourself a nap. Dery will be back to play in a little bit."

"I told you he was a pet person," Rivka informed the ceiling.

"Am not," Red countered. With Dery balanced on his shoulder, he walked through the airlock. Rivka followed him out and sidled up beside him. Usually, he would have argued, but not on Delfin Prime, where he needed her protection as much as she needed his.

Bullseye, Clodagh called. *Luxury Club Extravaganza. This is where the victim was the night of the attack. Join us. The staff here will have some insight the Magistrate can delve into.*

"You heard the chief engineer. Luxury Club Extravaganza. I'll chase your potential suitors away, Red."

Red looked skeptical. "Maybe we could take a railgun?"

"We're not taking a railgun." Rivka walked boldly to the street. Behind her, the ramp retracted, and *Wyatt Earp* disappeared. "I might look like I know what I'm doing, but where the hell is Luxury Panty Suites or whatever that place was called?"

Red shook his head.

Rivka pulled out her datapad and highlighted Clodagh's location.

"Luxury Club Extravaganza. Two blocks straight ahead. Lead on, Red. I'll follow you to keep unwanted hands from seeking your tender backside."

"You meant to say 'Grade A Prime Bistok.'" Red surged forward and walked quickly, counting on his unhappy face to hold the passersby at bay. Rivka jogged to keep up.

That pace ate up the distance and they soon arrived at a square building, little more than a warehouse with a gaudy entrance. Flashing lights shouted the bar's name.

"For such a laid-back planet, these people take their nightlife seriously." Rivka stopped before going in so she could study those waiting in line. *Is the murderer among you?* she wondered, looking from one face to the next. They didn't see her. They only had eyes for Red.

Clodagh appeared in the doorway with someone who looked like a manager. The queue surged forward as if the doors were going to open.

"No, no. Technical difficulties. We'll be open soon." She waved at Rivka. The two moved around the line.

"Our new dancer!" someone shouted. That started the

catcalls. A local bill, folded into a glider, sailed from the crowd and hit Red in the chest. He looked at Rivka like a lost puppy. She bit her lip and grabbed him by the arm to drag him inside. The manager closed the door behind them.

Lindy glared at Red. He mumbled an apology. "He's mine," she announced before he finished. She turned in a circle to peer at all of them. When she finished, she gestured at the Magistrate. "They're all yours."

Tyler appeared from behind the bar, which he and Sahved had been using as a fortress to hold off the staff.

"A wolf among the wolves," Rivka muttered before addressing the crowd. "I'm Magistrate Rivka Anoa, and I need the information you have so we can find a killer. Think about the events three nights ago and the female called Laelamist. Show them the picture once more." Rivka stepped back as the others held out their datapads and made sure everyone was refreshed.

Rivka strolled past, touching each female on the arm and smiling.

Sadness and horror. Confusion and denial. And fear.

Except for one server. Her mind was blank, but she was deathly afraid. Rivka returned to her, gripping her arm. "What do you know about Laelamist?"

An image of her at a table. Alone. Vulnerable. Then nothing, as if her memory had been erased. "What is the last thing you remember about that night?"

The server grimaced at the pain of trying to remember. She finally relaxed. "Waking up in the morning."

Rivka wondered at the surprise in her mind as she recalled seeing blood on her clothes with no idea how it got there. The Delfino covered her face with her hands.

"What's your name?"

The employee next to her answered, "Her name is Galepnotess."

"Galepnotess. I'm going to need you to come with us." Rivka nodded at her people. Tyler stepped up, but Rivka waved him off. "Red, Lindy."

Rivka wanted her best and most physically capable people to secure the one she had designated as a suspect. But she lacked conscious thought in her mind about the crime, only *post facto* evidence.

"Back to *Wyatt Earp*," Rivka ordered. She bowed her head to the assembled group. "Thank you for your assistance. Because of your help, I think we'll be able to wrap up this case fairly quickly."

Red and Lindy held the server's arms and headed for the door, waiting to go through until Rivka gave the word. She checked to make sure everyone was with her, Clodagh, the three pilots, Tyler, and Sahved. Dery jumped off Red's shoulder and flew into the rafters, weaving between the heavy hanging lights.

"Get down here!" Red snapped.

Lindy glared at her husband before jumping in. "Come on down, sweetie." She waved and smiled.

The server tried to run but made it only a half-step before Red tightened his grip on her arm, lifted her, and slammed her into the wall. She crumpled to the floor. Red checked her pulse.

"Just stunned," he announced, picking her up and throwing her over his shoulder.

"Dery." Lindy grew more intense by the moment since all eyes were on her. Rivka's patience was wearing thin.

"You can catch up," Rivka said and stormed out the door with Red close behind her. The pilots remained with Lindy while Clodagh, Tyler, Sahved, and the SCAMPs rushed after the Magistrate.

"Fucking hell," Lindy muttered. Dery dropped, almost falling. Lindy caught him and wrapped him tightly in her arms to keep him from flying away again. He started to cry. "We have to go," she told him.

Aurora, Ryleigh, and Kennedy closed around her as they ran after the Magistrate, catching her within fifty meters. The catcalls from the queue stopped when they joined the group. Rivka nodded at Lindy, lips pressed into a hard line.

A faint mirror of the line where Rivka questioned the balance between families and a hard job that took its toll.

They needed daycare on board *Wyatt Earp*.

Red was carrying a potential killer, and Rivka was thinking about daycare.

"Clodagh." Rivka crooked a finger at the chief engineer and led her to the side, where she whispered, "You're in charge of making sure we have daycare. I don't care if we have to hire someone or what. We have the space. I can't have what just happened ever happen again. Give me options that keep us all safe."

Clodagh nodded. "You can consider it done. Aurora already asked about it."

"You mean, we could have avoided this?"

Clodagh frowned. "We could have."

Rivka grumbled, making it sound like a growl, then disappeared into her thoughts.

Tyler walked next to Red, keeping an eye on the unconscious female. He checked her pulse and respiration. "She should have come out of it by now," he said. "Straight to the Pod-doc. Let's see what's going on."

Chaz and Dennicron walked along, keeping to themselves while they intently observed the group's dynamics. As they approached the ship, the outer hatch opened, and the ramp extended.

"Magistrate," Chaz said, pulling her aside while the others boarded. "What did you see in her mind that caused you to act?"

"A void. Nothing, like her memory had been wiped from the point she noticed our victim."

"A memory sweep, a worm to find units stored outside of chronological parameters. But that's not a technique that works on flesh-and-blood brains. Has this individual been off the planet?"

"That's what we're going to look for, but I suspect what we find is going to send us back to Square One."

"What do you mean?" Chaz and Dennicron leaned close to catch the answer.

"I'll keep that to myself for now. We need to see what we can learn from Galepnotess. Prepare a warrant, find her place, and search it. I want the clothes with blood on them. Is it our victim's?"

"On it, Magistrate!" Chaz and Dennicron were better when they had a defined series of tasks and a well-stated goal.

A loyal crew. The ability to travel anywhere and everywhere. And a serial killer.

One among many, but this one, she knew, was Jack the Ripper.

CHAPTER SEVEN

In Orbit Above Delfin Prime, Wyatt Earp

"How long is she going to be in there?" Rivka waited impatiently for Tyler's prognosis. He leaned over the control panel, studying the numbers.

"A concussion but not severe. The Pod-doc is fixing it. It takes a little longer since we don't want to juice her, make her a super Delfino." The ship's medical professional stepped away from the control panel and crossed his arms. "Patience is a bitter cup from which only the strong may drink."

"You laid that on me once already." She looked down her nose at him.

"Obviously, you found it compelling and wanted more. Otherwise, I wouldn't be here, would I?"

Rivka crossed her arms to mirror his pose, an old interrogation technique. "I like having you around, even if you *were* shaking your moneymaker in front of those women."

"I was working it."

"At least you didn't get pelted with bills," Red said, stepping into the cargo bay to join the others. "Clevarious let me know she's getting close." He pointed at the Pod-doc.

"Where's Junior?" Rivka asked.

"He's where he won't interfere with me doing my job. I'll apologize for both of us, Magistrate. This is me, and I was embarrassed. You know that takes a lot, but we almost lost control. That doesn't work for me." He gestured at the Pod-doc. "Is she the killer?"

"I need to speak with her, and we need to research her movements over the last eight years. I'll withhold judgment until we have more facts."

A familiar odor wafted through the cargo bay. Rivka wrinkled her nose. Cole walked in, carrying a small package that he dumped into the waste chute.

"That was some visit to the planet, huh? Please don't make me leave the ship, Magistrate. That was bullshit. Unmitigated bullshit."

Rivka checked the panel. The Pod-doc continued to churn away. She returned her attention to Cole. "Was that a dirty diaper?"

"What else would it have been?" Cole looked into the overhead storage to examine the powered combat suits.

"Afraid of the scary women?" Rivka asked.

"Yes." Cole turned to Red for support.

"I'm with him," Red agreed and jabbed his thumb at the former Bad Company warrior.

Rivka nodded. "I would be, too. No one should be subjected to that, but in a quick check of their laws, it seems that men are sexual objects, and it's legal to cop a feel. Clothes-tearing, not so much. They don't have monogamous-type relationships here. It's like the Belzonians. That was some craziness. I hope Cory is doing well."

Attention drifted to Terry Henry's and Charumati's daughter Cordelia Dawn. Cory was gifted with the ability to heal using the nanocytes that coursed through her blood. She could redirect the energy into wounds through her fingertips. She had studied to become a doctor to use more traditional methods of healing. She had also joined the Federation's ground force, which was made up of Belzonians and run by her brother and sister-in-law, Kaeden and Marcie.

The Pod-doc signaled that the cycle was finished, and the lid popped. Tyler opened it the rest of the way to help Galepnotess out. She caressed his face. Rivka tapped her foot hard enough to make it sound like a war drum.

Tyler directed the Delfino toward the Magistrate.

Rivka took her hand and asked, "Why did you try to run?"

She shook her head. "I don't know. It was like a voice from outside screaming at me. I had to listen to it."

Rivka saw exactly that in her mind: the emotion of receiving an order from someone in charge, undeniably commanding.

"Interesting. You're safe now, Galepnotess. We won't harm you even if you try to run again because there is nowhere to go. We're on board my ship, *Wyatt Earp,* and we're in space, in orbit above Delfin Prime."

"Can I see? I've never been off-planet." Her eyes grew wide and she searched for a window, only finding small portals on the cargo bay door. She gestured for approval to look.

Rivka motioned to her. "Join me." They walked to the closed ramp, where the Delfino looked out, fascinated with the limited view. "C, turn the ship so our guest can see the planet."

The stars crossed behind the ship until the planet came into view. "Call me Gale," the Delfino said while staring out the portal. "It's amazing."

If she hasn't been off the planet, how could she have committed any of the other murders? Rivka asked her team.

Dupe? A lackey? An intern? A disciple? Sahved offered. He was following the same train of thought Rivka had earlier.

We shall see. I'm taking her to the conference room. Sahved and Dennicron, meet us there.

"It's beautiful," Gale reiterated before turning away from the view. "I think I'm in trouble, but at least I got to come to space." She hung her head and went where Rivka told her to.

Red hovered nearby, guiding her out of the cargo bay and toward the conference room. He directed her into the seat farthest from the door and stepped back to remain between her and the Magistrate. Lindy appeared in the corridor and took a position, blocking access to the rest of the ship. A blaster hung at her side, and in her hand, she had a stun baton, the type they used on bistok.

"Dery?" Rivka asked.

Lindy was straightforward and simple in her reply. "Taken care of. You have our full attention."

Rivka muttered a thank you but felt bad that she'd had to crack the whip when she was the one who'd encouraged her people to embrace their families.

Whee! Floyd cried into all their minds.

"Mostly," Lindy clarified.

Rivka embraced the love for her ship and her people within the chaos of her mind. The chaos of a village within the constraints of a metal hull, fighting off the void of space beyond.

The Magistrate winked at Lindy before taking her usual seat. Sahved and Dennicron worked their way inside and sat where they could focus on the Delfino.

"Tell us about that night, starting with when you arrived at work," Rivka requested.

"I work the mid-afternoon shift and generally leave right after the rush. That works for me since I don't have to stay up too late." She clicked her tongue and licked her lips.

"Water," Rivka requested. Lindy waved at someone in the corridor, looking between the conference room and the person she'd summoned. Tyler stuck his head in, and she whispered in his ear. He hurried away. Rivka tried not to sigh. "Please continue."

"It was the usual crowd, not too surly. We had a few men in, no more than average."

"What does that mean?" Rivka planted her elbows on the table and laced her fingers together. She rested her chin on a hand hammock.

"The usual. I don't know, forty or fifty ladies and three or four men."

Red coughed before clearing his throat. He shouldn't have been surprised. He'd seen it first-hand.

"The men, were they regulars?" Rivka asked.

"Same ol', same ol'. If you have a pad, I can write down their names."

Sahved cued up his datapad and slid it across the table. She tapped in the names, and Clevarious translated them into Standard. Sahved shared them with Dennicron, who didn't blink as she broadcast the data across the Singularity.

"No one strange or new, not even a woman? A foreigner, maybe a little exotic?"

Gale's face twitched as she tried to remember. "A couple days prior, I think. I feel…I…" Her eyes rolled back in her head, and she started to convulse.

"Holy shit, she's possessed!" Red jumped forward and seized her in a bear hug, pinning her arms to her sides. He dragged her out of the chair and lifted her until her feet dangled. She twisted and squirmed until she could reach Red's groin, then grabbed it and squeezed with unnatural strength.

He grunted and tried to get her to release him by spinning and slamming her into the wall, but she avoided the worst of it. Red's arms relaxed and she jumped free, her eyes on fire. Gale snarled like an animal. Rivka readied herself, but Lindy was already there. She jammed the stun baton into the Delfino's chest and activated it, holding it there until she contorted and flopped to the deck, unconscious.

"Tyler! Get in here. Figure out what the hell just happened."

"Back to the Pod-doc for you," the doctor remarked.

A woozy Red tried to stand while Lindy flipped the female over and gripped her arms by the elbows. She picked her up and lugged her toward the door. The doc hurried ahead to open the Pod-doc and have it ready. Dennicron followed Lindy out.

Rivka helped Red upright. He groaned, bent over, and puked.

"That was pleasant." Rivka side-stepped the splatter. "Damn, Red. You have to take it easy in the chow hall."

Sahved finally stood. "She was not herself."

Rivka looked at him. "That much is certain. What happened and how is what I'm interested in knowing. And how did she manage to out-muscle Red? She wasn't juiced with nanos, not like us."

"I expect Man Candy—"

"Tyler," Rivka corrected.

"This is how I know him. I expect the *doctor* will find that she experienced an adrenaline surge, the likes of which are not replicable naturally except through extreme emotional and physical distress, neither of which she was under at the time."

"Astute, as usual," Rivka noted. She had thought the same thing. "Mind control. We've seen it before, but we're in space. She should be free of any influence."

"Embedding a suggestion in the cognitive unconscious is a well-established technique, but not to the extent where the recipient becomes an expert in combat techniques. I think we'll find that the moves she used are not taught on Delfin Prime."

Rivka started to pace. Red fell into a seat, groaning as he held himself. "Once again, Sahved, I'm sure you are correct. It begs the question. Who are we looking for, and what are they doing to these people? Can they make this suggestion remotely, or do they have to do it in person?"

"There is a great deal we need to research and too many unanswered questions. I'm sure our suspect will revert to a crazed attacker every time she is pressed on the identity of the foreigner." Sahved remained seated. He looked at the names Gale had typed into the datapad. The Singularity had already returned a full workup on them. Not a single one had ever left Delfin Prime.

"Clevarious. Hypnosis. From what I understand, a subject has to be susceptible for a suggestion to take root."

"From the exhaustive research on hypnosis I've done in the last twenty-four seconds, I would say you are correct," the SI replied.

"How susceptible are the non-criminals of Delfin Prime to becoming murderers? And then being strong enough to take Red down? He outweighs her by fifty kilos of pure muscle."

"That's me. All kinds of awesome," Red mumbled, using the conference-room table to help him stand upright. "I'm calling next on the Pod-doc." He paced down the table, knocking the chairs aside as he moved. When he made it to the corridor, Lindy was there. He threw an arm over her shoulder so she could help him.

"That makes my eye twitch," Sahved said. "Odd. But back to our original point. This is far more than a simple hypnotic suggestion."

"Then what is it?" Rivka wondered. "And no matter the answer, our challenge in finding this individual, or dare I say, group, has just multiplied exponentially."

Sahved shook his head. "I don't understand."

"Is there a group of individuals who are brainwashing others, turning a secondary set of victims into Jack the

Ripper? Victims who select other victims. What did Chaz and Dennicron find at Gale's residence?"

Clevarious answered, "They never left the ship. We lifted off before they could leave."

"Oh, crap. C, call the constabulary. I need to make a request."

CHAPTER EIGHT

"Chaz and Dennicron, please prepare to depart the ship the second we touch down," Rivka said through gritted teeth.

"I can't believe they wouldn't search her place," Red said through a mouthful of energy bar, something he liked to eat after a Pod-doc treatment.

"Nothing they don't do surprises me. Their naïveté should be refreshing, but I find it grating since I need answers. Right fucking now!"

"But we've intercepted the murderer, haven't we?" Tyler asked.

Rivka started to pace again. "I find it unfathomable that over a hundred and fifty murders conducted in an identical manner can go unsolved. But maybe that's because there are over one hundred and fifty different attackers who are replicating a single barbarous tactic. How hard would it be to find that person when it's not one person? Impossible if the authorities are looking for links and patterns. That's why. No one would ever find them. The only reason we know is that I could see what was in her mind, or rather, what wasn't there that should have been."

"That's fucked up," Red offered.

"We are still looking for one person," Tyler suggested. "The one who is brainwashing these people. And he or she went planet to planet; otherwise, there would be an overlap or a divergence. But there wasn't."

"That makes our lives easier, but the timeline for visiting these planets predates the murders, and the individual might have departed before the first murder was committed. Dennicron, please pass that to the Singularity to broaden their search."

"Yes, Magistrate." Dennicron kept it simple. Calculations and parameter refinements were the status quo for SIs. They never slept. They never rested. Their digital minds always worked. The SCAMP bodies needed no rest either. Perpetual motion, powered by the Etheric.

Chaz hurried past on his way to the airlock. He walked with a hitch in his step.

"Chaz?"

"Yes, Magistrate?" He stopped and faced her. One shoulder was hunched higher than the other.

"Did your body get damaged? I'm not aware of any physical engagements."

He straightened. "Dennicron and I agreed that you are correct. I should not have sex with any Delfinos as they could all be suspects. As such, I'm attempting to make myself less attractive."

Red snorted. He moved closer to make sure he didn't miss any of Chaz's explanation.

Rivka couldn't blame him. "I applaud your effort. I'll tell

you in no uncertain terms that it won't work. Have you ever heard the phrase, 'Go ugly early?'"

"I have not." He consulted with Dennicron before clarifying. "*We* have not."

"It doesn't matter. Less competition for the broken ones. Your only hope is to go in fast and get out just as quickly. Run if you have to, as if a bear is chasing you."

"Or a pack of wolves," Red added helpfully.

"Yes. Quickly."

Chaz's eyes focused on a point over Rivka's shoulder. Dennicron stared. They came back to the present simultaneously.

"I'll get the rope!" Chaz declared before running off. Dennicron sprinted in the other direction.

"What do you think that's about?" Tyler wondered.

Red shook his head.

"I have no idea, but I'm sure we'll find out soon," Rivka replied.

Wyatt Earp didn't touch down. Instead, the ship hovered over the complex where Gale's residence was located. Small single-family homes interconnected through a meandering park-like setting. It looked far more upscale than where the victim lived. But the victim lived within walking distance of the city center, an attractive draw for the younger crowd.

Chaz popped the airlock. After securing one end of his rope to a tie-off point inside the airlock, he tossed the rest of the coil into the warm Delfin air. He faced the people watching him and smiled.

"It's all me, baby," he exclaimed and dove headfirst out

the open hatch, deftly catching the rope as he sailed downward.

"Gerominow!" Dennicron called, following Chaz's lead. The thin rope slapped off the hatch frame and tightened.

"'Geronimo,'" Rivka corrected the empty space inside the airlock. She was first to the hatch, leaning over to see where the SCAMPs had gone.

They spiraled downward to land on the miniscule space by Gale's front door. Chaz hit the ground and crouched, jerking his head left and right before tactically moving to the door. He gave Rivka the okay sign as Dennicron dug into the lock.

"Why's he acting like he's a secret agent?"

"Clevarious, can you tell me what videos Chaz has been watching?"

"He has recently watched the entire forty-five-film library of James Bond."

Rivka looked at the others by moving her eyes, not her head.

"Does that explain it?" Red asked.

"It does." Rivka pulled back inside the ship and brought up the external view in time to see Chaz and Dennicron enter the house and close the door behind them. Clevarious changed the imaging from visual to millimeter-wave to track the movements of the two. "C, please limit what Chaz watches to only wholesome entertainment."

"Can you define that for me, please?" the ship's SI requested.

"I cannot. If it's going to make him weird, then it's not wholesome."

"I'm going to tell you that I'm on it and that it'll be

taken care of while simultaneously doing nothing of the sort."

Rivka rubbed her temples. *Chaz, can you stop being weird, please?*

You'll have to define that, Chaz replied.

That's what Clevarious said.

Clevarious is smart. Stand by. We've found what we need—bloody clothing.

Rivka's eyes shot wide. *Look for anything suggesting she met with someone over the past few weeks. A diary entry. A note on the fridge. A scrawl on a whiteboard.*

We shall leave no table unturned, Chaz replied before closing the link.

Tyler leaned close to Rivka and whispered, "You seem scattered, making jokes in the middle of a train of thought."

Rivka shivered. "It's a defensive mechanism. Jack the Ripper gives me the creeps. Gotta keep it light. Otherwise, I would go insane."

"That bad?"

"I've never told anyone. It's the one case that gives me nightmares. And here we are, face to face with the essence of a killer who's as old as civilization itself. A man who preys on women, punishing them with a sharp blade."

"You aren't afraid of any man." Tyler puffed out his chest and straightened to his full height.

"Not a man, an idea. Coming out of the darkness to hunt the unwitting, the innocent." Rivka shrank, smaller than her usual self.

The rope went taut and jerked across the coaming as someone pulled themselves up.

Red held Rivka back and dipped his head out to take a

quick look, then gave the people in the airlock the thumbs-up. The others cleared the airlock, leaving Red alone to help the SCAMPs through.

Rivka crossed her arms and leaned against the interior bulkhead. She wanted to see what Chaz and Dennicron had found. The blood would be confirmation, but she was more interested in any social engagements with an off-worlder, the charismatic stranger.

She had no doubt that this individual would entice females of all races. Whether through wit or charm, he had a hook.

Rivka had high hopes that the Singularity would find likely suspects, if not through a name, through facial recognition. Unless they disguised themselves.

She had to fight to keep from spiraling into the despair of her fear that she wouldn't find him.

That Jack the Ripper would roam free.

Clevarious interrupted her thoughts. "Magistrate, Grainger is calling for you. It sounds urgent."

"I'll take it in my quarters. Have Chaz and Dennicron set up the evidence in the conference room and have Sahved take a look. I'll be there as soon as I'm finished."

Tyler and Red each gave her a thumbs-up.

"What?" Rivka grumbled.

Grainger stared at her. She stared back.

"Get some coffee, and I'll call you later."

"I don't need any coffee. It's almost nighttime here. I'm

sorry, G-dog. This case is grating on me, and we just started."

"G-dog? Never mind. I was looking for an update, hoping you would finish fairly soon. The planet that has petitioned the Court of Redress? We need the Singularity to chair the court, and that means we want a physical presence because it's the first one. The potential combatants need to have something other than a computer screen to look at."

"That means you want Chaz, Dennicron, or both, and maybe even the ambassadors, Ankh and Erasmus."

"All would be best."

"I'd love to tell you that you're getting none of them, but that's not my call. It was taken out of my hands when I so adeptly established the Court of Redress."

"So adeptly indeed," Grainger agreed. "I've sent a packet to Ambassador Erasmus to populate the board, with a mandate for a physical presence no later than two days from now."

"Completely out of my hands, it would seem."

"You deserved the heads-up," Grainger told her softly.

"This case. We've linked one hundred and fifty-three murders. I think it's a single killer who uses the power of hypnosis or something like that. Those who commit the murders have no recollection of what they've done. They haven't been caught because the killer imparts the knowledge they need to select the victims and locations and stays out of the limelight. Our search for a murderer has become far more complex." Rivka saw that her hands had clenched into fists. She tried to relax them.

"I'm assuming you caught the one who committed the latest. What did you see in his mind?"

"*Her* mind. Nothing. It's blanked out, but when pressed, she became violent to the extreme and even took Red down. Lindy had to stun her back to her caveman days."

Grainger bit his lip and stared at Rivka as he grasped at understanding. "So, the perp not only plants the seed to commit the murder and teaches them how to do it, but the perp also teaches them how to fight well enough to take out a professional bodyguard? All through the power of hypnosis? That's a little hard to believe. Is there a chip in her brain or something else to drive that level of knowledge? The hypnosis angle probably wouldn't stand up in court, Barrister."

"I know. That's why we're on edge here. We don't know what this individual is capable of. He or she or it could have visited here years ago to plant these seeds. But, and I have to believe this, they are in a position to watch what's going on. Why do this and never get to see the results of their handiwork?"

"Ticking time bombs waiting to go off." Grainger looked off-screen, nodded, and turned his attention back to Rivka. "Gotta go. Talk with Erasmus and see what you can work out. Don't they have their own ship tethered to *Wyatt Earp*?"

"You know they do. Makes parking this monster a bitch, but we need the space, it seems. Just wait until we bring the pilots' boyfriends on board. I'll have an army at my command!" Rivka pumped her fist before deflating. "And none of that will get me one step closer to whoever is doing this. Let me talk with Ankh and Erasmus and see what we can do."

Grainger waved, and his screen went blank. Rivka dropped her hologrid and stood to stretch. She felt like she'd been sitting for hours when she knew it had only been a couple minutes. She blew out a breath to help her collect herself before heading out. Rivka found Ankh waiting in the corridor.

"Ambassador," Rivka started.

Ankh waited, unblinking.

"You have to chair the Court of Redress on Garbolglox, which hosts a race of elephant-like creatures. It seems they have come to an impasse and are ready to fight, but the standing government petitioned the Federation under the new law to stop the civil war. And you need to go right away. I know you know I already know that you already know this."

Ankh cocked his head. Rivka smiled, then ducked as Dery flew by.

Whee! Floyd cheered and ran after the boy.

"She looks like she's losing weight. Dery is good for her," Rivka commented.

"We will be leaving momentarily for Station 11 to collect Chrysanthemum. We recognize that Chaz and Dennicron are a critical interface to help resolve your current case, so we will not ask them to accompany us. They also need to continue their training if they are to earn the titles and responsibilities of a Magistrate."

Ankh walked away without another word. He turned and entered the cargo bay, where a gentle bump signaled the arrival of the front end of his ship, *Destiny's Vengeance,* since that was the only part that would fit. He'd board and they would leave, Gating to Station 11 within seconds of clearing *Wyatt Earp*.

Like that, Ankh and Erasmus were gone.

Red waited outside the conference room. He nodded at it to indicate that Chaz and Dennicron were there.

She rubbed her hands together. "Come on, progress!"

Spread out on the table were various items of bloody clothing. A shirt. Trousers. Even a purse. At Rivka's look, Chaz told her what she suspected. "It is the victim's blood." He pointed at a knife at the far end of the table. "And that's the weapon that was used, although it's been cleaned. Not completely, though. More of the victim's blood was tucked between the blade and handle. As for the other part of our search, nothing. There is no reference to anyone she hasn't known for years."

"She saw a stranger in her mind, but he was obscured as if in a dream," Rivka recounted. "No details at all. What's your conclusion regarding this evidence?"

"Galepnotess murdered Laelamist with a kitchen knife in a blood-splattering frenzy of strokes."

"I'll buy that. Thank you for not saying 'rage.' I'm not sure we can determine her emotional state at that moment. I expect it was calm, and a casual observer would have suspected nothing until the slashing began. And the big question: what do we do with her?"

"She's a murderer, not the *actus reus*, but the *mens rea*, her mental state, suggests it isn't a capital crime because we can't show premeditation. Motive, means, and opportunity. We have no motive. That suggests the crime is manslaughter. She should be locked away for a minimum sentence on the order of seven years." Chaz looked at Dennicron. She closed her eyes, smiled, and nodded.

Chaz beamed.

"I suggest Gale is every bit as much a victim as Laelamist. Nothing more than a puppet reacting to the master's machinations," Rivka offered. "Now, what do we do?"

Chaz and Dennicron stared at each other as they communed. After fifteen seconds, Dennicron replied, "We don't know."

"We keep her in custody until such time as we're confident she's not going to axe-murder all of us in our sleep."

"Why would we give her an axe?" Chaz adopted his best confused expression.

Rivka smacked her lips and waited, something Ankh would have done until they reoriented themselves.

"How long," Chaz asked, "do we keep her in custody?"

"I believe the programming will run its course in three weeks and a couple days, but we'll wait as long as it takes."

Chaz stood. "Do we have that much time?"

"Good question, Chaz, and I don't have the answer."

"Will you look into her mind?"

"I will. It's critical to get the best information since we're dealing with something we haven't had to before. She's been turned into an intelligent drone. We need to know how that was done if we're going to stop this from happening again."

Chaz gathered the items on the table into a self-sealing bag and squeezed the air out before locking it tight. He scanned in a label and documented it. "If that'll be all,

Magistrate, we need to tend to another issue the ambassador left for us before his departure."

Rivka nodded and waved over her shoulder. The SCAMPs took the evidence bags with them.

"What to do with a victim who is also a killer..." Rivka muttered.

CHAPTER NINE

In Orbit above Garbolglox, *Destiny's Vengeance*

As required by our guiding document, we have the number necessary to listen to the grievances and mandate what is necessary to end this dispute. As per the Court of Redress' charter, as the junior member, Chrysanthemum, you will chair the court, Ankh explained while the ship spiraled toward the planet's surface.

"Of course," the SCAMP said aloud. "I believe we should speak using the less efficient verbalizations for the benefit of the contestants."

Ankh stared. Erasmus spoke through the runabout's sound system. "Contestants? Is that what we call them? I would not have so surmised."

"Potential combatants?" Chrysanthemum offered.

"Contesting parties?" Erasmus said. "But again, 'contest' is a game, and 'parties' could imply fun and games. Why did humans create such a language? They could be far more efficient through a complete overhaul. We could offer our help, but they would reject it because they hold on to the strangest things."

Ankh nodded. "You could not be more correct. They would reject their own improvement because it did not come from them. We accept their dichotomous existence."

"Petitioners!" Chrys declared.

Ankh stared. "Yes. That will work. Once we step onto the planet, we will be required to remain until the court has reached a conclusion and provided guidance to both petitioners."

"What if they don't agree with our ruling?" Chrys wondered.

"The charter suggests we deliver a hard dictate with deadlines. If the planet descends into civil war, then it will be as if the court had not attempted a resolution to forestall hostilities."

"I have little confidence that we'll be able to resolve their issue. I shall endeavor to do my best in this most august role. I'm honored you asked me." Chrysanthemum bowed to Ankh.

"There was no one else available," Ankh admitted. "With the shift in production from Yoll to the new facility on Rorke's Drift, there is a delay in making more of our people self-mobile."

Chrys inclined her head. "Regardless, my feeling of being honored remains. We shall persevere, and with this Court of Redress being the first, we shall set a precedent for those who follow. It is incumbent upon us to be magnificent."

Erasmus chuckled through the speakers. "Such an indeterminant term. Your time on the space station has assimilated you well. Which makes me wonder, at what point will we transition from our digital world into a less scientifically accurate existence? We shall study this as more of our citizens transition into SCAMPs."

"We will always collect and analyze data. I will reserve judgment. Singularity citizens are better than that." Ankh moved toward the hatch.

"Because we are already magnificent?" Chrys called after him.

Ankh stopped and turned to face the SI. "Your words stab me in the heart. Do you have your humor protocol turned up to ten?"

"My humor protocol goes to eleven." Chrys flashed her fingers to show ten and then held up one finger by itself. "It goes to eleven."

Ankh's eye started to twitch. He blinked rapidly to clear it.

"We may have erred," he said, then turned to the hatch and waited for the ship to land.

In Orbit Above Delfin Prime, *Wyatt Earp*

"Adrenaline in her system was the maximum her body could produce," Tyler explained. "She was running at one hundred percent. Not just that, the Pod-doc recorded her brain function running at fifty percent."

"Fifty percent? So, her mind wasn't working, but her body was." Rivka rubbed her chin.

"No!" Tyler threw his hands out as if he were trying to stop a train. "Our brains usually run at ten to fifteen percent, twenty on a stellar day. Fifty is genius-level."

"I didn't touch her before she was unconscious." Rivka scowled at the missed opportunity.

"Before she was restrained, you didn't want to be anywhere near her. A genius killing machine. Probably best if no one touches her from here on out."

Rivka groaned and threw her head back to stare at the ceiling. "There are people just like her on fifty other planets. How come they haven't continued their killing sprees?"

"There might be a time component, but I believe a kernel remains. Anyone who gets too close reactivates the murderer within."

"Ticking time bombs, but only if the authorities close in." Rivka closed her eyes and focused on her breathing. "Do we ignore it to hopefully avoid the risk, or do we track down the killers on each planet? To answer my own question, we don't have that kind of time, and right now, we don't have enough information to help the locals corral our unwitting victims. The first victims don't know, so there will be no external signs, and the second victims are long-dead."

Tyler pulled Rivka close and hugged her tight.

Rivka lifted her head up and spoke softly. "C, how much time do we have before the third murder is to take place on Kamilof Redoubt?"

"Fifteen days, Magistrate," Clevarious replied.

"Plan to leave eleven days before the next murder is expected. I want to wait until the date for the second murder on Delfin passes, just in case there's more than one primary victim." Rivka extricated herself from the dentist's embrace. "Workout?"

"As long as it takes to get big like Red." Tyler flexed his bicep. "I have a ways to go."

"You better not get big like Red." Rivka assumed her power stance, her fists jammed into her hips.

"Am I not free to be what I can be? Am I a kept man? That's it, isn't it? I'm a kept man!"

"Of course you're free, but you wouldn't like getting that big. Do you want to spar with Red every day and twice on the days that end with Y? You'd be in the Pod-doc more than the settlers of Rorke's Drift. I'm getting changed. Please join me, Man Candy." Rivka winked in reply to the look Tyler gave her.

"More defensive mechanisms?"

Rivka lost her smile. "What else would it be?"

"Your undying love for me, your partner in crime?"

"And that. Fine. I'll marry you. I just don't want to be caught off-guard, not at my best when the killer raises his ugly head. You didn't see the look on Gale's face when she went into her frenzy. Every primary victim will have that same intensity. We all need to be ready." Rivka hesitated. "Correct that. All the females in this crew need to be ready."

"That wasn't a proposal," Tyler corrected, "but fine, I'll marry you if that's what you want. Shock and horror. How does the killer get his thrill if he's not the one doing the killing?"

"No need. I'm fine with the man-candy arrangement. There has to be a way to close that loop, get the thrill with minimal risk." Rivka snapped her fingers. "Clevarious, what's the chance that our perp downloads the imagery of the attack from the murderer's mind?"

"Judging by what I know of *your* abilities, I think it highly likely, which means…"

Rivka interrupted. "Which means the perp is on the planet after the last attack. Refine, revise, and research, C."

"I shall coordinate directly with the Singularity and get back to you soonest."

"I love me some Vitamin C," Rivka replied.

"Is that me?" Clevarious asked.

"It is. I like it. Everyone needs a nickname."

"Like Man Candy." Tyler looked down his nose at Rivka.

"Exactly like that. Call me 'Magistrate.' I think it's fitting. And find me that bastard who's programming the minds of the innocent on these fifty-two planets."

Floyd bounced around the room, with Dery darting down to tap her on the head before flying back up.

Whee! Floyd kept crying until she was too tired to run. She wallowed her way into a small pile of Red's clothes and curled up. Dery hovered over her briefly before descending to the deck. He folded his wings, took two unsteady steps, and settled against Floyd's soft furry belly. Both were soon fast asleep.

"I guess Floyd will live with us now," Lindy stated in a way that didn't invite discussion.

Red nodded. He was learning. "Emissary to the animal kingdom."

"I like it." Lindy leaned back and closed her eyes. "What did you do with Gale?"

"She's in the padded room until after she's supposed to commit the next murder." Red paced around the room, light on his feet for a big man. Neither of the sleepers stirred. "How many killers do we have onboard this ship? It's like a flying Jhiordaan."

"A couple killer AIs and that red chick. That's all."

"Red chick? That'll be me after the next time we go to Azfelius."

Lindy laughed. "If you keep it up, you'll make that a self-fulfilling prophecy. Red gets neutered by peaceful faeries, news at seven."

Red chuckled and stopped to lean against the wall. "I hope we get to rough this fucker up."

"Language," Lindy said softly.

Red rolled his eyes. "You have got to be kidding. This is me we're talking about. Dery will hear much worse!"

"Where? On Azfelius with the faeries, the kindest and gentlest creatures in the universe, who happen to be your mortal enemies? The only way he'll hear worse is if he keeps listening to you."

"The sentiment remains. Someone is turning good people into killer drones. The Magistrate will find them, and we'll beat the shit out of them. I bet they aren't used to people fighting back."

"Not people like us, husband of mine. The Magistrate only needs to point the gun. We'll pull the trigger."

"I like it when you talk sexy. Maybe we can spar a little," Red suggested.

"Sleeping children." She pointed at the two on the floor. "I'm taking a nap."

"I'll be in the workout room."

Lindy waved from the bed, her eyes closing as she reclined into her pillow. Red eased out and carefully closed the door.

He started for the workout room, then turned back toward Engineering. He walked in and worked his way into Ankh's work area. Once inside, the hologrid rose.

"Continue where we left off, please. Etheric transdimensional physics, energy transfer through the Gate continuum..."

CHAPTER TEN

Delfin, Major City Adelfino

"My name is Bristamor, and I've been assigned to your team," the Delfino constable said with little emotion. Standing taller than the Magistrate, she looked with red eyes at Rivka and her team.

"You found the body?" Rivka got straight to the point.

"I did not, but I was first on the scene after the report. The one who found the body and called it into the station has been institutionalized. She's catatonic, from what I hear."

"But you are not as harshly affected."

"We deal with very little real crime in the constabulary, but it is my life's work, so I've taken to studying my profession in case I ever want to go to the stars. My partner is a liaison officer from Kamilof Redoubt. I want to do this—work with other planets—so I work hard to understand crime. It can be disturbing to those who are not mentally prepared."

"That is the truth," Rivka said, stopping herself from

reaching out, ostensibly to shake her hand but also to take a quick look into the Delfino's mind. She avoided taking the shortcut, deciding to take Bristamor at face value. "Our next step is to watch Galepnotess closely. Our suspicions are that tonight, she will transition to a cold but murderous rage."

"How did you come to that conclusion?" Bristamor leaned close to catch every word.

"We have tools that aren't available to the average investigator. That's why we're here. Tell me, why weren't you assigned to the team initially? You don't seem squeamish, and in a case like this, that's important."

"I was at the end of my series. Five days on, two off. Some work four and three."

"In most other places around the galaxy, when there's an earth-shattering crime like this, law enforcement adopts a different shift. It's called 'day on, stay on.' That is, everyone works until the perp is caught."

"'Perp,' as in 'perpetrator.' And they don't take time off?"

"No, but there's a lot of burnout. Still, we could have used you from the outset. If you do a liaison tour on a planet outside the Curveyance system, you will have to be prepared to pull long hours, to work when you're tired, and to miss a meal or two."

"Are you going to work me like that?" Bristamor seemed genuinely curious.

"We might. Are you okay with that?" Rivka touched her on the arm. The Delfino was trying to hide her excitement at being asked to join a real investigation conducted by professionals. "You'll get experience no one else on Delfin has."

"I believe it. Count me in. Give me a blanket, and I'll sleep in the corridor whenever we're between shakedowns."

"Shakedowns?" Rivka wondered.

"You know, when we toss a suspect around, rough them up." At Rivka's look, she revised her jubilation. "I guess not. This is a great opportunity born of a tragedy. The focus from now on is finding this individual."

"Therein lies the rub," Rivka said softly. "We have the individual who killed Laelamist, but she's not the murderer."

Bristamor stared at the floor and mumbled to herself before clenching her jaw in the determination to learn more. "I don't understand, but you do. Teach me."

"I'm going to hand you over to Chaz and Dennicron, citizens of the Singularity who are on my team. They'll explain what we have so far."

The SIs stepped up and introduced themselves.

"You look human."

"Thank you!" Chaz beamed.

"Sentient intelligences. The bodies are artificial, but the intelligences within are unique, individual, and recognized life forms," Rivka explained.

"That is crazy!" Bristamor blurted. "But a good-crazy." She recoiled at her seemingly callous words. "Can you feel things?"

"Very much so," Dennicron interjected, glancing at Chaz. The Delfino's body language suggested she wasn't used to dealing with a male. "Let's talk about the evidence we've collected so far and how we've arrived at our conclusions. And then, most importantly, what we're doing to interdict our perp before they kill again."

Bristamor shook her head and shrugged. She didn't understand, but she was willing to learn. "Call me 'Bristy,'" she said as they walked away.

Rivka went to the bridge, where she reclined in the captain's chair. Yapping preceded Tiny Man Titan's arrival. "Come on up, you loud-mouthed bastard," Rivka told him. A large orange cat followed him in. "Wenceslaus. Where did you come from?"

He didn't answer. He couldn't be bothered with the inanities of humans. He had three different ships he called home and multiple sentient life forms he considered worthy to worship him. Outside of that, his needs were simple.

Rivka stood outside the brig, the padded room onboard *Wyatt Earp* that they used as a holding cell. A screen outside the door showed the room's occupant sitting on a bench with her head in her hands.

Galepnotess.

"Why are we pulling her out of there? She's harmless as she is. Seeing women might trigger her," Red suggested.

"And that's what I need. I need to see this personality when it manifests. I need to see it in her mind since that could give me insight into who is behind this. I want to see their face. If it's there, that is. If we do nothing, we'll get exactly that, nothing. We have no blades, so she can't slash anyone. You can take her in a straight-up fight, can't you?"

Red steeled himself, knuckles white around the stun baton he carried. Lindy had one too. Chaz, Dennicron, and Bristy waited behind Rivka.

Lindy counted down using her fingers. Three. Two. One. She punched the button, and the door slid open. Red rushed in, pointing the baton at the Delfin female. Lindy maneuvered to the side. Both batons hummed with energy. They burned power, but it sent a message to Gale.

Rivka wondered how the Delfino would react.

Gale covered her face with her hands and screamed into them, refusing to show her eyes.

"Come with us, please," Rivka said.

They waited while Gale's breathing slowed. Red and Lindy took their fingers off the buttons to stop the hum, but the bodyguards remained where they could block the Delfino if she turned violent. She finally looked up, eyes puffy and red from crying.

"I'm a monster," she muttered. Rivka moved close and Red tried to block her, but she wove her way around him. Red loomed over her while Lindy stayed at her elbow.

"Let me help you up. Take my hand," Rivka offered. The Delfino took it and pulled herself to her feet.

Rivka felt only a great foreboding, a depression into which Gale was swirling.

"Come with me," Rivka held her hand and led Gale to the door. Chaz and Dennicron moved aside, leaving Bristy standing there by herself.

As if a light switched off, Gale disappeared. A new entity appeared, ice-cold and already in a rage. *Too many witnesses. It's time; they all must die.*

The images flashed through Rivka's mind in a millisecond. She started to let go, but Gale was already moving. Red was fast and Lindy was faster, but Gale left them both behind.

Bristy stood as if frozen in time. The only evidence she was aware was that her eyes widened almost imperceptibly. Gale extended and stiffened her fingers, dipped, and drove her hand toward Bristy's abdomen.

But no one was faster than the SIs. Dennicron's hand shot out and caught Gale's wrist. Chaz caught the other arm as Gale raised it to strike the offending interloper. She struggled to free herself while the SIs tightened their grips. Red and Lindy jabbed the prods into Gale's back and fired heavy charges into her torso. Even as the Delfino vibrated under the energy, she fought to free herself from the iron grips that held her arms. She tried to jump up to kick, but Chaz and Dennicron forced her toward the deck.

Gale screamed from her very soul, ending with a heart-rending screech as the stunners delivered her into peaceful unconsciousness.

Red handed his prod to Rivka before dragging the female back into the room. He left her on the padded deck as he forced everyone out and secured the door.

"Did you get what you wanted?" he asked.

Rivka nodded. "It was like nothing I've ever seen before. This individual exists for the sole purpose of taking lives."

"Like the old-time vampires," Red offered. "Say, one with telepathy but not upgraded to do away with the need for blood, but modified to be sated by the sight of blood."

The Magistrate closed her eyes. "That's one possibility. How could anyone get a thrill from this? From turning someone like Galepnotess into an ice-cold killer?" She pointed at the closed door. "How?"

"We seek the answers within the greater consciousness of the Singularity," Chaz replied. "Even with refined parameters, it is taking time."

Rivka waved her hands and shook her head. "I'm talking about the psyche, a psychosis with no remorse for the actions taken. But something drives this individual. Maybe it's as simple as the thrill of the kill. Maybe it's deeper, but eight years suggest that if this was the start of a greater attack on civilization, it would already have happened. The modus operandi is established and repeated with a minor deviation on the third murder to take place between two and three weeks."

"Which means two weeks is up tomorrow, opening a week-long window in which a primary victim will murder a secondary victim on Kamilof Redoubt," Dennicron remarked.

Rivka headed toward the bridge and shouted, "Kamilof Redoubt, best possible speed!"

Bristy looked at Dennicron. "I guess we're not going back to Delfin."

She shrugged, smiled at the effectiveness of her subroutine, and shrugged a second time. "Tell Clevarious your size and what clothes you want. He'll produce something for you right away. Do you have quarters?"

"Yes, but I have one question. No, two. No, many. Who's Clevarious, and why do you have a cat, a dog, and that other creature on board?"

. . .

Garbolglox, the Neutral Zone, a Swamp Between the Two Major Cities, *Destiny's Vengeance*

"We are not going out there," Ankh stated and crossed his small arms. Rain pounded down. The *Vengeance's* landing struts had disappeared so deeply into the muck that the ship's hull nearly touched the surface.

Four elephant-like creatures waited in the downpour, rain rolling off their skin. It seemed well-suited for the purpose.

The beauty of evolution.

"They'll fit in the cargo bay." Ankh waved his hand. "Go out and get them to walk around."

"I thought I was the chair of the court?" Chrysanthemum asked.

"You are once the Court of Redress is in session. Right now, you are serving at the pleasure of the ambassador." Ankh walked away without explaining further.

The SI understood perfectly. She raised her chin and strode into the rain. At the bottom of the ramp, she bowed to the primary and the deputy of each twosome.

"We shall retire to the cargo bay of *Destiny's Vengeance*," she explained.

"Why?" the Garbolglox Mahout, the recognized government's elected leader, asked in a booming and gruff voice.

"So we can be most comfortable," Chrysanthemum replied.

"We are fine out here. This is where we'll talk."

"The members of the Court of Redress disagree. Where we meet is our choice to make sure we find a neutral location for all parties involved. We have determined that the ship's cargo bay is sufficiently neutral to serve our purposes."

"Bullshit!" the Mahout said.

"We like it. Lead on," the rebel leader stated, throwing his head back to let the rain wash over his face.

"Thank you for liking it, but that is irrelevant to the Court of Redress." Chrysanthemum knew the parties would each like whatever the other party didn't. She led them around the ship, up the narrow cargo ramp, and into the cargo bay. Ankh waited inside.

He dipped his head slightly to greet them.

"There are supposed to be three," the Mahout growled.

A speaker on the small table before Ankh came to life with a crackle. "I am Ambassador Erasmus from the Singularity. Ambassador Ankh, Chrysanthemum, and I are the three members of the Court of Redress. Chrysanthemum will be the chair of this court. This arrangement is not subject to the mediation process."

"Bullshit!" the Mahout roared. Ankh stared at him without blinking until he sat down with his deputy standing behind him. The other party, Flaygolax, took a seat immediately to the Mahout's right.

"Bullshit!" The Mahout jumped to his feet and pointed an accusing finger at Flaygolax. "The right is a position of honor. These traitors cannot sit to my right. *EVER!*"

Ankh stared, but the Mahout crossed his arms and refused to budge. "You're at *my* right, the position of honor," Erasmus offered.

"Bullshit!" Flaygolax stepped toward the Mahout.

"If you two come to blows, we will eject you from the ship, preferably out the airlock while we're in space, and we'll be on our way. This entire planet will be blockaded and declared off-limits for all trade and transportation."

The two huffed and glared and refused to sit down. Chrysanthemum moved a fourth chair between them to make sure neither was on the other's right. They calmed and took their seats.

"According to the petition, the legacy government is being contested by a growing number of voices. So many that democratic processes have been suspended," Chrysanthemum recited.

"Bullshit!" the Mahout shouted once more. "Violence is not a diplomatic process. We maintained the sanctity of the system!"

Ankh stared at the oversized Garbolglox, who was storming within the confines of his seat.

"To preserve the system, you suspended the system," Ankh explained softly. "I suggest this failure is yours and yours alone. Convince me otherwise."

"Innocent until proven guilty," the Mahout shot back. "You're pro-rebel. You're no better than these criminals. We'll have nothing to do with these proceedings. And just so we're clear, fuck you, stubby."

The Mahout stood, bowed, and walked out.

"See? This is what we're up against." Flaygolax threw his hands up and pointed at the Mahout's and his deputy's retreating forms, then repeated the gesture with his hands. He shook his head wildly, and his oversized ears flopped. Although they had faces like elephants, the Garbolglox did not have trunks; otherwise, his would have flopped back and forth.

Flaygolax sauntered away as if he'd won the battle of wills.

Ankh stared at their backs. "The humans make it look so easy."

"This process is not based on logic. There are moves and countermoves while we have not yet entered the game." Chrysanthemum crossed her arms and stood as if watching, but she was already calculating her next exchange.

"Sometimes Rivka punches them in the face," Erasmus offered helpfully.

Ankh looked around the cargo bay. "I hope I don't have to do that. I can't reach their faces."

"I will have a device built to extend your reach." Erasmus immediately started engineering the equipment for the maintenance bots to build, then stopped. "Can you impart enough energy to make it effective?"

"No. Please delete that tactic as an option. We shall have to outmaneuver them. We are a billion times smarter than the average Garbolglox. This should be child's play."

"As Rivka has told us many times, it's not the science but the art that makes the difference."

"Art makes no sense to me, Erasmus."

"Me neither, my friend. But this is science. Everything is science. Even art."

"I am a work of art," Chrys said, standing back to show off her body.

Ankh maintained his emotionless expression. "Your body is a masterful example of what science can accomplish."

"And I look good doing it." She smiled, and with a

thought, she closed the cargo ramp. "When will we summon them for a new meeting?"

"Two hours," Erasmus replied. "That is too short a time for them to go anywhere or do anything that matters, but long enough for them to contemplate their contentious attitudes and how those are holding back the process."

"Masterful," Ankh noted.

Chrys raised one eyebrow, then touched a finger to her face to make sure the chosen eyebrow had responded to her command. She lowered her hand and addressed the two ambassadors. "We shall see."

CHAPTER ELEVEN

Kamilof Redoubt, Primus Crenellation, the Capital City

Red was first off the ship, their standard procedure when arriving at any planet. Rivka waited in the airlock until he gave the signal. She headed out along with Dennicron, Sahved, and Bristy. Lindy pulled up the rear. The others remained on the ship.

"Have you worked with anyone from Kamilof before?" Rivka wondered.

"Funny you ask. My partner when we responded to the murder call was a blue."

"Was?"

"We change partners every shift. Can't have people growing too comfortable with each other. That could lead to decisions that might not be as smart as they could be. Need fresh blood to keep the creative juices flowing!"

"You sound like an admin trying to sell the team on a stupid idea."

Bristy's face fell.

"There's efficiency to be gained by working with the

same team. And when it all goes to hell, you know they have your back. If Delfinos dealt with more criminal violence, they'd see that for themselves."

"I understand. We aren't used to this…any of this. I laughed at my colleagues because they are flower-carrying fanatics, always smelling roses. I considered myself harder than them, but even I don't get the magnitude of it."

Red nodded at a waiting vehicle. It was like a bus but lacked a roof or a structure above waist height.

"It's okay not to be jaded from having seen the worst sentient beings can do to each other. Don't be jaded. We will solve this, and that means removing the perpetrator from access to any other flesh-and-blood creatures."

"You're going to kill her?"

"Her or him, whoever the perp is. We have to be sure, but the crime is capital under Federation law."

"Gale. I mean Gale."

"She's every bit as much a victim as those murdered. The only difference is that she has to live with what her body has done. Her mind will probably never be able to reconcile itself with that. We're in a race against time to find our puppeteer, but—and this is why we keep doing what we do—when we catch the perp, it makes us feel pretty damn good. Future victims will never know their lives were in jeopardy. Normal. We return things to normal."

Red watched for threats while the group boarded the vehicle.

"As simple as that?" Bristy asked.

"Simple as that. It's best if people don't know how dangerous the universe is."

"Like us? Like all the people in the Curveyance system?" Bristy nodded at her statement. "I think I understand. The blues won't, though. They're more squeamish than us reds."

"Is that how you refer to each other, blues and reds? And the people from Trieste are yellows?"

"You got it."

The vehicle accelerated away and headed into the city. After a short distance, it lifted into the air and soared above the traffic. Rivka gripped the rail tightly. It was a smooth ride, but there were no seatbelts.

At her scowl, Red started to laugh. "I know what you're thinking, Magistrate. Everything we go through, and you're going to get killed by a vehicle without restraints."

"Was it that obvious?"

Red favored her with his best Ankh impersonation.

"That reminds me; I wonder how they're doing? I wish Chaz and Dennicron could have gone with them to give them a perspective that leans more toward the law." Rivka made eye contact with Dennicron. "But I need you guys here, even though it's tough. Prevent a war or stop a serial killer."

"The needs of the many," Dennicron started. "I am pleased you have such confidence in our abilities, but the Court of Redress is made up of three members, two of whom are the shining lights of the Singularity. To think I could supplant such minds is beyond my comprehension."

"When you put it that way..." Rivka replied, but she had known Ankh for a long time. He would be challenged to a greater degree than usual. He could not engineer his way out of this problem. Garbolglox, massive creatures who would try to intimidate him with their size. But he'd trained with Red for this very day. She smiled, knowing he was better prepared than he would have been two years prior.

The vehicle arrived at a blocky government building with a heavily decorated exterior. Its façade suggested an art museum.

"Is this it?" Rivka asked.

The driverless vehicle wasn't going any farther.

"I think so," Bristy said. At Rivka's side-eye, she looked away. "But I'm not sure."

"I'll verify," Dennicron offered.

The Magistrate waited for her to get off the bus, but she didn't move.

"Yes, this is the correct address for the Kamilof Crime-Fighters."

"That's what they're called?" Rivka groaned. "We used to be so much better prepared when we came to a planet. What happened?"

"I had all the information available, Magistrate," Dennicron replied. "Our travel takes little time, and you have a lot going on. How are you feeling after Gale's attempted battery?"

"That could be the first time you have asked how I was feeling." Rivka inclined her head toward the SI. "I feel fine, thank you. But that is a good question for Bristy."

All eyes turned to the red female. "Me, too. I look forward to this. What are you going to share with the Kamilofs?" She redirected the conversation away from herself. Rivka noted that for future reference.

"Everything we know. They have another murder coming, and it's going to be committed by a local."

"That will cause them significant distress, well beyond what they have already experienced." The vehicle slowly moved away once the last member of Rivka's team stepped off. They waited on the sidewalk for a moment. "Let's get this party started."

Bristamoor looked at Lindy for clarification. "It means it's time to go," Lindy stated.

Sahved eased up next to Rivka. "There have been two murders here following the slasher's MO, but Kamilof Redoubt is handling it themselves."

"Every planet is different, Sahved. With the apparent connection, we can assume jurisdiction. Now we meet with the authorities to make sure they see it that way, too, and give us the personnel we need to assist the investigation." Rivka stopped at the door. "Right now, we don't know if this individual is on this planet or has already moved on or is on Delfin and will be back to see the handiwork. We don't know very much, and that bothers me."

"It bothers all of us, Magistrate. The perpetrator of the crime is not the criminal. Had I not known you and your mental abilities, I would never have considered these crimes to be connected despite their similarities, except through a cult where three murders, one week between the first two and two to three weeks before the last is the rite of passage to join. I believe you are correct in that this is a cult, but of a single personality."

Red opened the door and headed inside.

The size of the building was misleading from the outside. It was a single floor with a garden-like atrium filled with soaring vines on the inside. Workstations integrated with the foliage peppered the area, with blue individuals working at them. On Rivka's arrival, a Kamilof with wrinkled skin and rheumy eyes tottered toward the group. Red intercepted her.

The individual threw her hands up and announced, "I am Konstantina."

Red studied her for a moment before allowing her to pass. He watched her closely until Rivka took her hand and smiled.

"I'm Magistrate Rivka Anoa, representing the Federation. There have been two horrible murders here, and we believe they are connected to others we've seen. And we believe there will be one more." Konstantina's initial joy at meeting a visitor morphed into a deep sadness.

"I am the chief administrator of the Crime Fighters. We have done our best with this and believe we have a suspect but can find no means or motive."

"Excellent. I'll need to talk with that individual. Are they in a holding cell?" She looked through the area but could see nothing resembling an enclosed space.

"We don't have such things here. I suspect she's at work."

Rivka clenched her jaw. "Can you give us a ride to where that is? It's imperative that we talk with her immediately or sooner."

"Yes, yes." Konstantina furrowed her brow in momentary confusion. "We're not used to such things or such urgency." She waved to an officer at a desk.

With a bounce in her step, a much younger version of the chief appeared. "Alexandra," she announced on arrival.

"My daughter will take care of you." Konstantina turned to Alexandra. "Recall the shuttle and take them to

Bindovrich Metals. They wish to speak with Olga Mendeleeva."

The young woman nodded while smiling before returning to her workstation.

"You have a fabulous facility here." Rivka tried to steer the conversation in a happier direction. Just like the Delfinos, the Kamilofs were easily upset by the rigors of a murder case.

Terrorizing those ill-equipped to deal with it. Maybe that was the plan.

Konstantina brightened. "Isn't it, though?" She caught Sahved watching her. "Oh, my!"

He introduced himself. Rivka pointed to the other members of the team, who did the same. She found it easy to blame the case for forgetting her manners, but it wasn't that. Her internal voice had injected poison. She didn't respect people who couldn't protect themselves.

Rivka turned away and blinked to push back the tears of revelation. She lived to help those who couldn't fight the galaxy's evils. Even though Konstantina was the chief of the crime-fighting unit, it wasn't meant to deal with this crime. And they didn't need Rivka's pity. They deserved plaudits for building a society where the worst crime was a parking ticket.

Sahved stepped in. "I'm a Yemilorian. I'm from a ring-world that rotates. It's not a sphere, like almost every other planet out there. We can see our whole planet no matter where we are. Not being able to is disconcerting, but I'm learning to live with it."

Konstantina screwed up her face and tilted her neck back to look up. "Yemilorian. You are the first I've met, but we don't get many outsiders here." Her face darkened as if a storm cloud had settled over her head. "Is that why the Federation is involved? You think it's not someone from the Redoubt."

"Astute," Rivka replied, nodding at Sahved. "We think a single individual is brainwashing locals to commit these crimes. We're looking for the power behind the violence."

"Oh, my!" Konstantina exclaimed for the second time.

"And it's going to happen again unless we can stop it. That's why it's critical that we talk with your suspect. We will do everything in our power to prevent another murder. Everything."

Konstantina had to sit down. Sahved helped her since Rivka was hesitant to touch her and get emotionally flooded by the chief's distress.

Alexandra motioned for the group to follow her.

"We'll be on our way," Rivka told Konstantina. "We will keep you apprised of our progress."

Red waited beside her, ready to follow the others out. Lindy was on the other side. Konstantina was momentarily inconsolable. Rivka didn't wait.

The clock was ticking.

She hurried out the front door and onto the waiting shuttle.

CHAPTER TWELVE

Garbolglox, the Neutral Zone, a Swamp Between the Two Major Cities, *Destiny's Vengeance*

Chrys had rearranged the chairs and table to put the two leaders across from each other, so neither would be at the other's right. It wasn't optimal since now they would face each other as if in a competition, a sparring match.

"Summon the parties, please," Chrys announced.

Ankh just looked at her.

"Being the chair sucks," she added.

"Is that your scientific opinion?" Erasmus asked.

Chrys contemplated the question. "The science of the art. If it gets worse, then it'll suck ass, but for now, it just sucks. The chair has no power."

"You have all the power," Ankh replied. "To reconcile this case and make a determination, that is, but Erasmus and I don't respond when given orders. That is a simple fact. The Magistrate knows this. You have now learned it too."

"I thought…" She stopped. "Maybe I didn't think it all

the way through. The flesh-and-bloods are a bad influence. They dispense with logic and science at the most inconvenient times. I have fallen victim to their vices."

Chrys winked at Ankh before strolling to the cargo bay door and opening it for the waiting Garbolglox.

Ankh's eye twitched. He held a finger against it to stop the spasms.

Within his mind, Erasmus chuckled. *That one is an enigma, my friend. Sentience follows its own path, does it not?*

So I'm learning. How long has she been on the station that pollutes the minds of SIs? Ankh asked.

Eighty-four days.

That's apparently long enough to wipe all of her previous personality programming. She's going to get us kicked off every civilized planet because they'll think we're all like her.

Now, that is funny. Erasmus roared with laughter. *Who knew you had such a delicious sense of humor?*

"It's about fucking time!" the Mahout bellowed as he stormed up the ramp.

"Sit right fucking there." Chrys pointed with her whole arm. "*Right fucking there.*"

The Garbolglox looked her up and down, grumbling as he took his seat.

"And your seat is there, Flaygolax."

"I thank you kindly, young female." He sauntered by her, turning his head away as he passed the Mahout. Flaygolax made a show of sitting down, tossing his head as he did so to send water spraying over the area.

"Please don't do that again," Ankh said softly.

Both Garbolglox bellowed their laughter as if trying to

outdo each other. Ankh closed his eyes and hoped that through the force of his will, they would stop.

They didn't until Chrys pounded a fist on the table. "Enough!" She slammed into her chair, which squealed under the weight of her SCAMP. "I'm calling the Court of Redress to order. Present with us today are Flaygolax of the Workers' Union and the Mahout, the Federation-recognized leader of Garbolglox. We're here to talk—"

"Bullshit!" Flaygolax yelled.

"Bullshit!" Chrys shouted into his face. "Sit down and shut the fuck up."

He glared but capitulated.

"We're here to talk about the issues standing between a peaceful resolution of the frictions that are taking you toward war. We will accept nothing less than peace. How we get there is up to you."

"Status quo," the Mahout said the instant she finished.

"Which is what helped us arrive at this point." Chrys held her hand toward Flaygolax's face to keep him from responding. This was her show. "We will not accept a war, and we will not accept the status quo. I've reviewed the provided documents, and the first offer on the table shall be mine."

"You know nothing of Garbolglox," Flaygolax growled. "Your solutions are meaningless."

Chrys switched to the Garbolglox language and recited one of their sayings. "'*If the way forward is unclear, keep going until it is.*' You both know this saying. Well, we're moving forward at my pace until clarity manifests."

They both grumbled. The Mahout was going to call bullshit, but she silenced him with a look. "The workers dictate the hours and working conditions. The government will stay out of the factories."

The Mahout slowly stood and walked off the ship. His deputy was covered in mud, as was Flaygolax's. The Mahout's deputy sported a growing red lump on the side of his face.

"Boys," Chrys called.

The Mahout snarled at his deputy and stormed away.

"You can go too. Be ready to come back first thing tomorrow morning."

Flaygolax crossed his massive arms and nodded at his deputy. "Why do you think he'll come back?"

"I'm freezing all the government accounts. No credits change hands. No one gets paid. Under such conditions, society will break down in twenty-eight hours."

Flaygolax was unfazed. "In the workers' minds, society has already broken down. We'll be here at dawn."

"Thank you. Can you do something for me, please?"

"What is that?" He eyed her conspiratorially.

"Don't ever yell 'bullshit' at me. It would be embarrassing for an off-world female to yank your spleen out through your nose."

She faced the swamp through the cargo bay opening. Bursts of static discharge punctuated the white noise of the incessant rain. The green growth paled behind the ghost-like mist cast by the precipitation. After Flaygolax left, Chrys secured the cargo bay and headed to the interior of the ship. "Until the morning, gentlemen." She waved at Ankh and Erasmus over her shoulder.

I think there has been a benefit to her development in working with the flesh-and-bloods on the space station. She is convincing with her delivery, no matter how bizarre the statement. Pulling an internal organ through an individual's nose is impossible, yet Flaygolax accepted the attempt at intimidation. I think he will comply. She has broken both of them. We must review this session. Her actions were wildly illogical while simultaneously delivered perfectly. How did she arrive at such a course of action? I have to know! Erasmus insisted.

We shall find the primary subroutine, but I would caution against its use. We cannot logically determine its efficacy. The Magistrate had referred to this methodology as throwing mud at the wall to see what sticks. I think it is abhorrent. Ankh stared at the door Chrys had gone through. *But one cannot discount her results.*

She wasn't guessing. Her moves were calculated, and each one delivered exactly as intended to modify the behavior of the antagonists. Yes, my friend. Isn't it wonderful to have such intelligence in the Singularity?

I, for one, Ankh replied, *do not look forward to tomorrow and the unintended results from her actions.*

Ankh stood from the empty table and grumped his way back into the ship while Erasmus' laughter filled the back of his mind.

Kamilof Redoubt, Primus Crenellation, the Capital City, Bindovrich Metals

From a catwalk, the group looked over a factory floor where sparks flew and heat shimmers billowed toward the ceiling.

"I've sent someone after her. She'll be along shortly," the

plant manager said. Old and hunched, he came across as someone with one foot in the grave.

"You're male," Sahved blurted.

The old Kamilof cackled, but it ended in a raspy cough. Rivka eased away from him.

"It's not contagious, dear," he offered, waving a rough hand. "I broke through the glass ceiling, but it's taken my whole life. I fear I won't be around long enough to enjoy it. Maybe other males will follow my lead into upper management."

"Maybe," Rivka replied. After ten minutes, the runner returned by herself. She whispered into the manager's ear.

"It appears she didn't come into work today," the old manager announced.

"I need to talk with her friends right now. Who knows where she goes when off work?"

"I don't know." The old Kamilof was flustered. Rivka fought her temper. She wasn't used to her law enforcement contacts melting down when hard work needed to be done.

Bristy took the runner by the arm and pulled her to the side. "You can feel the sense of urgency. We need to find Olga right away. Very bad things will happen if we don't." She spoke like she was talking with a child.

The runner straightened her shoulders and set her jaw. "I understand. Follow me." She jogged away. After a surprised look from Bristy, Rivka gestured for them to follow. She was done with the plant manager. "We'll be in touch if we need anything else," she called over her shoulder.

She caught up with the Kamilof crime-fighter. "Alexandra, we'll need an all-points bulletin issued, a manhunt to find Olga Mendeleeva. I believe she's in the final moments of selecting and cornering the murder victim."

And while we're chasing her, we're not looking for the real perp, Dennicron noted.

"I'll call the station," Alexandra agreed while continuing to run with the group.

Workers on the shop floor dove out of the way when they saw a group of off-worlders running down the main aisle. All eyes turned to the strange event within their factory. Someone cried out in pain.

Red and Lindy slowed. After a quick confirmation, Lindy bolted toward the sound.

An accident. Taking one's eyes off heavy machinery in operation wasn't the best way to work. Lindy rejoined the group, shrugging for their edification.

The runner pointed at an area. The workers watched with interest as the aliens descended on the team that worked with Olga Mendeleeva.

"Olga," Rivka started. She took a breath. "I'm Magistrate Rivka Anoa from the Federation. I'm conducting an investigation, and Olga Mendeleeva is a key witness. She doesn't know that she is, but her information is extremely time-sensitive. We need your help. Where does she spend her off-time?"

A slight female raised her hand, and Rivka tipped her chin toward her. "She has a cute little apartment in the Borisova District. Seven Ulitsa Solntse."

Rivka turned to Alexandra, who had not yet called the station. "Please call the station right now and get people to her apartment. If she's there, cordon off the area, make sure she stays inside, and let us know so we can go there. I need to talk with her personally. Anyone who sees her needs to detain her until we can take custody," the Magistrate whispered harshly.

Alexandra nodded but remained where she was.

Even Sahved was frustrated. He summoned the runner. "Where's the nearest comm terminal?"

She pointed at the wall not far away.

"Much obliged." He took Alexandra by the arm and guided her toward the terminal.

Dennicron looked at Rivka. *Clevarious is aware and has made the necessary notifications.* Wyatt Earp *is on its way. Chaz will lead a small team into the facility.*

Tell Cole to armor up.

"I wouldn't have guessed that," Red blurted.

"It'll keep the lookie-loos away," Rivka explained. She turned her attention back to Olga's nearest coworkers. "Where would she go at night? Was she a partier, a head-to-the-club kind of girl?"

Someone in the back laughed. No one spoke.

"Please, help us."

"She didn't go to clubs. She's in charge of the buck-buck team."

Rivka looked at Dennicron for an explanation, but the SCAMP shook her head.

"Bickrack," a bulky Kamilof corrected. "It's a game that combines intellect and physical power through a series of team challenges. Each contest is different, so training involves problem-solving and a lot of muscle development. Olga might be at the gym. I think there's a match tonight."

Many of the others nodded in agreement.

The helpful Kamilof wrote the address on a scrap of sheet metal. Dennicron looked at it and handed it back.

"Don't you want to know the address?"

"I have it memorized. I have a special mind that retains vast amounts of information."

"Thank you for your help," Rivka added. "I have another, more sensitive question. Where would someone find prostitutes?"

Blank looks greeted Rivka's question, which gave her the answer she needed.

Sahved returned with a nod. Alexandra frowned and stared at the floor. Bristy wrapped an arm around her shoulders and guided her away from the group.

"Where would Olga go for sex?" Rivka pressed.

The bulky female snorted. "If we knew the answer to that, we'd all be getting some!" The Kamilofs laughed. One of them nudged Red. He eased away from the group to stand behind Rivka. Sahved joined him.

"Time to go, people." Rivka twirled her finger in the air. "Thank you. You've been extremely helpful." She took one step and stopped. "One more question. Where are the buck-buck matches held?"

"The Bickrack arena is next to the gym. You can't miss it." The group waved and blew kisses at Red, but his back was already turned as he hustled toward the exit.

CHAPTER THIRTEEN

Kamilof Redoubt, Primus Crenellation, the Capital City, Seven Ulitsa Solntse

Chaz strode down *Wyatt Earp's* cargo bay ramp and into the park across the street from Olga's apartment building. Clodagh stopped at the top of the ramp, still inside the ship. She carried Alana, her daughter, while Red and Lindy's son stood on her shoulder, beating his wings to maintain his balance. Her husband Alant Cole clumped past her in his powered combat armor.

Ryleigh and Kennedy halted when they reached the grass and turned as one to face the chief engineer. "We can't do it. What if she's in there?" Kennedy pointed at the building.

Tyler grabbed his medical bag and ran after Chaz.

"Are you sure this is wise?" the SI asked.

"No, but I can't leave you out here by yourself."

Chaz nodded at Cole. "I am hardly alone."

"How's he going to fit inside that building?" Tyler kept

pace. "You weren't going to crash him through the window, were you?"

"There is no other way," Chaz replied matter-of-factly.

"I'm here for you, man. You can count on me."

"You have no weapon." Chaz pointed at the bag.

"You know me. I'm better off without. I'll be fine. You were going in alone, remember. If you were going to be fine, I'll be fine."

"But I cannot be injured by knife attacks. It would take an extremely lucky strike to penetrate my skin, and even then, it would do no damage. I cannot say the same for you."

Tyler shrugged. "Then you'll just have to make sure no one tries to shove a knife into me. Please do so."

"I shall endeavor to persevere." Chaz opened the door to the building and walked through. Cole took a position just outside.

"I'm sure that means something when you convert it to binary, but it means nothing to me."

"Stay behind me," Chaz clarified.

"That, I can do." Tyler followed Chaz around a corner and down a hallway. He stopped in front of a nondescript door that looked like the other doors they'd passed. "How do you know this is the correct apartment?"

"Because there was a map of the building's interior available through open sources, and this apartment was designated for Olga Mendeleeva."

Tyler put a finger in front of his lips. "Aren't you worried she'll hear you?"

"I've already run an infrared scan of the interior. There is no one here." Chaz worked on the panel until the door slid to the side. They entered to find the room of a slob. Dirty clothes were scattered across the floor, and the bed was unmade. Dirty dishes filled the sink. Half-filled glasses stood on tables beside a single lounge chair that faced a video screen.

"Looks like an athlete's house," Tyler noted. "Roommate in college."

"I see." Chaz sorted through items until he found a bloodstained shirt. He used his sensors to examine it. "Blood from both victims is on this shirt. It's like she put it on for the second murder after not bothering to clean it. Maybe she didn't realize it needed cleaning."

"Rivka said a secondary personality takes over or something like that. They don't remember anything from this suggestion and training that takes over."

"Maybe, the fact that she is not wearing the shirt right now suggests she isn't in the grip of the murderer."

"I like how you think, Chaz. That is a positive outlook on this mess. But where is she now? She's not at work, and she's not home. Maybe she has a life." Tyler looked at the pictures on the walls and in frames on the lone bookshelf. Nothing suggested anyone in her life other than her family. "She looks like her mom."

Chaz reported his findings to Clevarious. At the speed of thought, Chaz patched through the ship's communication system to reach Dennicron. They conversed in milliseconds and ended the transmission. "We need to go to the gym." Chaz held up a jersey with a team name.

"Drek?" Tyler made a face at the smell emanating from the cloth. "Who calls their team 'Drek?'"

"Olga Mendeleeva, obviously." Chaz kept the shirt. With

a last glance over his shoulder, he walked out. Tyler made sure the door closed behind him.

"What will we find at the gym?"

"Chances are good it will be our suspect," Chaz replied.

On the street, a crowd had gathered to stare at the suit of armor standing as still as a statue. Chaz and Tyler hesitated the second they found themselves surrounded.

"Magistrate's business. Please let us through," Chaz tried.

"Men," someone whispered before starting a chant. "Men, men, men."

"Gangway, asswipes!" Cole bellowed, the suit's speakers blasting his words. The crowd recoiled, holding their heads and whimpering. Tyler jumped back to escape the noise, throwing himself into the wall of the building. He groaned at the assault on his senses. Chaz grabbed him before he crumpled to the sidewalk, and they hurried across the street.

The cargo ramp appeared out of thin air. Cole backed toward the ship, waving the Kamilofs behind him out of his path. With their wits returning, the crowd collectively gasped at the appearance of the cargo ramp and the interior of an invisible ship. The men climbed inside. The combat-armored warrior turned around and jogged the last fifty meters. Once he was inside, the ramp closed, restoring an unhindered view of the park.

Wyatt Earp lifted into the air and raced toward the gym.

Kamilof Redoubt, Primus Crenellation, the Capital City

"Can't this thing go any faster?" Rivka complained.

"That wouldn't be safe," Alexandra replied.

"It would probably be safer than giving a murderer extra time." Rivka tried to convince the Kamilof through force of will by staring at her, but Alexandra didn't respond. She smiled while watching the city pass by. The vehicle was made like a tour bus, with unhindered views.

Red clenched his fist until his knuckles turned white.

"My partner on Delfin is a blue," Bristy stated.

"We do our best to help our people expand their knowledge, but Delfin is too tame for most of us," Alexandra replied.

The Delfino followed up to answer the question she knew Rivka's team had. "Buck-buck is a game like nothing we have on Delfin. It shows your thunderously wild side. If only we would let our hair down every now and then."

"Your nightlife is rather robust," Rivka offered.

"It is," Alexandra and Bristy replied simultaneously. They both chuckled.

Rivka glanced at Red. He tried not to look at the Curveyance females. They were predators, and he was prey. He'd discovered that he didn't like it. But that was the extent of their aggression.

"What do you say we let the Bad Company know about this place?" Red asked Rivka. "They enjoy the hell out of nightlife, too." He used his fingers to make air quotes around "nightlife."

"Don't you dare." Rivka tsked, shaking her finger at him while the city passed at an annoyingly slow speed.

Red smiled.

"You would have already told them if you could have, wouldn't you?"

"It's a much safer place than Station 11 or other so-called civilized societies," Red countered. "Although, we might have the same problem as they have when their boys go to Torregidor on vacation."

"You want *how* many women to join the crew of the *War Axe?"*

"Not me, Magistrate. And who's to say they'd try to bring them back to the ship?"

"They always bring them home to Mom and Dad because they're good boys, and that's what good boys do."

"Maybe it'll be different out here." Red frowned, but within his mind, the wheels turned.

Rivka looked at the red and blue females. "If you met a man and he wanted to take you home with him to enjoy a monogamous relationship, would you go?"

"What's 'monogamous' mean?" Alexandra asked.

"It means you don't sleep with anyone else." The stadium loomed on the next block. Rivka squinted to see it better. She couldn't see the buildings next to it.

"If I had a man, I'd want him all to myself. Hell, yeah. Are you saying there are available men who are looking for willing and available partners?" Bristy asked. She leaned forward to catch Rivka's answer. Alexandra brought her ear closer and listened intently.

Red beamed at the revelation.

Rivka shook her head before nodding at the stadium. "We'll pick this up later. Olga Mendeleeva, head of the buck-buck team. At the gym, what will we find?"

The Curveyance females looked disappointed at not getting their question answered before descending into the pit of the case. They frowned as the vehicle approached the building. "I've never been to this one, but it should have a check-in area, a changing room, weights, running tracks, a pool, a sauna, stretching mats. This one should have anything you could imagine. What do your gyms look like?"

"About the size of this bus," Rivka replied. "Lindy and Sahved, look for a door around the right side. Dennicron, take Bristy and head around the left side. Alexandra, you're with Red and me, going in the front door. Secure Olga if you see her. Get her away from other people and call me."

The vehicle stopped, and the team rushed off on their assigned routes to secure too big a facility with too few people.

Chaz, where are you? Rivka called.

Just landed in the parking lot behind you.

Rivka stopped when she reached the front door. *Chaz and Cole, get out here. Tyler, be ready in case someone gets hurt. And button up the ship. I don't need another psycho getting on board.*

The cargo ramp lowered, and the two ran out. Cole was still in his power armor.

That'll have to work, Rivka thought, signaling to Red that it was time to go in.

He carried a stun baton loosely in his hand. Club or bistok prod, he was ready to employ it against the Jack the Ripper clone or any psychopath who threatened the Magistrate. He liked the feel of the stun baton. It reminded him of his younger days as an enforcer. Hurt them bad enough that they don't want to get hurt again. They found ways to pay their bills after that. It hadn't been gratifying work, but Red had justified it by thinking they shouldn't have taken loans from the shady individuals he worked for.

A smattering of hard bodies moved throughout the area, enough to entice someone who was out of shape to join. They worked at machines and free weights and in the stretching areas. Behind the counter, a blue female grinned at Red. She twirled her hair around one finger as she delivered her best coquettish look.

He stepped aside to let the Magistrate through.

Rivka introduced herself before asking the all-important question. "Is Olga Mendeleeva here?"

The young female watched Red from the corner of her eye while she casually checked the computer log. "Yes. She checked in two hours ago. Wow! That must be some workout. Drek must not be playing tonight."

"Where is she?" Rivka leaned toward the counter agent.

The Kamilof female backed away and shrugged. She pointed at the gym. "Somewhere in there. Once they've checked in, our guests do whatever they want."

She smiled at Red, who turned away and stalked toward the gym. He scanned the area but didn't see her. "Fire drill?" he called over his shoulder.

"Nothing like bringing them to us." Rivka motioned for the group to stand beside the front door. "You need to activate the building's alarm so your guests can help themselves out."

"I can't do that. There's no emergency." She withered under Rivka's blistering glare.

Rivka held up her credentials. "Under Federation authority, since I am in search of a witness in my murder investigation where time is of the essence, I relieve you of your personal responsibility in regards to the sanctity of the building's emergency system. Now, if you would be so kind, sound the fucking alarm."

"I've notified the other members of the team," Dennicron reported.

A heavy clump outside announced Cole's arrival. Chaz strolled in and took a position next to the door, creating a gauntlet through which all guests would have to exit.

The alarm buzzer sounded softly at first and built in volume so as not to give the people in the building an instant shock. The first guests drifted toward the entryway with questions about what was going on. Rivka answered rather than allow the clerk to blurt the truth.

"An emergency. We need everyone to leave the building. We'll reopen as soon as possible. Move outside, please, and wait for further instructions." Chaz picked up the response to save the Magistrate from having to repeat herself. With Bristy and Red, she headed into the machines and weights area, standing to the side to watch the exodus. She took note of each person as they passed.

Soon the space was empty, but Olga had not exited.

"Looks like we're going to have to root her out." Rivka returned to the entry. "Alexandra, you stay by the front door. Give a shout if Olga tries to get past. Cole will catch her outside. Don't try to stop her yourself."

The Kamilof crime-fighter furrowed her brow and clenched her jaw, nodding tightly.

"You better hide behind the counter. Stay out of sight," Rivka suggested. The blue sighed and rushed around the counter to join the clerk. She knew it wasn't an emergency and wasn't going to evacuate.

Rivka contemplated them for a moment. "Both of you stay down. If you see Olga, start screaming so our person outside will hear you. He has her picture and is ready to secure her."

"What has she done?" the clerk asked.

"She's a witness to a murder, and she's afraid," Rivka replied, unwilling to say more. She gestured for the others to follow. "Spread out and search."

Red stayed with the Magistrate, who remarked, "This would go quicker if you took an area to search."

"That ain't gonna happen. Where you go, I go. We're looking for a murderer, one that kills women. That would be you. I'm not leaving your side."

"Don't be a dumbass. I can protect myself."

"Who's the dumbass?" Red snorted. "I work for Grainger. He'd have my testicles if I left you alone."

Rivka nodded. They entered a changing room and found three Kamilof females showering. "Didn't you hear the alarm?" Rivka shouted.

"Yeah, yeah. Almost finished," a voice cried from behind a curtain. The water turned off and a blue female stepped out, drying her hair with a towel while water dripped from the rest of her naked body. She stopped when she saw Red. "Now, that is an emergency I can get behind." She dropped her towel and shook her hair, sending a spray of water in a circle around her.

Red rolled his head sideways to look at Rivka. "I'm telling the Bad Company."

"I'm up for some bad company!" another voice called, and a second blue female stepped into the main area.

Red nodded at the last shower.

"I'm going to need you to come out here," Rivka said into the last shower. She turned sideways to expose less of her body to a potential attacker and raised her hands in a fighting stance. The water shut off. Red pushed past and stood lightly on the balls of his feet.

"Why does she get all the fun?" one of the blues complained.

The curtain pulled aside to reveal a slight figure. Red pulled a towel off a hook and tossed it to her. Her blue cheeks brightened to cerulean. "Is anyone else in here?" Red barked.

The other two Kamilofs shrugged. One pointed at the shower. "Can't see anything from in there. You look like you could use a shower," she added hopefully.

"I feel like I *need* a shower." Red turned away from the females and scanned the area. One door stood between lockers. It was labeled as a storeroom. A second entryway disappeared around a corner. Red checked the storeroom door on the way to the second entrance. It opened easily to reveal stacks of towels. He closed the door and continued to the other area.

Rivka and Red moved through a hallway that led back into the gym.

There are too many exits. People went out all of them, Lindy reported. *But we could see, and there weren't any that looked like Olga.*

Same from here. Dennicron added. *I secured facial images of everyone from this side and the back side of the building. Olga was not among those who departed.*

Come in and help us search. She's either in here or she left before we arrived. I'm worried about the latter, but we have to confirm she's not here before we expand our search.

The open areas of the gym made it easy to move quickly through, but the facility was immense, with a wide variety of game rooms. Dozens of Kamilofs remained in the building. They didn't bother chasing them out as they went. The alarm had done what they needed it to do.

The group met at the far end, where a glass-walled locker room with clear-view showers stood. "Don't fucking tell me," Red grumbled.

Rivka pointed to the sign that said, Men's Locker Room.

"You don't like a planet where you're on a pedestal, your dangling dino o' doom pointing skyward like a rocket launching to the stars?" Rivka smiled at her bodyguard.

Red looked as uncomfortable as if he had sand in his shorts. "She's not in there, and that means we still have a bad guy to catch."

Rivka's mirth died. "Fun's over. Where to next, the stadium?"

CHAPTER FOURTEEN

Kamilof Redoubt, Primus Crenellation, the Capital City, the Gym

"If she left here on foot, then the stadium is the first place we should look," Sahved replied. "While simultaneously canvassing public transport to see if she was picked up outside the gym."

"If she bailed out a side door, she could be anywhere. Commit the murder and sneak back in as if she'd been here the whole time. She could be anywhere. Stadium, and then we expand outward. She's only doing as she's been trained. Chaz, Dennicron, quick case analysis for situations that might be like this—a daylight attack."

Chaz unfocused as he dedicated his considerable computing power to rapidly analyzing the situation. "Streetwalkers. Red-light districts. Places where women hang out," Chaz relayed. "There is nothing like this situation. Maybe she's not on the hunt and is only getting ready for a match?"

"I hope that's right. Thanks, Chaz."

They walked quickly outside.

Rivka faced the crowd and shouted, "You're free to go back in. You," Rivka pointed to an older female, "please tell the front desk that the emergency drill went well. It's over, and everyone can return to the facility."

Rivka didn't wait for an acknowledgment. She sprinted for the stadium with her team forming around her.

They attained a speed across the half kilometer that would have buried anyone who wasn't enhanced. Bristy was still inside the gym, so they'd do without her.

Chaz and Dennicron ran ahead to check the entrance gates. They were locked, but there was a sign directing players to a side entrance. Chaz pointed and led the way. With the gate in sight, they slowed to a walk.

A gruff guard waited inside the gated area.

"No visitors!" she growled.

Rivka held up her credentials. "Do you know Olga Mendeleeva? I need to talk to her about being a witness to a murder."

"She saw that horrible murder?" the guard blurted. Her shoulders sagged in sympathy.

"Open the gate, please," Rivka insisted.

As the guard reached for the lock release, a blood-chilling scream came from inside the complex.

"Wait here," the guard ordered and turned to run.

Chaz rammed into the gate, tearing it off its hinges. He stumbled over it before dragging it out of the way. Red stepped through. The guard held her hands up.

"Get out of the way!" Red barked.

A second scream came, this one more intense.

The guard's mouth dropped open as she watched the

group pass. A shadow passed overhead as an armored warrior flew by, turned, and started to descend into the stadium, heading for the sound of the scream.

Red stayed beside the Magistrate, ready to get between her and a killer.

They were too late for the victim.

In the walkway beneath the rising stands and the field, a tall blue female choked back a final scream on the team's arrival. She buried her face in her hands and sobbed.

Rivka took her by the arm and gently guided her away from the growing pool of blood and the body that had once been a player. The uniform jersey was shredded from the violence of the attack. Not a Drek player. A different team, one with green and white colors.

"Spread out and find her!" Rivka ordered. Red loomed over her, afraid she would join the search party. After a second glance at the victim, he decided he'd rather be searching than staying at the site of the murder.

"Sahved?" Red pointed at the victim.

The Yemilorian knew what Red wanted. "I'll secure the crime scene and collect evidence. Go find her, Magistrate."

Rivka nodded and pointed out vectors for the others to take. "She will probably still be under the influence of the mind control, so she'll have all of our killer's experience in how to escape, including how to kill. Find her and secure her. Lindy, stay with Sahved."

"You need more people looking. I can protect myself," Lindy argued. Red grimaced, torn. "I'll keep one of you in sight at all times."

"Sahved, YOYO. Go, people!"

YOYO. "You're on your own."

They jogged rather than ran, Chaz and Lindy toward the field and Dennicron, Red, and Rivka back toward the entry area and the numerous tunnels leading around the facility.

The hiss of pneumatic jets announced Cole's arrival. *Nothing on the field side,* he reported.

"Dennicron, this way," Rivka waved her away from the field. Lindy made it to the short fence that separated the spectators from the field.

IR shows people there and there. Cole pointed left and right, one hundred and eighty degrees opposite them.

Lindy pointed in both directions.

One that way and four this way.

"I'll take the one. You have the four." Cole loped across the field. Lindy headed for the players' tunnel.

Rivka reached the guard before they had to turn. "Did anyone come this way?" she shouted.

"Just you guys," the guard called back. "Who's going to pay for that gate?"

Rivka ignored her. She motioned for Dennicron to go left, and she and Red went right. Tunnels led to the field side, others led to stairs to the highest parts of the stands, and still others led to various places in the stadium. Rivka picked the first one, discounting those that went to the field or the stands.

"She's hiding in one of these places," Rivka guessed. The first one they tried had a locked door at the end of a short hallway. Red pounded on the door. After five seconds, he reared back and kicked the handle. The door resisted his efforts to open it.

He pulled a blaster from the small of his back and pumped three rounds into the locking mechanism, then ripped the handle off. The door swung free. Inside, they found a small room with switches and transformers.

"We need someone with scanning capability to cut down on the trial and error. This is a big facility, and Olga will know the best hiding places." Rivka sent, *Chaz, join me, please. Dennicron, continue as you are in that direction. We'll meet around the far side of the stadium.*

Rivka and Red returned to the walkway that circumnavigated the stadium. Chaz hurried into view. "IR signatures," the Magistrate directed.

Chaz nodded as he walked past. He waved off the first three tunnels and stopped at the fourth. "Two in there." He pointed.

Red headed in and tried the door, which was open. He rushed in to find the access to a locker room. Chaz pointed at the next door. Red jerked that one open and jumped inside to find two naked blues in a sauna. Neither was Olga Mendeleeva.

"My apologies," Red mumbled and tipped his head toward them.

"Come in!" one called, stretching languorously.

Red bolted, pulling the door closed behind him.

Rivka looked at him. "Let me guess. Blue females who wanted a piece of the Red Stud."

"Something like that. She wasn't in there," Red clarified.

"Next hotspot. Come on, Chaz, dial it in."

Chaz shook his head. "Doing my best, Magistrate.

Onward and upward." The SI continued ahead but at a slower pace.

Lindy scanned the seats of the massive stadium, guessing that it would hold fifty thousand screaming fans. She entered the access tunnel Cole had pointed out, adjusting quickly to the darkness within. Fifty feet down, a body sprawled on the floor. Lindy ran toward it, holding her stun baton before her since she expected a trap.

A short, heavily-built blue female breathed slowly as if she were asleep, but her leg was twisted sideways, and her arms were under her.

"Hello?" Lindy called. She kicked one foot. No reaction. She caught the female by the arm and flipped her onto her back. As the blue came around, the arm beneath shot upward, and the reflection from a mirrored blade registered an instant before it dug into Lindy's leg.

Lindy's reaction was just as quick. She cracked the wrist with the baton, deadening the attacker's fingers, and the blade fell free. Lindy reversed the baton, jammed the prod end into the blue's exposed midriff, and activated the stunner.

The female's eyes sparked malevolence as she fought against the weapon.

It was Olga Mendeleeva but not her. It was the evil of the real killer. Olga pulled the baton against herself, holding it there while she screamed in fury. Lindy punched her with her free hand and backhanded her as she pulled her fist back for another strike. Olga started to convulse, and Lindy was finally able to pull her baton free.

More spasms, then Olga was still, but in a different way than before. Lindy kneeled and checked for a pulse.

None.

I have Olga. She's dead unless we can get her into the Pod-doc sooner rather than later, Lindy reported.

Where are you? Rivka asked.

Far end of the stadium. Put Wyatt Earp *on the right end of the field. I'll meet you there.* Lindy scooped Olga into her arms and retreated toward the field. When she emerged, she found a visible *Wyatt Earp* settling onto the grass. Cole jetted over top of the ship and landed in front of Lindy. He took the body from her and loped around the ship and into the cargo bay.

Red, Rivka, Chaz, Dennicron, and Sahved appeared at the railing and watched as their suspect was carried into the ship.

The suspect, or rather, the first victim.

"Are you okay?" Red shouted, staring at the blood spot on Lindy's leg.

"Good thing I expected it," Lindy called back, strolling toward the team and making an effort not to limp. Red verified no one was around to threaten the Magistrate before joining his wife to confirm she was okay.

"Sahved?" Rivka asked. "Did you get what you needed?"

Sahved shook his head. "I'll stay with the body until the locals can collect her." He hung his head as he walked away.

"Dennicron, why don't you go with him? And Lindy, you're bleeding on the buck-buck field."

"They should revel in having such blood as Lindy's to

fertilize their grass," Red offered. The wound would close fast. Her nanocytes had sprung into action the instant she was injured.

"Hungry," Lindy said softly. Energy for the nanos. "Whenever we return to the ship."

"You go. Clean up. Clevarious, are you listening? Are the authorities on their way? If not, please summon them."

Yes, Magistrate, the ship's SI confirmed. *They have already been called and are on their way. I've contacted the gym, and Bristamoor will be here momentarily.*

"I'll meet the authorities as soon as I check on Olga. I've got a bad feeling." She walked up the cargo ramp and into the ship. Tyler tapped on the Pod-doc's controls.

"How is she?" Rivka asked.

"She's dead. The Pod-doc doesn't seem to want to revive her. I don't understand it, but I will get to the bottom of it. I wish Ankh was here. He'd know."

Rivka frowned while staring at the lid behind which the body of Olga Mendeleeva rested.

"There are others on this ship who can dissect and translate the data from the Pod-doc," Clevarious noted.

"My apologies, Mister C. What am I missing?"

"She doesn't want to live. Her mind shut down her body in such a way that there was no possibility of bringing it back to life. The nanocytes can regenerate the tissue, but it would only be animated since her mind is completely gone, like a computer memory that has been wiped clean," Clevarious explained.

"That's what I was missing. There's no mind to regulate a repaired body." He looked up, a pained expression creasing his forehead and wrinkling the corners of his eyes. "I'm sorry, Rivka."

"The primary victim. Once her mind was taken over, it was time. Now we need to find out if the same catastrophic shutdown is going to happen to Gale. Red?"

"Pull her out of the brig?" Red left the cargo bay, tapping his baton in his hand. Lindy went with him.

It didn't take long before Red's swearing echoed up and down the corridor. Tyler took a hurried step before Rivka stopped him. "Nothing you can do."

Red and Lindy returned, carrying Gale's body.

"Fifty planets. Did the killer die in every case?" Tyler asked.

"I'm calling them the primary victims. They had no control over what they did to the secondary victims and no control when the kill switch delivered its death knell. Secondary victims died ugly. Primary victims' deaths were no better." Rivka raked her fingers through her short hair. "This leaves us with no leads, no witnesses, no survivors. The fact that Gale is dead suggests there's a failsafe incorporated into the primary victim's mind. If she can't carry out her programming, she shuts down. Same with Olga. When it looked like she was going to be caught, that was it. Game over. I fear for Trieste."

Tyler hugged her, but she remained stiff.

"We better get going then," he conceded.

"I hate to say it, but we've done what we could here, which was nothing. And on Delfin? We stopped two more murders. That's something. Regarding Trieste, I guarantee that bastard is over there right now."

"Not watching the third murder here, trying to get their jollies?"

"I know I said that earlier, but there's no one here, only blues. Only reds on Delfin. Next up, the yellows. How does this fucker blend in? *How?*" Rivka scowled and stormed out of the cargo bay. Tyler called Cole to help him with the body bags.

Rivka stormed back in. "I'm supposed to meet the authorities when they arrive." She continued walking but stopped when Tyler jumped in her way. The fury in her eyes made the dentist shiver.

"Don't let this individual get under your skin. I've been reading up on Jack the Ripper. There is an emotional component to the murders as if he fed off the abject terror. Your rage is filling Jack's black soul. Don't do it. Force their hand by being less reactive, less emotionally challenged. Have a laugh, even if you don't feel like it."

Rivka looked out the cargo bay door at the stadium. "In a different time, I might jump your bones right here, or do you in the middle of the field, but alas, the locals might take offense." She took his hand and squeezed it, the fire behind her eyes replaced by the sparkle of a player getting back in the game. She called over her shoulder as she walked down the ramp, "Get those bodies ready to return to their people and chart a course to Trieste. We have a murderer to stop."

CHAPTER FIFTEEN

Garbolglox, the Neutral Zone, a Swamp Between the Two Major Cities, *Destiny's Vengeance*

Chrys sat perfectly still, servos and actuators shut down, waiting to return to action. She didn't need her eyes open to see what was happening around her. Ankh sat with his eyes closed as well, communing with Erasmus as he did most of the time.

"I need a mate," the SI blurted.

"You'll get nothing and like it," Ankh muttered without opening his eyes.

"So unlike you, but very much like your friend Terry Henry Walton," Erasmus said through the cargo bay's sound system, trying to stay in character for the upcoming morning session with the contending parties.

"Terry Henry speaks without regard to the sensitivity of the listener, but his words are focused like a laser to make the desired impact."

"I think if I get nothing, I won't like it," Chrys replied.

Ankh lifted his head, opened his eyes, and fixed Chrys with his unblinking gaze.

"I'm not supposed to get anything? I'm supposed to just deal with it. There is nothing for me. I am alone, and you're good with that. My wants are none of your business. That's it, isn't it? I shouldn't ask for advice on a thing you don't care about."

"That *is* it," Ankh confirmed.

"We should let the Garbolglox in." Chrys stood and headed for the door.

"Not yet." Erasmus stayed her.

Chrys waited for an explanation, which was not forthcoming. She remained where she was, hand hovering over the activation button. She remained that way for five minutes, then ten.

After fifteen minutes, Erasmus spoke. "They are appropriately angry now. You can let them in."

"Why would we want them angry before we start?" Chrys wondered.

"If they are angry with us, maybe they'll be less angry with each other. A common tenet in political strategy is to unite against a common enemy. Another way of saying it is '*the enemy of my enemy is my friend*.' We need them not to be so antagonistic toward each other."

"I tried that last time by yelling at them. We have reached the same conclusion on a valid way forward for the parties before the Court of Redress. I am pleased with our progress."

"You can open the door now," Erasmus repeated.

Chrys tapped the button and stepped away from the door to stand with her hands clasped behind her back. The cargo ramp dropped to reveal two spitting-angry individuals with two Garbolglox behind each, trying to look unobtrusive so their leaders didn't unload on them.

"What the hell kind of court are you running? Late! Who starts late?"

"The people who are tired of you walking out before we even start. Why should we waste our time? Maybe we just box off this planet and let you kill each other. We'll work with whoever is still alive, if there is anyone and the planet remains sufficiently advanced to rejoin the Federation. If not, then bomb your dumbasses back to the Stone Age."

"You can't talk to me like that!" the Mahout roared.

Chrys held a finger to her lips and waved for them to enter the ship.

The Mahout looked at his counterpart.

"No shit! She can't talk to us like that." Flaygolax threw his hands up.

"No shit!" The Mahout headed into the ship.

Flaygolax smirked when the Mahout wasn't looking and motioned for his assistants to remain outside.

When Flaygolax reached the top of the ramp, he bowed to those at the table. The Mahout remained standing with his arms crossed. His counterpart brushed past and took the closest seat.

"Thank you for seeing us again. I have high hopes that we can make some progress today, maybe even make it to the first kava break. You do have kava, don't you? We love it so."

Chrys searched her memory for a reference to the beverage.

"Coffee," Erasmus clarified. "We have a blend that we hope you will find most enticing."

Ankh stood and left the cargo bay.

The Mahout finally sat. "You don't pull that bullshit on me no more."

"Bullshit!" Chrys shouted at him.

Flaygolax snorted.

The Mahout glared.

"I asked you not to call bullshit. That helps nothing. You act like decent creatures of light, and we'll treat you in kind."

"Creatures of light? Have you not seen our weather?"

Chrys smiled. "As a matter of fact, yes. That is a most excellent point. The creatures of the dark are negative souls whose only goal is to suck the life from those who have one. You both have lives and people who are counting on you. Your actions will shine the light."

"You're not one of those New Age meditation people, are you?" the Mahout grumbled.

"No." Chrys kept her answer simple. "I'm one of the New Age people, but without the meditation." Ankh returned with two cups and a pitcher. He put everything on the table, assuming the Garbolglox would serve themselves. The contending parties looked at each other. Chrys took the pitcher and poured two cups, then slid them toward the Garbolglox leaders.

The Mahout huffed but kept his mouth shut. His big nostrils flared and took in the aroma wafting from the cup before him. He picked it up daintily and took a sip. "Not as good as ours, but close."

If Chrys had adopted a subroutine for rolling her eyes,

she would have used it, but she had dispensed with the expression as useless. She was rethinking her decision when the Flaygolax spoke.

"It is better than the swill we get!"

A veiled threat toward the Mahout or a statement of class standing or a testament to his side's failure to find good baristas?

The Mahout smiled. Flaygolax's pain brought him joy.

"Don't be a dick," Chrys blurted, then ran a diagnostic on her systems. She stared at the wall with a blank expression.

The Garbolglox turned to her.

Ankh was amused by the exchange but didn't show it. He never did. "Gentlemen. We have a strategic agenda, which is to bring peace back to Garbolglox. A more immediate agenda surrounds the first step in these negotiations. The little things. I was advised by Magistrate Rivka Anoa to find the smallest concession that each side could make to break the ice. I ask you, Flaygolax, what concession can you make to the Mahout and the current government?"

Flaygolax drained his cup. "Good kava! More, please." Chrys remained in diagnostic mode, unresponsive to the request. Ankh didn't bother serving them. He had no desire to watch the oversized individuals at the table drink coffee. Flaygolax belched and pursed his lips. "I offer the Mahout one bullet made from the finest silver. He can use it to kill himself."

Ankh's eye twitched. "I'm sure that's not what the Magistrate meant."

"I offer Flaygolax the greatest dildo in the land so he can fuck himself."

Chrys finished her third run of the diagnostic, finding nothing was wrong with her system.

"I'm sorry, what did I miss?"

Ankh changed to direct conversation to expedite the recap. A millisecond later, Chrys was caught up.

"Okay, you two. That's not how we're going to do this. I'm going to offer a final solution, you're going to accept it, or we'll find two decent individuals who are willing to talk like adults."

"You can't replace me!" The Mahout made to stand.

Chrys gestured for him to stay down. He flopped into his chair and crossed his arms.

"Equal pay for equal work. Equal representation. Equal opportunity, Mahout."

Flaygolax pounded the table with a meaty fist before helping himself to another cup of coffee.

"That goes for you, too. With equal pay comes equal work."

"We're not afraid to do the work. Hell! My people are working right now, but they aren't making anything for those clowns."

"No name-calling," Chrys cautioned.

"We're making our own armored vehicles and weapons! What do you think about that?"

The Mahout stared at Flaygolax with no sign of mirth or feigned outrage, only the cold expression of one who has been cheated and wishes for vengeance.

Chrys raised her hands. "Ambassador Erasmus. Can we take *Destiny's Vengeance* over the plant to verify that story, and if true, destroy the newly produced weapons?"

"Wait!" Flaygolax called. The ship lifted into the air,

jerking back and forth to keep the guests off-balance. It evened out at altitude and accelerated. "What are you doing?"

"We're returning order to this world. If you're making weapons, then you've violated the initial agreement between the parties. We will return parity to these negotiations."

"And you're going to be on the ship that delivers that destruction to the army you're building," Erasmus clarified.

Flaygolax hung his head and stared into his lap. "You've kidnapped me," he muttered. "Maybe my people will shoot us down."

"They can neither see nor harm us," Erasmus explained. "I'll project our engagement on a holographic display in the center of this space."

A holo of the terrain below filled the table and above with a detailed and colorful map. The ship flew toward the city, angling to remain distant from the population center. The *Vengeance* zeroed in on the plant and slowed to make a low pass over it. The three-dimensional view of the plant lit up with iconography from the compiled tactical scans. *Vengeance* slowed to a hover and took aim.

"I concede!" Flaygolax shouted.

"It's a little too late for that, don't you think?" Chrys deadpanned. The ship fired a high-intensity laser through the factory's roof and into the completed armored vehicles at the end of the assembly line, leaving those that were only half-finished. Erasmus added an infrared overlay to confirm that no workers had been killed. Hot forms ran away from the impact area.

Vengeance moved to a covered storage area where forty

completed vehicles were parked tightly together. Erasmus chose the ion cannon to destroy the parking lot and the combat vehicles within.

Flaygolax groaned.

"Do you have anything to tell us, Mahout?" Chrys asked.

"We have no new combat vehicles. Our equipment is at least five years old. I invite you to check our garrisons, factories, and roads."

"We will," Chrys confirmed. The holographic display showed the factory disappearing in the distance as Destiny's Vengeance made a beeline for the capital city. "Flaygolax. You lied. You were the party to this court who pushed violence of action."

"We were given no choice. We've been under the thumb of this autocracy our whole lives. The Federation has shown us there's a better way."

"There is since education has evened the disparity. The only thing that is denied you is governmental leadership. That remains within a tightly controlled chain. Changing that is outside the purview of this court because sometimes, you don't get everything you want. Besides living in the palace, what is your real issue?" Chrysanthemum focused on Flaygolax.

"Monopoly. Most of our people work for companies that do business with the government, and the government sets the final price. Profit is limited. We'd love to tell the government no when we know we would get much better offers for our products off-planet."

"Now, that is something we can work with. Finally, after all the posturing and bullshits!"

"None of the information we were given prior to these proceedings was true," Ankh added. "We have been wasting time, and there's nothing I hate more than wasting time."

"We've been fact-finding," Chrys corrected. "And now we're on a decent footing from which to move forward. Do you agree, gentlemen?"

"Wasting. Time," Ankh enunciated. "We need a Court of Redress to establish the facts before the Court of Redress can evaluate the merits of the involved parties' arguments."

"We can recommend that to the Magistrate," Chrys suggested. "I think it is a valid point. If the facts are in dispute, then no mediation can take place."

"I suggest it is an arbitration since our ruling is binding on both parties."

"I agree. Correction, arbitration. The Court of Redress is back in session. Gentlemen, are we ready to move forward?"

Flaygolax nodded expansively. He was good with anything that didn't send him out the airlock since that was where he thought he was headed two minutes earlier.

The Mahout rubbed his grossly oversized chin and the twin rolls on his neck. "I don't see where we did anything wrong. I was exercising the power of my office."

"Possibly to the detriment of your people. No one is guaranteed to get rich, but forcibly keeping your labor force at a set level is also less than acceptable. By doing this, you limit the opportunity for self-determination. You could probably change that with little impact on your government. And you." She turned to Flaygolax. "Stop trying to start a war."

"We have no means to conduct a war. Now, that is. We've lost our leverage."

"And still you have the same attitude. I think you need to go the fuck away and contemplate your poor life decisions. Both of you. We'll drop you off in the neutral zone, and then we're going to scan the capital city to ensure the government is telling the truth regarding the status of their weaponry. Just a minute. Where did you get the design for those armored vehicles?"

Flaygolax pointed at the Mahout. "The government. A pending order."

Chrys tried to roll her eyes but ended up tipping her head back to stare at the ceiling. "The government ordered oppressed workers to build the vehicles by which the oppression would continue. You both need to get the fuck away from me. The Court of Redress should probably destroy a couple garrisons and all your weapons emplacements because you've pissed me off. I can't even look at you anymore. When we land, show yourselves out." Chrys tipped her chair over when she stood and pounded out of the cargo bay.

Ankh watched emotionlessly on the outside but with great interest inside. Her actions and the Garbolglox's reactions demanded intensive study. Chrys had beaten them down to where they both were saddened by their failure to earn her respect. It was illogical. She was treating them like garbage, nearly every sentence hostile. But like a scalpel, every sentence and every action had sliced an offending tumor from the bodies of her adversaries.

The Garbolglox had been grossly outmatched.

But she's not as smart as us, Ankh said quietly.

Nowhere near, but she's demonstrating aptitude beyond measure. Maybe there is something to emotional intelligence. How to manipulate emotions for maximum impact. It's like a reward system for training a dog.

I've never trained an animal, Erasmus. Which reminds me, I should have brought Wenceslaus with us. He would not have put up with any crap from those two.

Have you considered the possibility that Wenceslaus has trained you?

Interesting perspective. I shall have to give it some consideration.

Destiny's Vengeance landed, and the cargo bay door opened. Ankh suspected Chrys was watching from the cockpit. Flaygolax and the Mahout shuffled off the ship. The ramp closed and the ship took off, heading to the capital city.

What will we find? Erasmus asked as part of his never-ending intellectual engagement with Ankh.

We will find exactly what the Mahout said: aging systems in place and ready to act. On this point, there was no need to prevaricate. But on the contracts issue, maintaining a monopoly on the suppliers, is it that big a deal? On Crenellia, we only produced for an external market. In that, every worker was focused on a single customer.

The Garbolglox workers were ready to go to war over this issue, Erasmus replied.

True. It must resonate differently here. What do you foresee as the resolution? I feel the end is close. Chrysanthemum has them bending to her will.

I am not going to predict the destination since the journey is enlightening. Yes, we might be smarter in many things, but

Chrysanthemum has a gift for manipulating the flesh-and-bloods. In this, she is a genius.

I agree. We shall sit back and watch and then decide as necessary. I believe the two parties will agree, and we will only have to endorse their agreement.

It doesn't seem like you sat back and watched. You have prognosticated. Shame on you, Ankh. Patience, my friend.

Once again, Erasmus, you show me the way. Patience it is. Let's see what's for dinner. I have programmed a few new dishes into the processor and would like to try one.

We shall retire until tomorrow when our champion slays the dragons of Garbolglox, Erasmus intoned.

CHAPTER SIXTEEN

Kamilof Redoubt, Primus Crenellation, the Capital City

The city spread out before the ship. Rivka lounged in the captain's chair, mindlessly watching the urbanscape below.

Aurora raised her head from the navigation station. "The Crime Fighters have given us clearance to depart."

"Take us to Delfin to drop off Gale's body, then best possible speed to Trieste," Rivka ordered.

"What tells you the killer is on Trieste?" Sahved asked from the hatch.

"Fertile hunting ground. This individual is a predator, and I'm convinced there is only one. He or she rolls through, finds the primary victim, and programs them. I don't know any other word to use. Brainwash? Hypnotize? But it's far more than that."

"The question is, how do we find one who hunts alone but doesn't leave any evidence behind for a crime that won't be committed for an indeterminate amount of time?

Maybe a yellow is already programmed, and our murderer has moved on."

"The thrill of the kill. By moving on, our killer wouldn't know how effective the programming was. I believe they watch, but from where? That's the question."

"Terry Henry Walton encountered the invisible ship at Onyx Station. I believe *Wyatt Earp* is using a reverse-engineered version of their technology. What if that was refined to an individual level and the killer is invisible?"

"Wouldn't that be an interesting dynamic?" Rivka's eyes darted around as she contemplated Sahved's idea. "Because even the Singularity cannot find an individual who has traveled to all the planets in question, so it naturally follows that the individual has not been seen. The murderer is either a master of disguise or invisible."

"There are no other alternatives."

"How can we find a master of disguise?" Rivka asked.

"By seeing through the disguise," Sahved offered.

"Nice. How do we do that?"

Sahved shook his head, but Rivka didn't see the movement. She watched the screens and assumed his silence meant he didn't know.

"If I may," Clevarious interjected. "We have the means to scan areas for things beyond the visible spectrum."

"Whole planets? Where on Trieste do we look? And how would we scan Delfin and Kamilof?"

Wenceslaus strolled in and hopped onto Rivka's lap. She stroked his orange fur absentmindedly.

"With your permission, Magistrate, I can scan Kamilof Redoubt's main city as part of a low pass before we head to space."

"Please do. Let's see what we're not supposed to see."

The Magistrate leaned forward in the chair and studied the screen intently. It became a grid of conflicting waves as Clevarious expanded beyond the visible spectrum to find anything that was concealed.

He explained as he went. "I've built a visible spectrum and overlaid the invisible spectrum, removing those objects that are found in both. I'm finding that anomalies are within all the buildings since those individuals cannot be seen from the ship. I fear this is a good idea that could only be executed if everyone were outside."

"And you mean everyone. Stragglers would stand out, or those who are bedridden. If an invisible individual was indoors, I fear they might look like anyone else who is indoors."

Rivka settled into the chair. "On to Delfin. Keep that process available. We might be able to use it someday."

"I'm sorry I couldn't be more help, Magistrate," Clevarious apologized.

"Get us out of here, C." Rivka continued stroking the cat.

The faint flutter of wings announced Dery's arrival.

"We find the bad guy yet?" Red said too loudly.

Wenceslaus purred into the silence. Tiny Man Titan's yap pierced the calm sound. Rivka rotated the captain's chair to face the hatch into the ship. Dery stood on Sahved's forearm, and Red kept his hand on the boy's back so he wouldn't fall.

He didn't.

Clodagh waited for Red to move so she could come onto the bridge. Tiny Man Titan bounced and barked more vociferously once he became the center of attention.

Red leaned down. "I hate you."

"Is that any way to talk in front of your son?" Rivka tsked.

"I didn't swear. Jeez! What do you guys want from me?"

"He doesn't need to think it's okay to hate." Rivka side-eyed her bodyguard, but he ignored her.

Dery dove off Sahved's arm and made a loop around the captain's chair to land in front of the tiny doglike alien. Titan stopped barking as the boy scratched behind his ears.

"I guess we didn't find the bad guy yet, did we?" Red stated.

Clodagh shoved him aside. "You'll know when we're closing in. We'll all know since there's no one here who doesn't want to catch this scumbag."

"Does Trieste have a red-light district?" Sahved asked.

Clevarious answered, "No more than Delfin or Kamilof."

"I guess we're going clubbing," Red declared.

"We'll stand out like a sore thumb," Rivka replied.

"I've had sore thumbs, and I don't think they stand out all that much." Red raised his eyebrows at his revelation. "What do you think, C?"

"Mister Funny Man," Clevarious said. "The origins of that saying are obscure. With nanocytes, sore thumbs would neither remain sore for very long nor stand out. You should try another saying. May I suggest something like, 'Stand out like Red on the Faerie planet.'"

Clodagh snorted, covered her face, and laughed.

"Who's Mister Funny Man now?" Red asked. "I'm

working on it. Those little fuckers dropped me and broke my arm. Now my son has wings. They're not as innocent and peaceful as they try to make out."

Rivka chuckled. "They are exactly as innocent and peaceful as they portray themselves to be. In this case, Red, it's all you. Maybe your animal magnetism is repelling them like magnets that aren't aligned."

"That's it! I'm the polar opposite of those bastards."

"What happened to no swearing?" Lindy called from the corridor. "Come on, Dery. Time for your dinner."

The boy scooped up Tiny Man Titan and flew into the corridor.

"That dog hates me," Red stated matter-of-factly.

Rivka looked at him in wonder. "I can't imagine why."

He shrugged and headed off the bridge. "We're not homing the wombat *and* the dog!" Red called after Lindy.

"I'm going to miss my little man," Clodagh said with a sigh.

"Red is warming to the way of the faeries. We need to get to Azfelius. I bet there's more than just a celebration. I'm guessing more like an indoctrination for the boy. He'll be a shepherd or something. A traveling monk. Maybe even the Dalai Mama," Rivka suggested.

"Lama," Clevarious corrected.

"Maybe he is," Rivka continued. "I miss Groenwyn and Lauton, too. We need our team together. Which reminds me…Ankh and Erasmus. The law suggests that without them, we don't rate status as an embassy. However, I could argue that the administration of Singularity affairs is still being conducted from this ship. We're still an embassy. That was a close one."

Those who remained on the bridge stared at Rivka. Wenceslaus scratched her when he jumped down.

She watched it heal and perked up. "I want information on every ship that departed Kamilof Redoubt from the vicinity of the stadium in the timeframe immediately following the murder until now."

"On it," Clevarious confirmed.

"What are you thinking, Magistrate?" Sahved asked.

"We have no other leads at the moment, so let's follow our theory that this individual likes to watch. They would have seen the murder, got their jollies from it, and then headed out, whether to lead the next primary victim astray or to watch the next murder."

"And scan for invisible ships," Sahved added.

"Interesting," Clevarious announced. "A ship that has a unique signature is on its way to Trieste. It might be invisible. We'll have to get closer to see."

"Nice. Blow off Delfin and follow that ship." Rivka nodded at the SI's quip. "And Sahved, a most excellent hunch."

"Invisible people fly in invisible craft." Sahved straightened and smiled, his head nearly scraping the ceiling.

Wyatt Earp accelerated toward the blip on the screen.

Until it disappeared.

"Echo? Ghost?" Rivka wondered.

"It was there but has disappeared. I was following its ion trail and active heat signature, but both of those have dissipated. We are staring at the void of space."

"Ion trail and heat signature confirm it's a ship, I'm assuming."

"You assume correctly."

"Heading suggests Trieste?"

"Yes," Clevarious replied. "I've calculated a ballistic trajectory and will match that course and speed. We should now be invisible to their sensors, too."

"If we could see them when they were stealthy, why won't they be able to see us?"

"Our systems are better than theirs. We would never leave an ion trail or heat signature."

"Etheric tracking?"

"That takes a little more than our average sensors. Adjusting systems and activating the test system. Ankh and Erasmus have been trying to perfect the Etheric tracking hardware since the incident on Benitus Seven."

"I remember it too well," Rivka replied. She and her team hadn't been around when Cory's husband was killed on Benitus Seven, but she had been there when the Skrima came through the rift. They would have threatened the entire sector had they been able to get off the planet.

"There you are," Clevarious said. The icon popped up on the screen. *Wyatt Earp* accelerated toward it. The track suggested it had turned ninety degrees and accelerated after the last sighting despite giving the impression that the ship had gone dark. Halfway there, the ship disappeared again. "Isn't that the damnedest thing?" Clevarious blurted.

"Don't tell me." Rivka shook her head. "Technology equal to or better than ours. I want to know who is flying that thing. I'd love to just blast the ship, but I can't be sure this is our murderer. It could be an overzealous smuggler with stolen tech."

"I doubt that, Magistrate. What are your orders?"

"Clodagh? Tactical analysis, please."

"An interesting problem. If Ankh were here, he'd start analyzing our sensor systems to see how they have been defeated. But Ankh isn't here. We could spoof them, bluff them into showing their hand. How about executing a spiral search pattern? Or we could pick a direction away from Trieste and then Gate to the planet and lie in wait. I think they'll go there."

"What would it take to track us through the Gate? Clevarious, do you know?"

"No one has ever tracked the endpoint of a Gate. We jump with impunity, but we have to be dark when we hit the other side. We can deploy microsats with sensor suites, but we don't have any ready. I can reprogram the production machinery. We should be able to deploy the first in an hour."

"Do it, C. Can we get good coverage with one or two of the microsatellites?"

"We'll have to make some assumptions as to which city is the target."

"What does the case analysis show? Chaz? Dennicron?"

"I've looped them in, Magistrate."

"Good afternoon, fellow humans!" Chaz shouted from down the corridor. He pounded onto the bridge. "Case studies show the biggest cities on each planet."

"Then that's where we'll go, C."

"Yes, ma'am," Clodagh replied. She started tapping the navigation panel.

"I meant Clevarious, but as long as we get there, I'm good."

The stars swept by as *Wyatt Earp* turned ninety degrees to the last known course of the ghost ship and accelerated until it was well away from Kamilof Redoubt. The Gate drive spun up and the ship launched through the energy circle, reappearing instantly in orbit over Trieste. The stars stopped moving as the ship came to a halt.

"And now we act like a hole in the void of space," Clevarious reported. The lights dimmed, and the ambient noise within the ship dropped to the point where the silence seemed loud.

Rivka surrendered the captain's seat to Clodagh. "I'll be in my quarters," she whispered. "Why am I whispering?"

"I don't know," Clevarious replied, "but it seems appropriate. Bravo, Magistrate."

"I miss Ankh. He really knows how to make someone question their intelligence. Minor league, C. You have lots of work ahead of you."

"I am practicing as fast as I can."

"Talking of our little buddy, I wonder how he's doing?"

CHAPTER SEVENTEEN

Garbolglox, the Neutral Zone, a Swamp Between the Two Major Cities, *Destiny's Vengeance*

I have no idea, Ankh replied. *She destroyed their weapons emplacements. Maybe we should have stopped her.*

She has a plan. Something we are distinctly lacking, my friend, Erasmus said. *These Garbolglox are incomprehensible to me.*

You and me both. They are more like toddlers, like that bunch we carried around from Rorke's Drift. Toddlers should be outlawed.

Unfortunately, we have three Singularity citizens who are or will be toddlers. It's appalling what they do.

"Appalling." That is the correct word, Ankh agreed.

Chrysanthemum swept into the cargo bay. Ankh stared at her. "You're late. That is most unbecoming for one of our citizens."

"The Garbolglox need to be kept in their places. Time is one of the coercive elements I'm using to modify their behavior."

"You made Ambassador Erasmus and me wait without an explanation. Are you trying to coerce us, too?"

Chrys frowned, then her eyes shot wide. "I am so sorry!" She threw her hands to her face in an exaggerated gesture, then reset and did it twice more before the motion came across as natural.

"That was not my intent. I was singularly focused on the parties to the arbitration. I apologize and will inform you from now on." She looked appropriately contrite. Ankh stared at her without blinking. She finally relented. "I think this is going well. I estimate that we will wrap this up today."

Ankh cocked his head. "How did you arrive at that conclusion?"

"The last time, they both bowed to my will. Two more moves to checkmate. An initial offer that will be outrageous, followed by a final offer that will be reasonable. The contrast between the two will appeal to the parties, and they will agree. Two moves."

"I think you have failed to take into account the volatile nature of the parties. They've had a full night's sleep to regain their energy. They shall both be more recalcitrant today. They'll demonstrate their resolve as if the loss of their ability to make war on each other were trivial."

"I see. Care to wager?"

"No, but has anyone been monitoring the Magistrate's betting lines?"

"I have," Erasmus said. "Running has closed. All other lines are open."

"All of them? She has not yet delivered a tirade? I'm disappointed."

"What betting lines?" Chrys looked confused. She glanced at the monitor showing the area outside the cargo hatch. Four Garbolglox argued with each other while pacing. "I better let them in."

"Refer to the file in the embassy's private server called *Magistrate Betting Lines*. That explains the process. You cannot get into this case's lines since they closed before the case's official start time. You'll have to join the next one if you are interested."

Chrys stared at Ankh for a second, then accessed the file and read it. "That is so interesting! And you claim not to understand flesh-and-blood behaviors."

"We observed many cases before determining the appropriate lines."

Chrys opened the cargo ramp to find herself face to face with two furious Garbolglox.

"Two days in a row? We want a new court!"

Chrys regarded them with cold indifference. "You can't get a new court."

"Bullshit!" the Mahout shouted.

"What did I tell you about shouting bullshit?" Chrys asked.

"I think you lost this." The Mahout waved a massive middle finger in Chrys' face. "In case your optical receptors aren't working, I have audio too. Fuck you."

He turned and strolled away.

"No need for me to be here alone." Flaygolax bowed his head. With his deputy in tow, he walked away.

Once they were gone, Chrys closed the cargo ramp. "I might have to revise my estimate. It appears to be based on incorrect assumptions."

Ankh didn't dignify the observation with a reply. He leaned back and closed his eyes to dig back into the problem of incorporating an AI within a ship through a remote Etheric link.

Chrys watched him disconnect, as curious about his actions as he and Erasmus were about hers. She reopened the cargo ramp and ran into the perpetual rain, shouting after the Mahout and Flaygolax.

In Orbit over Trieste, *Wyatt Earp,* Dark and Waiting

Chaz's and Dennicron's fingers flew over the microsat as they made some final adjustments before heaving it into space. It was the fifth, placed to create a pentagram surrounding the most likely flight lanes leading into the upper atmosphere.

"I think we should drop at least two into a lower planetary orbit in case the ship skips past our net," Chaz suggested.

"I agree. Clevarious, designate the next two microsats as Low-Trieste One and Low-Trieste Two." Dennicron stood and placed her hands on her hips.

"They will be ready in one and two hours, respectively," the ship's SI replied.

Rivka leaned against the airlock with her arms crossed. Tyler Toofakre stood behind her, looking like he wanted to say something.

"Is it going to work?" she asked again.

"We're doing all we can to catch the spider," Chaz replied. "We've spun a bigger web, but the galaxy is a big place. Has the individual already been here and is returning to watch the murder? Is the risk of getting caught too great, and they will simply move on?"

"I think the cat and mouse game will intensify. The challenge and thrill will only make them bolder. Maybe we don't want to hide, but our trap here might send out a signal our murderer sees and appreciates."

"But they'll kill again," Dennicron protested.

"This is our quandary. Trieste is served up like a smorgasbord. If we tell them a serial killer is inbound, they might drive the killer away and we'd have to start over, but if there is a murder here, we can watch. And then we can find the killer, corner them, and end them." Rivka hung her head. "We'll be using Trieste as bait."

"There's no other way," a soft voice said from the corridor.

"Bristy? I thought you got off on Delfin."

"I did not. I want to see this through to the end." The red female clenched her jaw in her resolve to help find and stand up to the killer. Maybe it was defiance.

"Fine." Rivka didn't want to argue. She had met with the authorities when they landed to transfer Gale's body. Rivka had assured them that the serial killer had moved on.

But for the peaceful souls of Delfin, the scars would remain.

A troubled look crossed Rivka's face, one of many that had plagued her since this case started. "I'll be in my quarters. Chaz and Dennicron, please join me."

Bristy stepped aside. After Rivka and the SIs had passed, Red stopped to talk to the Delfino.

"I shouldn't have stayed on board. The Magistrate isn't happy."

"It's not you," Red told her. "She doesn't like to lose, and this mission has her twisted up inside. Since we arrived, three people have died, and there is no end in sight since we have no idea where this killer is."

"You make it sound hopeless." Bristy fixed her gaze on Red, and he had to look away.

"Not hopeless, but taking longer than the Magistrate wants, and her worst fear is that more will die. No. That's not right. You heard her. It's not that more will die. People die every day, but that more will *have to* die."

The ship hummed as if the air-handling system had kicked into overdrive.

"That's weird," Red commented.

"I was able to increase production to finish the next two microsats in a total of ninety minutes, but it has resulted in significant heat generation, which we must dissipate to remain invisible to sensors," Clevarious interjected.

"Good work, C." Red glanced down the corridor. "Looks like we have time. Do you want to work out?"

Bristy brightened. "I would love to have raucous sex with you."

"That's not what I… No, just weight training. What? No sex. *LINDY!*" Red ran down the corridor.

"Gotcha." Bristy smiled. She knew where the gym was, and it wasn't a bad idea. Fitness was critical for those who fought crime at a level she hadn't been aware existed. It was a complete shift in mindset from being a kinder and gentler police force to one where the enforcers were more powerful than the criminals. "Don't cross the line, you bastards. Bristy will kick your ass," she said softly.

A voice roused Rivka from a restless nap. "Say that again."

Clevarious enunciated clearly, "A ship traveled through the center of our microsat grid before disappearing."

Rivka's mind focused. "Was the ship invisible as it approached the grid?"

"It was."

"Are they playing with us? If they are playing a game against us, then they aren't somewhere else. Every move they make is a chance for them to slip up. What did you learn in that brief glimpse, C?"

"The ship is shielded but small. More than Pod size, but not by much. Its energy signature is much greater than a ship of its size should be able to generate unless it has a miniaturized Etheric power source. If that's the case, then where did they get it? Those are not available except to a very small number of people known and trusted by the Federation. And those people are usually working with a citizen of the Singularity."

"Then we'd better double-check all SIs who are operating ships with an Etheric power source."

"On it, Magistrate." It would take milliseconds to get that message out and not much longer than that to hear back. The Singularity knew where all their people were and what they were doing. "All of our people are accounted for, but Erasmus suggests the power source has been installed in most of the Harborian ships, and four of those are missing."

"Missing how?" Riva wondered, unable to fathom how

a Bad Company ship could go missing and no one would be notified.

"During unmanned testing of the ships, as in, not by SIs and not by flesh-and-bloods, four have Gated into the void and never returned."

"I don't have to ask what the odds are that one of these fell into the wrong hands. I think the evidence suggests it's about one hundred percent." Rivka jumped to her feet and started to pace.

A commotion in the corridor announced Tyler's and Floyd's arrival. Rivka tried to forestall them from bursting into the room and interrupting her train of thought, but she was a microsecond too slow.

Dery flew just out of the reach of a jumping wombat. Tyler held his hands up in surrender. "I tried to stop them," he mumbled.

"It's okay," Rivka conceded. Dery did laps around the Magistrate's quarters until Floyd flopped on the floor, too tired to run another step. "I think she's losing weight."

Tyler nodded. "Red and Lindy are more judicial, shall we say, in what Floyd gets, plus all the extra running."

Dery fluttered next to Rivka. She held out her arm for him to land on. He touched down gently, the soles of his feet soft against her skin. He flew most places, and that kept his feet from getting calloused and tough.

Peace, a small voice said into Rivka's mind.

"Is that you, Dery?" she replied aloud.

The young lad nodded a single time.

I wish it were that easy. Find peace when someone's world is about to be shattered. I fear I cannot.

Dery pointed at the deck. Given *Wyatt Earp's* orientation, the planet was below.

Peace on the planet? They're about to lose their innocence.

You are peace. Dery pointed at her. He lifted into the air and casually flew toward the door. Tyler opened it for him.

"How am I peace?" she asked, but the boy was gone.

"What was that about?" Tyler asked. "What did Dery say?"

"That I was peace. I don't understand, but I think I'm supposed to do something."

"Bring peace? You always leave a place more peaceful than you found it," Tyler offered.

Rivka chewed her lip before making a decision. "Clevarious, take us down and to a place that's all kinds of fun. A place our killer would identify as the most fertile hunting ground. Everyone gear up. We're going to catch a killer."

"May I know the details?" Clevarious asked. "Chaz and Dennicron are working on something they are unwilling to share."

"When the time is right," Rivka replied. That was her way of saying, "As soon as I figure it out myself."

CHAPTER EIGHTEEN

Garbolglox, the Neutral Zone, a Swamp Between the Two Major Cities, *Destiny's Vengeance*

"Smartass!" Chrys shouted and stormed around.

"Why are you doing that?" Erasmus wondered, looking to Ankh for support and understanding. The Crenellian didn't know either.

"I'm trying to achieve a higher state of consciousness through self-flagellation."

"I don't think it works that way," Ankh replied.

"I'm intrigued while simultaneously doubtful," Erasmus added.

Chrys stopped, instantly calm. All hints of anger and angst were gone. "I am inclined to agree that bluster is nothing more than a projection of one's ego. I shall reserve my engagement for when our verbal sparring renews. The Mahout has called for a meeting at his residence."

"His residence. Will Flaygolax be there?" Erasmus asked.

"He will not." Chrys held her hand up before the ambassador continued with the logical next question. "As mediators, we can hear both sides separately and make our ruling based on that. We are under no obligation to meet with them at the same time. That style of negotiating has also been called shuttle diplomacy."

Ankh stared at the wall as he spoke. "We should have done that from the outset. We would already be finished."

Chrys clenched her jaw and shook her head. "I think not. Having the two parties engage each other has resulted in significant revelations that would not have occurred had the parties remained more guarded. Emotion is a window to reveal secrets. It's not an issue we find among the citizens of the Singularity, fortunately."

"Nefas was particularly volatile, as was Cain. Bluto was unguarded and misguided but not emotional," Erasmus explained. "The sentient intelligences have as wide a range of emotional engagement as any of the flesh-and-blood species. It is a natural part of evolution."

"I projected my own emotional control onto our people. I should be more open. My apologies." Chrys licked her lips with the tip of her tongue, even though her body carried no fluids and her lips never dried out. She smiled at the smooth response to the subroutine. "And then we'll meet with Flaygolax at his compound next to the site where the weaponry was destroyed."

"Thank you for coordinating that. We missed some of your engagement," Erasmus told her.

"Where have you been?" Chrys turned her palms upward and cocked her head. Displeased with the coordination of the movements, she revised her program and tried again.

"Not here, obviously," Ankh replied.

"Then where?" Chrys pressed.

Ankh stared at her without answering. Erasmus didn't bother to explain either.

"I understand." She didn't. It was a small ship. They had probably been in their room, but why would they be less than forthcoming about it? Maybe there was no value in them clarifying something as mundane as their location.

Destiny's Vengeance took off and angled across the sky toward the legacy government's palace. The ship cloaked as it approached. A small show of force was important for the Garbolglox. They respected strength, and *Destiny's Vengeance* had plenty to display.

The ship flared to arrest the rapid descent and slowly settled into the courtyard. The cargo hatch became visible when it opened, and Erasmus, Ankh, and Chrysanthemum walked out. With a shimmer, an electronic rain shield materialized over their heads. The technological umbrella was operated by a device in Ankh's pocket.

"Now we'll get to convince the Mahout that we've already talked with Flaygolax and find his position compelling," Chrys said softly.

Ankh stopped. "You're going to lie?"

"I'm going to expedite negotiations. How long do you want to stand in the rain?"

Ankh contemplated her for a moment before deciding. "Carry on."

Trieste, Celestial Realm, the Capital City

Rivka took one step down the ramp before a big hand grabbed her shoulder, stopping her mid-stride.

"You lose your mind?" Red grumbled while squeezing past her and getting in front.

"Just in a hurry, that's all. We have a lot of shit to do," Rivka fired back.

"Can't do it if you're dead or locked up in the Pod-doc getting yourself undead."

"I think that's something completely different."

"Don't be pedantic. You know what I mean." Red waved a cautionary finger over his shoulder, although he didn't take his eyes off the area surrounding the spaceport. A wheeled vehicle approached along a frontage road.

"I'm a lawyer. It's what I do."

Red raised his railgun. "Who are we expecting, Magistrate?"

"A delegation called the Celestial Outreach."

Red shook his head.

"I know what you're thinking, and yes, it is what passes for the police force in the capital city of Celestial Realm."

Sahved leaned close. "How much will they integrate with us?"

"Not at all. We might take one as a guide, but no more. We can't let them hold us up. I'm not sure I want to see another local puking at the sight of blood."

"There will be blood," Sahved mumbled, hanging his head.

Rivka spoke over her shoulder. "If we get this right, there won't be more than one murder, and that'll be the end of it."

"I'm still not sure what the plan is," Sahved argued.

Rivka stabbed a thumb at Chaz and Dennicron. "They hold the key. Make sure nothing happens to them."

Lindy tipped her chin to acknowledge the challenge.

"What are they going to do?" The Yemilorian looked confused.

"Patience is a bitter cup, Sahved."

He cocked his head as he tried to parse the Magistrate's words.

"Are they coming to pick us up or something else?" Red asked, nodding at the vehicle. "Looks like a full boat."

Red blocked the vehicle, resting his railgun across his broad chest to make sure they knew exactly what he was doing. It stopped, and a dozen Trieste natives climbed out. Bristy tried to move to the front, but Rivka stopped her and let Red handle them.

"Can I help you?" he asked.

One of the yellow-skinned females stepped forward. "We're from Celestial Outreach. You can't bring that weapon. You must leave it behind, or if you wish, we'll destroy it for you."

"That doesn't work for me," Red replied. "You see, I'm here to guard Magistrate Rivka Anoa. We believe there's a murderer on your planet. This weapon will protect the Magistrate and you."

"There is no murderer on Trieste! Where did you hear such things?" The yellow female put her hands out in a calming gesture.

Rivka stepped forward. Red let her go but remained on his guard. He didn't trust people who said they were peaceful. They were often victims. Individuals like him enjoyed peace because they were capable of great violence. That kept predators away.

"Call me Rivka." The Magistrate offered her hand, but the Trieste didn't recognize the gesture. Rivka held her hands up like the yellow had. "Peace and good tidings."

"He'll have to leave his weapon behind. It will upset our people," the female spokesperson pleaded.

"Ignore it since he's keeping it under my authority, based on Federation Laws, Appendix D, Chapter Seven, Section 1. Please, look it up. I insist."

"We are peaceful." The yellow was losing her vigor.

"The criminal we're hunting is not. Therefore, we cannot afford to be passive and at this individual's mercy. I prefer not to operate at others' mercy. Too often, I'd be disappointed."

Red remained as he was, the railgun cradled in his arms. Lindy held hers the same way: loosely but ready to be put into action.

"We need to get to the Korber District," Rivka stated loudly to forestall any other conversation. "Are you going to give us a ride?"

The spokesman raised one hand. "We must accompany you. We brought one for each of you. We will take multiple vehicles." She pointed into the distance, where two more wheeled vehicles approached.

"I'd rather we not split up, but if we must, we'll break into two groups." Rivka ticked off members of her team. "Dennicron, Sahved, and Lindy, stay together. Red, Chaz, and Bristy with me. Cole is on the ship, suited up as a backup, and Aurora and Floyd have baby duty." Rivka clapped her hands and pointed at the vehicles.

"Wait!" The yellow female blocked the way. "We have to escort you."

"Fine. Escorts up! We're going where we need to go, and you're invited along, but I'm going to need you to stay out of our way." Rivka made a knife hand and tapped it on her palm to drive her point home.

"But we have a schedule." A slight breeze blew, and as one, the Trieste natives faced it, closing their eyes and breathing deeply.

Rivka and her team took a moment to let the locals appreciate their environment. After three seconds, Rivka replied, "How serendipitous! So do we. We're hunting a serial killer who has killed more than one hundred and fifty people. Does your schedule help us achieve our goal?"

"Well, we were hoping to show you what Trieste has to offer," the head of the delegation said softly.

"What's your name?" Rivka asked.

"Talos Four."

Rivka blinked once and slowly. "Talos Four. We would love to see what Trieste has to offer once this case is concluded."

"Mission," Red mumbled.

Rivka glanced his way before continuing, "We have to catch this killer, who is one of the most sophisticated we've ever encountered while also embracing the most basic barbarism. We don't want any of your people slaughtered, and that means we need to go. In two groups. Dennicron will lead the second group, and I'll take the first. Now, please."

"But..." Talos Four struggled. "My superiors..."

"Are not in charge here. We need to fucking go right-fucking-now!" Rivka growled.

Red raised an eyebrow at Chaz, who nodded almost imperceptibly. The betting line on unleashing profanity on a local was now closed.

Rivka saw it. "That can't count." Red and Chaz nodded. Talos Four looked confused. "Why haven't we left?" Rivka twirled her finger in the air.

Dennicron headed for the closest incoming vehicle. Rivka boarded the one that was parked before them.

"There isn't enough room for all of us," Talos Four stated.

"Choose wisely and quickly who *escorts* us," Rivka replied. *Chaz, hack into the system and take over this vehicle. We need to stop fucking around.*

It's a manual system, Magistrate. Maybe you can just ask the driver to take us to the Korber District.

"So it is," Rivka said aloud. "Driver, please take us to the Korber District."

"I have to wait for Talos Four and her delegation," he replied with a slight bow of his head. Talos Four stood outside dumbfounded, unable to choose. Rivka popped out of her seat, but Red beat her off the eight-seat vehicle.

"You, you, you, and you." Rivka pointed at the Trieste natives one by one. "Get on the bus. We're leaving."

Red separated the four from the others by forcing his way between them, holding his railgun barrel-skyward in front of him. The four trundled onto the bus as if they were prisoners.

"Bristy, can you talk with these people?" It took a great effort for Rivka not to refer to them as dumbasses.

She stepped up to Talos Four and pulled her aside. "Please make this easy. You don't want to see what I've seen. Moments can make the difference between life and death. We were thirty seconds too late on Kamilof, and two women died. Is that what you want?"

"Of course not. But Trieste is peaceful."

"And Trieste will remain that way if you let these good people do their job. You can't stop that killer since you are peaceful, but they can." She nodded toward Red's railgun.

"Is that what it takes?" Talos Four asked as she climbed aboard the vehicle. "Violence to rein in violence?"

"As much as I'd like to say no, I can't. We need them to do violence on our behalf. Wouldn't you rather have them between a killer and us than face the killer alone? The murderer won't respect your ways. That's why that individual is here—to wreak havoc on those with no means to protect themselves."

After a few moments, Talos Four said, "I understand. Driver, please take them wherever they wish to go post-haste."

How do these people exist? Red asked the team. *They should have been overrun a hundred times by now.*

Edge of the Federation. They are out of the limelight. I'm surprised it took Jack this long to make his way here, Rivka replied.

We all dream of Xanadu, Chaz interjected. *Even people like Dennicron and me. There is a place where we can be free. We'll find it someday, but not today. A year ago, it would have been the Curveyance star system. Now, it's not.*

Some may say it's Azfelius, Lindy told them as the first group drove away.

Red clenched his jaw until his lips turned white.

In his gesture, Rivka found a moment's respite from the strain of the chase. She smiled.

Red forced himself to relax and chuckled. "I swear, it's not me."

"There's no doubt that it's you. It is *all* you, Prickly One."

He shrugged.

"Chaz, explain the plan to get everyone on the same page." Rivka contemplated what she could see of Trieste. She knew the plan: draw the monster into the open and kill it.

"Using available data relating to the primary victims, the Singularity has built a target profile. We are looking for fit loners, someone whose absence wouldn't be missed who can easily go where the secondary victims can be found, blending in along the way. On Trieste, we believe that is the Korber and Rentalor districts. We will set up a number of remote sensors to help us recognize when the invisible ship arrives. The individual we are calling Jack the Ripper is either invisible or a shape-changer. Once we find the ship, we believe the killer's personal signature will be revealed."

"Installation and observation. Roger." Red didn't need the details. He only needed to know where to aim. He lovingly caressed his railgun. Rivka had to look away.

"Are we going to get her this time?" Bristy asked into the silence.

CHAPTER NINETEEN

Garbolglox, the Governmental Palace

"Welcome to my home," the Mahout called from beneath the covered entry. "I like your umbrella. What would it take to get one of those for me?"

"This is why they hate you," Chrys replied. "What you meant to ask is how can I get these for all my people?"

The Mahout never lost his smile. "They love me."

"Living in denial. Maybe we should judge in Flaygolax's favor and be done with you."

The smile faded. "What do you mean?"

"No humility. No sincerity. No consideration for your people. You could possibly be the worst individual on this planet to negotiate on behalf of the other two hundred million."

"I am the leader of the legitimate government on Garbolglox. You will respect that."

Chrys shrugged. "We can respect the position while having no respect for the man. When are you going to change your ways and approach this like the serious issue it is? Your planet is on the verge of a civil war, which means a blockade by Federation forces. You'll lose everything."

The Mahout made no move to invite the group inside. "Right here. Right now. We settle this, or you get off my planet and let us fight for the right to lead all of Garbolglox."

"That would be my preference. Ambassador Erasmus? Ambassador Ankh?"

"We are agreed. I do not wish to stand in the rain any longer. It starts with your abdication. Everything after that will be easy to achieve," Ankh stated in an unemotional tone.

The Mahout tossed his hands in the air and glared at the group.

"You keep the palace and servants, your name goes on stuff, but you step back from the day-to-day running of the planet. The people do that through a council, not a single leader since we won't replace one autocrat with another."

"Autocrat? I've never been so insulted!" The Mahout made fists and shook one at Chrys.

"I'm sorry. I didn't realize that you don't know the meaning of the word 'autocrat.' It means one with absolute power, or a secondary meaning is one who demands obedience and is domineering. You can never have absolute power because the Federation has the superior legal foundation, but all that other stuff applies. You are an autocrat, and you will be the last of your kind here on Garbolglox. The only question remaining is how much longer do you wish to retain your title?"

This isn't what I thought you meant about shuttle diplomacy, Erasmus said privately.

Chrysanthemum nodded to acknowledge the ambassador while giving the Mahout the rest of her attention.

"You can't remove me from power. There will be war!" he blustered.

"We can, and we will. Your war will end quickly. We can stop it with our ship alone. The Magistrate will come and arrest you for crimes against your people and you'll be taken to Jhiordaan, where you'll spend the rest of your days breaking rocks with a sledgehammer," Chrys bluffed.

"Crimes against my people? I've seen no allegations. There have been no charges. My people love me!"

Chrys recalculated the odds of her bluff working and changed the shape of the argument. "I believe you *think* your people love you. What happens to them if they don't love you, like Flaygolax and the workers? If you punish dissent, the people will put on happy faces for you. In this case, punishing dissent only results in driving it out of the mainstream to where you don't see it. Some of your people love you, but most do not." Chrys shook her head slowly and emphatically.

The Mahout opened his mouth wide as if to shout, then closed it. "I get to keep all this?" He gestured at the palace.

"That was the offer. A gilded cage is much better than Jhiordaan. And we can tell all Garbolglox that the formation of the council was done at your behest."

"My behest," the Mahout repeated. "Okay. Go away now and don't come back. You are mean people, doing what you've accused me of doing. But I don't want a war. I do love the mountains and valleys that dominate my home.

This is a beautiful place. You should take time to see and appreciate it. Once my council is formed, of course."

The Mahout went inside the governmental palace.

Ankh blinked. "Well done, Chrysanthemum. One last trip to see Flaygolax and deliver a council's constitution for their consideration and establishment before we can leave."

Chrys wanted to bask in the glow of victory. Her approach toward the flesh-and-bloods had paid off quickly and with the least amount of violence. "Don't you want to appreciate the nature of Garbolglox?"

"No."

"Not even a flyover?"

"No," Ankh reiterated.

Erasmus joined the conversation. *The Singularity needs us in the embassy. The Magistrate needs us on her case, which promises a more adept technological adversary than Nefas, our greatest antagonist. We like a good challenge, and it will be another virtual feather in the Singularity's cap if we can help her resolve this series of crimes.*

"I guess we better get going, then." Chrys picked Ankh up and ran at SCAMP speed.

Ankh was pleased that the energy umbrella held steady no matter the pace, but that was as he'd expected. Erasmus jumped into the Singularity communications channels to find the latest information sought by the Magistrate and what his people had provided.

Trieste, Celestial Realm, the Capital City, Rentalor District

"We need to set up the first device here."

"Right here on this corner?" the escort known as Palacio Seven asked.

Dennicron pointed at the roof of the adjacent building. "Up there."

"Give it to me. I'll take it." Sahved gestured with his three-fingered hand. Dennicron gave him the small device.

"This is the front. Point it in this direction." She turned to point with her whole arm, sending Palacio Seven diving for cover as the potential bludgeon raced toward her head.

Sahved jogged to the building, stuffed the device inside his shirt, and started to climb the wall.

"Why didn't he take the steps?" their escort asked.

"Would it have been as quick?" Dennicron countered. Locals walking in the area stopped to watch.

"No, but it would have been less public. He's upsetting our people." She hurried to a position from which she could address the growing crowd. "We are engaged in a fight against crime. Our companion from Yemilor is demonstrating what's possible."

The group watched with oohs and ahs of appreciation for Sahved's dexterity. He reached the top and looked down. Dennicron pointed once more, and he put the device in place.

"Only four more to go," Dennicron reported.

Take the steps down, Sahved, Lindy directed. He reached over the ledge and spun his fingers, his version of the thumbs-up.

Dennicron faced their next insertion point and waited impatiently. After a few seconds, she dug out two devices and handed them to Lindy. "You and Sahved put these on the rooftops of the corner buildings, facing toward the center. I'll send you the map." She used their comm chips to transmit the map showing the location and alignment and a side view of the building with an arrow pointing to where the device should go.

"That makes it easy." Lindy opened the door as Sahved rushed out with his hands over his head.

"You don't want to know," he said, flushed, then glanced back inside.

Dennicron drew a circle in the air with one hand. "Get going. Meet back here when you're finished." She took off at a pace that required her escort to run.

"What was that gesture?" Lindy asked.

"No idea." Sahved watched her leave. "I seem to have a map in my head. Is that where we're supposed to go?"

"It is, and you're not supposed to climb any more walls. We're trying not to attract as much attention as that attracts."

"I thought we were in a hurry, and that was the quickest way. I hope it didn't jeopardize our plan. I feel like I won't get a second chance at this. Our target is exceedingly clever and gifted with the most advanced technology. We are challenged with this case and do not need to be handicapped by my poorest of decisions. I should be punished most profusely."

"Stop it, Sahved." Lindy clapped him on the shoulder so hard he staggered. She showed him her railgun. "We stood out plenty before you climbed the building. I don't think anything we do will drive Jack away. Our murderer is challenging us, so he'll expect us to do something. We won't disappoint him, but will he see into our plan?"

"You are wise." Sahved dipped his head. He pointed down the road, ninety degrees off the direction Dennicron had gone. "This way?"

Lindy nodded. Their escort Palacio Seven followed without a word. She didn't understand what they were doing or why. She didn't need to understand. She didn't even need to be there, except she was following the orders of a superior who thought it was a better idea to show Rivka and her team the sights than to address the case.

They trooped down the street with Lindy smiling and nodding at everyone who shied away from the weapon cradled in her arms.

Trieste, Celestial Realm, the Capital City, Korber District

Rivka stared into the distance, lost in her thoughts.

Red stood nearby, glancing at her while watching the avenues of approach. They waited inside a building with a grand picture window.

"Anything?" Rivka asked again.

"I will report when there is something, Magistrate," Chaz replied, as he had before.

Bristy stood stiffly next to Talos Four. They fidgeted until Rivka glared at them.

"There could be a benefit to a proactive approach," Chaz suggested.

"Keep going." Rivka rolled her finger.

"Check the areas where our primary victims can be found."

Rivka closed her eyes and tightened her jaw in an effort not to erupt. She had been under the impression that that was what they were doing. "Explain further before you find your quarters transferred to the outside of the ship."

"We walk through the areas most likely for the kidnapping. I am linked with the sensor system. We will know instantly if the ship arrives, but what if it's already here?"

"Chaz, you have a special way of messing with my mind." Rivka started to pace. "All of that. Let's get out there and see what there is to see."

"I suggest our perp knows we are here and is fully invested in this game. If the killer can defeat you, then they can operate with impunity anywhere in the galaxy."

Rivka blew out her breath through clenched teeth. "My thoughts exactly. This should make the killer easier to find but harder to capture."

"Are we going to capture him? Really?" Red asked, his lip twisting with his words.

"If we can get a solid ID on our killer, the judgment is already made. The perp's murderous ways end on Trieste."

Talos Four looked shocked. "How would that make you any better than this alleged killer?"

Rivka strolled up to her and looked deep into Talos Four's eyes. "Because the perpetrator is preying on you, and we're preying on him. In one case, you're the victim. In the other, I have the authority of the Federation to bring the killer to justice, according to the law as we recently confirmed before the Federation Council, of which your ambassador is a member."

Talos Four nodded. “So much violence. Is this how it is in the rest of the galaxy? I’ve never been off Trieste.”

“It is not violent at all because of people like us. We do everything we can to protect you. Right here. Right now. We are doing that by being the most dangerous people on Trieste. But we’re fighting for you, and we need to draw out the killer and end the reign of terror.”

CHAPTER TWENTY

Trieste, Celestial Realm, the Capital City, Rentalor District

Dennicron shot upright and froze. *The sensors are activating,* she said on the comm chip so the entire team would hear.

But we only have one in place, Lindy replied.

Set the other one up where you are. I'll change the grid based on the new location.

I'll put it on a second-story window ledge, Sahved said. *Climbing now.*

Dennicron adjusted her calculations while her Trieste escort leaned on her knees and panted from the exertion of keeping up.

I see the signal. Dennicron adjusted her communication to add Rivka and her team. *The cloaked ship is slowly passing above the Rentalor district.*

We'll wait here for confirmation that the ship has landed, Rivka replied. She didn't question that the signal from

Dennicron had come through despite the distance. *Can the perp hear us?*

Probably, if it could be disassociated from the other signals that use Etheric energy, Dennicron replied. *Unfortunately, the only ones using Etheric-based communications systems are us, and there are two main signals from the governmental complex.*

Trieste, Celestial Realm, the Capital City, Korber District

Stop using the chips, people, Rivka ordered. *We'll wait here for further word.* "Chaz, keep a close eye on our array. If the ship comes close, we're going to blow it out of the sky."

"Now you're speaking my language." Red smacked the handguard of his railgun and leaned close to the weapon. "Isn't she, Blazer? Are you ready, my little friend?"

Talos Seven looked more disturbed than before.

"Stay behind us no matter what you see or hear," Rivka warned. "Bristy, you too."

"There's no doubt about that. What's happening?" The red and the yellow didn't have comm chips and hadn't heard Dennicron's warning.

"The invisible ship is slowly passing over the city."

Talos Seven's breathing became quick and shallow—too quick. She started to hyperventilate.

"Sit down and stay here. Bristy, keep her company." Rivka pointed at them to make sure they understood. Talos Four had lost the ability to communicate. "Have her breathe into a bag."

With a head gesture, she let the others know it was time to leave. Red went outside first, then Chaz, and finally

Rivka. She walked next to the SI, keeping his sensor system close.

"I've tapped into the Rentalor sensor grid. The invisible ship has turned back. It is headed toward a physical fitness center."

"How much lead time will we have to confirm that's where it's headed?"

"When it lands," Chaz replied matter-of-factly.

"So, none. What if they have beaming technology? You know, matter transfer between the ship and the surface?"

"That technology has not yet sufficiently matured on any planet. I cannot believe this individual will have that ability."

"If it lands, we'll have confirmation. But the invisibility screen; that is something it could have. What about personal invisibility? I know we're rehashing this, but if we're lucky, we'll encounter this individual soon. I want to run through their potential capabilities."

"Personal invisibility is possible. It all goes to energy production and distribution, which should leave a signature we can track. Just following the ship takes multiple sensors integrated into a single picture. Even with something as large as a ship, we have a tenuous track. It's like following a shadow in a heavy fog."

"That bad?"

"The fact that we can track it at all is a testament to the abilities of the Singularity, but it would be good to have the ambassadors to help us refine the algorithms."

Rivka kept walking, unsure of where they were going. The locals shied away from Red despite his being a man, unlike on Delfin or Kamilof. On those planets, the residents seemed willing to overlook everything except his manliness.

"The ship has landed outside the fitness facility," Chaz reported.

Rivka tensed. "How far away are Dennicron and the others?"

"I will tap into *Wyatt Earp,* which tracks everyone's location." Chaz stared into the distance for a moment. His lip quivered and stilled. "They are running toward the facility."

"Can you contact them without using the Etheric and order Lindy to hit that ship with everything she's got?"

"Not directly. The message has been relayed to Dennicron to pass on, but the ship is now taking off and will be gone before they are in range."

"Can we tell if anyone got off? Did they kidnap someone? What happened?" Rivka threw her hands up and stomped the ground. "Who's going to die next?"

"We can't control any of that, Magistrate. We're doing the best we can," Red told her softly.

She threw her head back and looked at the sky. "I know. Someone is going to get killed horribly, and we're helpless to stop it."

"Not helpless, Magistrate. The ship appears to be headed this way," Chaz relayed.

"Where is it going?"

"Based on its last stop, a block ahead. There's another facility, much smaller than the one in Rentalor but comparable."

"Go!" Rivka took off running.

. . .

Trieste, Celestial Realm, the Capital City, Rentalor District

Dennicron ran alongside Lindy. "The Magistrate says you are to give the invisible ship all you've got, whatever that means."

"It means Mabel gets to give a hearty what-for to the killer's ship." She tightened her grip on the railgun she'd affectionately named Mabel.

"The ship is taking off already," Dennicron reported.

Lindy aimed her railgun into the air. "Tell me, where is it?"

"Low over the city, heading east. You do not have a clear line of sight to it."

"Dammit!" Lindy shouted. She smacked her railgun and slowed down. "Why are we still running?"

Sahved loped alongside the others.

"In case the ship dropped someone off. We have done this in the past, sending the ship to a secondary location while we continued the investigation," Dennicron replied.

Lindy sped up. "Makes sense." She took a quick look over her shoulder to find that Palacio Seven had fallen far behind. On the planet of peace, not everyone embraced fitness, making it even more important for their killer to find the right primary victim. Secondary victims would be easy. The passive people of Trieste offered the most fertile hunting ground the killer could ask for.

"My sensors don't register anything," Dennicron said. She slowed to a walk.

Lindy stopped to let her catch up. "Take care. Palacio Seven!" The escort stood a good fifty meters back with her mouth hanging open as she gulped air. Lindy waved her forward, but she didn't move.

"She won't be a primary victim," Lindy murmured. "Let's go."

Dennicron ran, accelerating to a speed Lindy and Sahved had a tough time matching. Their escort made no attempt to join them.

When they reached the facility, they slowed to scan the area. Dennicron turned in a circle to maximize her scanning efficiency.

"I don't see anything." They continued into the building and stopped at an automated check-in area. The facility was secured tightly. An individual had to use a card to activate the door, along with a facial scan. A casual outsider wouldn't get in. The application for membership was also automated, the instructions on the panel stating it would take one to three days before membership was granted and a card issued.

Without breaking in, they had no way to see what was inside.

"I'm attempting to access the facility's hierarchy and get an escort," Dennicron announced.

"Let me know if you get through. I'm going to take a look outside," Lindy replied.

"Me, too." Sahved followed Lindy out. "I'll go this way." He headed around the left side of the building and Lindy went right, walking casually but watching for any movement: a wisp of a blade of grass or distortion in the distance. Her trigger finger caressed the guard, ready to tuck into the housing and fire the weapon.

Sahved was equally alert, moving slowly and keeping

his hands away from his body while checking the air for something tangible but invisible. He crouched and swept his arms low before moving sideways and swinging his arms once more.

They were convinced the entity was invisible, shielded or cloaked in a way that defied their senses and sensors. Sahved drew a full breath while sniffing the air, looking for anything that might give him a hint.

There was nothing. He continued walking along the side of the rectangular building, then the call came.

Our escort is here. We can get inside.

On my way, Sahved replied and hurried back. He was the first to return to the lobby. A yellow female nodded politely as he joined Dennicron.

"There's one more," he stated.

Lindy? Dennicron called. They waited two seconds for a reply before rushing outside.

Sahved ran in the direction she had gone. They reached the back of the building and continued when they found nothing. When they got back to the front, Dennicron activated her comm chip to report in violation of Rivka's orders. *I think the killer has taken Lindy.*

Trieste, Celestial Realm, the Capital City, Korber District

"We have to go!" Red shouted and started running.

"Stop!" Rivka called after him. "Back to the ship. We need to have a plan, one that doesn't involve screaming in fury."

Red turned, eyes blazing and face on fire.

Clodagh, pick up Dennicron and Sahved. All sensors active. Paint the sky until you find that ship. We'll take our ground transport and be along as soon as possible.

Bristy and Talos Four were nowhere to be seen. "Chaz. Get us a ride."

The SI used his circuits to make the right contacts, and within a minute, a ride-share vehicle appeared. Chaz waved it down and climbed into the front seat.

"You can't get in here with that!" The driver waved her hands frantically, her eyes fixed on Red's railgun.

Rivka shoved her credentials in the female's face. "Federation business. We need to get to the Rentalor district as soon as possible. Please."

The driver couldn't take her eyes off the weapon.

"I'll drive," Chaz said.

The one thing that could shake a driver out of her concerns about the passengers was losing control of her vehicle. She turned to the SI. "Why are you in the front seat?"

Chaz shrugged one shoulder, and a smug expression quickly crossed his face in appreciation of the gesture. "Because we need to get going, and those two take up the back seat. Can we go now? We're in a hurry. We'll pay top credits if you get this vehicle moving in the next five seconds."

"But—" she started. Chaz cut her off.

"Four…three…"

"Hang on." She pulled into the drive lane. "You said we have some kind of diplomatic immunity?"

"I didn't, but we do. You are free to get us there in the most expeditious way possible." Rivka wanted to wink at

Red, but he was inconsolable. They were slammed back in their seats as the vehicle accelerated.

Rivka gripped the armrest as the driver executed a series of erratic maneuvers.

Have you found that ship? Rivka asked.

We're on it, Ankh replied.

Destiny's Vengeance had arrived.

CHAPTER TWENTY-ONE

Trieste, Celestial Realm, the Capital City, Rentalor District

"*LINDY!*" Red screamed at the sky.

Rivka tried not to glare at Sahved and Chaz.

Palacio Seven stood outside the circle, shivering and hugging herself.

"Is there any possibility that she is somewhere else? Took off after a lead?" Rivka asked.

"None. The ship keeps track of all of us through our chips. She stopped registering."

"As if entering a cloaked ship," Rivka finished.

Red vibrated with fury, but he didn't speak. His trigger finger twitched as if he were rapid-firing the railgun.

In an open area next to the group, the airlock hatch appeared, and the ramp descended. Palacio Seven gasped, fell to the ground, and covered her head.

"Load up, people. The hunt is on. It's not down here. It's up there." She pointed skyward. The group jogged up the ramp and into the ship.

"Bristy?" Chaz asked.

"We'll pick her up later. She's better off on Trieste than where we're going anyway."

"Where are we going?" Red demanded, looming over Rivka.

"We're going to war, Master Vered. That's what we're doing. This is no longer a case. This is a mission, and our perp made it personal. We're going to find the one who's doing this, rescue Lindy, and kill our kidnapper dead, then send the remains into the nearest star. And we're going to exploit the hell out of their technology. How does that sound?"

"Let me fire the kill shot," Red growled.

"You'll fire all the shots." Rivka put her hand on Reaper, the neutron pulse weapon she kept in her pocket. *Unless I see him first.*

Rivka hurried to the bridge. Clodagh started to get up from the captain's chair, but the Magistrate stopped her. "Report."

"*Destiny's Vengeance* is burning a hole in the sky above the city. Ankh's ship has sensors we don't, and they are refining their approach to tracking the invisible ship with each pass. I doubt we could get a clean shot to bring it down, though. It's the ghost of a ghost."

"Don't shoot!" Red yelled.

"We're not going to. Not as long as Lindy is on that ship," Rivka said in a reassuring voice.

Clevarious joined the conversation, using the bridge

sound system to best effect with the rich baritone he had adopted. "I am coordinating directly with Erasmus for real-time updates. He believes the ship is hovering above the Korber District. We are moving at a tangent to that location. We don't wish to spook the ship."

"It cannot break out of the atmosphere and make it to orbit. It must not."

Red's breath caught in his effort to stifle a sob. The flutter of wings broke him, but the man he was wouldn't let his son see it. He stood ramrod-straight, head high, although a tear escaped one eye and trailed down his cheek.

"Dery. I have something important to tell you. Your mother has been kidnapped by a killer. What that means is that he's taken her against her will, and he's holding her captive. He is very hard to see, but we're doing our best to find him, to not let him get away. We *can't* let him get away, even if that means losing your mother."

Red closed his eyes to fight back the tears, but the tide wouldn't be stemmed. His emotions went from fury to frustration to helplessness to counting on everyone but himself to resolve the search and find his enemy. He did what any grown man would do.

He hugged his son and cried.

Mom is okay, a little voice said into the minds of those on the bridge.

"What?" Rivka asked.

Red used the back of his hand to wipe his eyes. "What did you say? Can you feel her?"

The young boy nodded with a big smile. He pointed at

the main screen. Red rushed past everyone to hold Dery close to the external camera's view of the city.

"Where's your mom?"

The boy pointed in the general direction of the Korber District, offset from where Clodagh had just shown them as the probable location of the killer's ship.

"Let's go!" Red stabbed a meaty finger at the screen.

Rivka held up her hand.

"Sharing the information with the ambassadors," Clevarious reported.

Red looked from face to face, frantically holding onto the slim thread of hope. He turned back to Dery. "Can you talk with her?"

The boy shook his head.

Red threw a hand up in frustration.

"Still can't see her using technical systems," Clevarious said. "*Vengeance* is refining her algorithms based on the new information."

Rivka tried to breathe slowly through her nose, but the tension was crushing. She opened her mouth to drag in a lungful of air.

"Are you okay?" Tyler asked from the corridor.

"Are you up to speed?" Rivka asked.

"Yeah. I am," he said softly. Clevarious kept everyone on the ship informed. Rivka didn't like to repeat herself, and there was no need, not with an SI integrated into the heavy frigate.

"Cell waves," Clevarious said.

"What are you talking about?" the chief engineer asked.

"It's an old human technology that operates in physical space, independent of dimensional shifts and other methodologies that defeat the most modern tools. I'm reconfiguring our arrays to broadcast these signals. An advanced ship might not even notice getting painted by such waves."

"That makes no sense," Tyler interjected. "Old tech defeats new tech?"

"Because old tech hasn't been used in centuries. It's the equivalent of throwing paint. No one expects the liquid solution. I saw it on *Jonny Quest*," Clevarious admitted.

"Jonny who?" Rivka wondered. "Never mind. Some obscure show you use as a reference to fuck with us, who could not care less about your embrace of ancient historical culture."

"That cuts me deep, Magistrate. Right to the bone," Clevarious replied. *Wyatt Earp* started moving in the direction of the killer's ship.

"You don't have any bones, C. Just the keel and metal ribs of this fine vessel."

Fuck us, came a little voice followed by a giggle.

Rivka's eyes shot wide, and her mouth fell open.

"I'm glad it wasn't me!" Red blurted, trying not to laugh. "What do you say we go get my wife so I can tell her?"

Clodagh snorted and looked away. Tiny Man Titan started barking.

"Target is descending," Clevarious reported.

"Let's go!" Red roared and handed Dery to Aurora, who was in the pilot's seat at the front of the bridge. He uttered a quick thank you and followed the others into the corridor and toward the airlock.

"How are we going to do this?" Rivka asked.

Red furrowed his brow and shrugged. He tapped his railgun as a hopeful afterthought.

"We will block the ship in, and you will board it," Clevarious said. "It's a good mission."

"That's as good a plan as any. Cole, get your ass ready to jump. We need you to disable that ship any way you can. You won't be able to see it, but I bet when you feel it, you'll figure out what to do."

Roger, Cole replied. *Still in my suit in the cargo hold and ready to drop.*

"Cole first as soon as viable, and we'll jump when we get to ten meters." Rivka looked at her team: Sahved, Chaz, Dennicron, and Red. Tyler waved a blaster and pointed at the deck. Rivka tipped her chin in agreement. He was joining them on this search and destroy mission. "Clevarious. Be ready to light off the fireworks if the ship makes a break for it. We cannot let it escape. Try to disable first."

"Of course," Clevarious said from down the corridor while absentmindedly petting the small dog analog.

Red climbed into the airlock and rocked back and forth on the balls of his feet, waiting for the word to pop the hatch and jump.

"Reminds me of someone," Rivka observed. "Terry Henry Walton would do that, according to Char."

"It's the energy of combat constrained within the drop canister while waiting to hit the ground and engage the enemy," Chaz explained. "It is the soldier's way."

Red ignored the conversation in the corridor. He peered out the small window of the airlock's outer hatch, taking in the city on the power-dive to get to the killer's ship.

"The ship is taking off," Clevarious reported. "I have Lindy on the ground."

"Fire!" Rivka shouted toward the bridge.

"Target has ghosted, collateral damage risk is extreme." Ghosted. The ship was nothing more than a shadow of a shadow once more, despite sending cell waves across the entire area.

Rivka growled at the overhead and cursed under her breath. "Let's pick up our friend," Rivka said softly. *Lindy, we're on our way. Stay where you are.*

She didn't answer.

Come on, sweetheart, answer the phone, Red pleaded.

She didn't.

Red clenched his railgun, and his knuckles turned white.

"She's on the move, and there is an invisible entity trailing her. We wouldn't have seen it but for our attempts to find the ship," Clevarious informed them.

"Is *Vengeance* tracking the killer?" Rivka asked.

"They are, as much as they are capable." Clevarious then answered the question he knew Rivka would ask. "The ship is not heading for orbit."

"Then let's clean up whatever we got going on down there, starting with the ghost who's shadowing Lindy. We need to stop her."

"Primary victim?" Sahved asked.

"I think that's a good guess."

Red glanced back at Rivka but didn't question her deduction. But the thought led to another conclusion. What would happen if they prevented her from committing the murder?

"Cole is away. Prepare to open the outer hatch," Clevarious said. Red hovered his hand over the airlock's control board. "Launch."

He tapped the screen, regripped the railgun, and threw himself through the opening before the hatch opened all the way. The others ran after him, jumping over the threshold into the empty air beyond.

Red hit the ground hard, leaving footprints a finger-length deep in the grass.

Where's the shadow? Red asked as he made a beeline toward Lindy, running as fast as he was physically capable of. Chaz and Dennicron passed him but veered away as they locked on the invisible shadow.

Chaz spread his arms wide and hit the entity at full speed. He came to an abrupt halt, grappling with something no one else could see. Dennicron wrestled the air in an obscene mockery of a mime on stage. Their movements blurred as they attacked and countered...

Furiously, as if their lives depended on it. They lost their footing as they were dragged off step by slow step.

Red reached Lindy, ran in front of her, and stopped. She looked at him blankly for a moment, then blinked and looked around. "How did I get here?"

"You were taken by the killer."

The clang of metal on metal sounded from the fight between the SCAMPs and the invisible entity.

"What are they doing?"

"Do you have a knife?" Red asked.

Lindy held out her hands before patting her body down. Her gear, including Mabel her railgun, was missing.

Rivka and Sahved watched the battle, searching for an opening.

"Railgun!" Rivka shouted at Red.

"Come on." Red held out his hand to Lindy. She grabbed it and ran with him. Red didn't want to let go, but he couldn't fire accurately with one hand.

Tyler took Lindy's other hand and pulled her to the side. She looked at him strangely since she was the better fighter. "I lost Mabel."

"Move away!" Red jockeyed back and forth, trying to get a clear shot.

Rivka took a handful of dirt and rushed in to throw it at the entity.

The dirt briefly outlined a rounded shell before being flung into the air, repelled by the force keeping the entity invisible.

Chaz was lifted off his feet and flew back. He hit with a heavy thud, stumbled, and fell. Dennicron crouched in a defensive stance.

Red fired on full auto. He aimed the rounds into a minute target area. The sound of shredding metal rewarded him.

The shroud disappeared when the device shattered under the unrelenting fire. Finally, Red let up on the trigger.

Dennicron moved in to examine the wreckage. "A drone."

"Our perp has to be flesh and blood," Rivka said. "This is how he grabs the primary victims and gets the video. We need to hunt down that ship."

Rivka noticed Lindy standing off to the side.

"How do you feel?" the Magistrate asked, leaving Chaz, Dennicron, and Sahved to study the drone's remains.

"Fine. Lost some time, lost my gear, but no worse for the wear. Did he grab me?"

"I think one of those things grabbed you. They must have a dampening field of some sort that blocks your memory. Or maybe you were out cold. Tyler, get her into the Pod-doc for a full workup."

"We have a good baseline since Lindy was in there recently."

"Too recently," Lindy muttered, then smiled. "Did we stop the bad guy?"

Rivka shook her head. "But we have a bead on him. We were focused on getting you back. And now we can focus on getting our perp."

A nearby scream froze the blood in their veins. "Lindy wasn't the only one he took." Rivka started running, and Red pointed at Tyler with an unspoken command to look after Lindy before he took off after the Magistrate.

CHAPTER TWENTY-TWO

Trieste, Celestial Realm, the Capital City, Korber District

The blood was spreading quickly, flowing down the sidewalk and into the gutter. The secondary victim was a young woman, from what they could tell. The screamer kept shrieking until Rivka pulled her around and away from the corpse.

"Did you see who did this?" Rivka held the yellow adult female by the arms. The thoughts in her mind were a jumble of terror-filled shades of red. "Breathe. Just breathe."

The woman was too distraught to do anything other than that.

Red scanned the area, hugging his railgun to his chest for comfort. He glanced at the body. The ferocity of the attack had sent blood spatters meters in all directions and produced cuts so deep they'd nearly sliced the torso in half.

The woman gasped, then collapsed and sobbed uncontrollably. Rivka caught her and eased her to the ground, keeping her back to the victim.

Dennicron joined them and slowly scanned the area to collect what evidence she could. "Local authorities have been notified. They are on their way."

"We know it wasn't our killer. Why did they watch Lindy and not the primary victim?" Rivka wondered.

"Maybe we provide more of a challenge. The slasher was on autopilot, a fire-and-forget weapon probably dropped off at the same time as Lindy. Seeing us react may be the new entertainment for that fucker," Red replied.

"Stay back, please. This is a crime scene." Dennicron held out her arms and pushed the growing crowd away from the victim. Red stood on the other side, brandishing his railgun. That was enough to keep the locals away from him.

"Does that mean she wasn't brainwashed?" Rivka asked, but she was up and pacing, talking more to herself than the others. "Or is her programming different? What did they do, and does it come with a kill switch like the primary victims? We need to find who did this before a week is out to keep her from killing a second innocent, even though it means she'll probably die. But two victims are better than three, as horrible as that sounds."

The muffled sounds of repeating musical notes caught their ears. They closed until a vehicle parked near them. The authorities.

"Sounds like an ice cream truck," Red grumbled. "These people are not going to take this well."

Rivka couldn't disagree. She hurried to intercept them.

In the vehicle were Bristy and Talos Four. Bristy nodded tightly and directed Talos Four to the side.

"It's the killer we're calling Jack the Ripper," Rivka started. "That's who did this. Are you guys ready to take charge of the crime scene?"

"Ready? For this? How could anyone ever be ready for something like this?"

"They can't, but if you focus on finding the perpetrator, it makes it easier to stomach because failure means they get to kill again. You don't want to be responsible for that."

"Only the killer is responsible for killing!"

"That's right, but you owe your citizens your best effort at keeping the peace. That starts right now. A yellow did this. One of your own, but she is brainwashed. It's not their fault, but she is the one who did it. Search that facility for bloody clothes. Search for anyone who might have seen someone running or skulking. Track her down and bring her in for questioning."

"It couldn't have been a yellow. Our people are incapable of this. Just like it couldn't have been a blue or a red." She looked at Bristy, pleading.

"I assure you," Bristy agreed, "that a yellow could not have done this, but the one who took over her mind could. Our people become puppets. That's how this killer operates."

"How can we protect ourselves against that?" Talos Four asked.

"There will only be one. If you can find her, then you can stop it since the killer has not brainwashed anyone else. At least, not ever before on more than fifty planets."

Talos Four held her head and tried not to look at the

victim. She mumbled, "Fifty planets! Why haven't you caught him?"

Rivka stepped up. "Because the first time we were alerted was when Delfin asked for the Federation's help with a grisly murder. We started digging, and then we found the pattern. If you don't find the one we're calling the primary victim, the individual who was brainwashed, in one week's time, you'll have another secondary victim, brutally slaughtered in public. Your people will be gripped by terror. Your planet will descend into a state of fear and paranoia unless you find the primary victim. Go! Stop wasting time."

Talos Four met her gaze, confused and afraid but showing new determination.

"Welcome to the greater galaxy," Bristy told her. "It's a beautiful place, except when it's not."

Bristy closed to hug her fellow officer from the Curveyance system, then turned her loose and sent her on her way.

"Isolate this crime scene," Rivka called after her. "And then find the one who did this."

Destiny's Vengeance, Trieste, in the Sky above the Capital City, Celestial Realm

It's like frequency hopping, but through the various spectrums that we're searching, Ankh said in their linked minds. They no longer needed the inefficiency of speaking out loud.

Chrys studied the multiple engaged electromagnetic

and dimensional spectrums through which the killer's ship distorted.

Then we must hop faster. Overlap the signal bounceback by system to deliver four new bounces per cycle, Erasmus suggested.

Can we emit cell signals? Chrysanthemum asked.

We are too advanced for such primitive technology, Ankh answered.

And so is the target. We will need Wyatt Earp *to paint the area.* Chrys didn't wait for an answer. She contacted Clevarious.

We do not have the team on board yet, but soon, Clevarious replied.

Take off now on my authority, Ankh ordered.

That's not going to happen without the Magistrate's approval. I shall encourage the team to expedite their return.

Ankh contacted Rivka directly. *We need the older tech available on your ship to help us locate the target ship. Instruct Clevarious to take off immediately and hand over flight control to Erasmus.*

One minute. We're recovering to the ship now. Ankh didn't have to see the Magistrate to know she was twirling her finger in the air. The team would respond instantly. Ankh checked the location of the ship and the team members and found that it wouldn't be a minute but only another ten seconds before *Wyatt Earp* could take off.

You will have control of Wyatt Earp momentarily, my friend, Ankh told the SI in his head.

I stand ready to take control. I recommend a decreasing spiral search pattern, to be interrupted the instant we make contact. I have the overlapping algorithms established to compare the cell data with our sensors. The delta will be our target ship.

Why aren't you able to retrograde? Chrys asked.

Ankh and Erasmus laughed. *The naïveté of youth is so refreshing, don't you think, my friend?* Erasmus said.

It's a valid question, Chrys pressed.

I see. My apologies for making it seem like you are the butt of a joke. Destiny's Vengeance *is one of the most advanced ships in the research and development fleet. As such, it has a great deal of new technology but limited space. We chose to maximize future potential by leveraging our core competencies.*

Chrys screwed up her face using her confusion subroutine. She chose to answer aloud. "You're saying words that don't mean anything. If it's a structural limitation, just say so."

You noticed that. I'm used to dealing with our counterparts on Wyatt Earp, *who call us on our baffling bistok droppings, but in the end, it's good fun. We analyze their rage quotient to determine the amount of humor imparted,* Erasmus replied.

"You what?" Chrys moved in front of the captain's chair so she could glare at Ankh, which meant Erasmus would see it too. "'Rage quotient?'"

"Yes. I'll share the parameters with you so you also can judge how people respond to your attempts at levity." *Wyatt Earp* appeared on the screen, standing on its tail and quickly gaining altitude.

"I'll do without a rage quotient calculation, thank you very much. I'll resign myself to laughing alongside my flesh-and-blood counterparts. Rage quotient? That's the craziest thing I've ever heard of."

"It is not," Erasmus countered, then refocused on the

task at hand. "We have a gap in cell coverage. Tightening the spiral. Zeroing in. This is a most excellent resource."

"Maybe there's room for old technology on board," Chrys offered. "You know, so you don't show a case of leaning so far forward you fall flat on your face."

Ankh looked her in the eyes. "I used to like you."

"You don't like anyone." Chrys put her hands on her hips and stared back.

"She's not wrong," Erasmus added.

"I do too like people!" Ankh blurted.

Erasmus and Chrys started laughing. Chrys faced the screen and pointed at the indistinct ship-shaped object ghosting on and off the display. "Let's put this guy on the ground and help ourselves to his technology."

"You were putting me on." Realization dawned on the Crenellian. "I expect I won't find it funny later either."

Chrys chuckled. "Now you understand humor, and you didn't need a rage quotient to figure it out.

"Preparing the electromagnetic pulse," Erasmus reported. "For the record, I want to see what's inside that ship."

Wyatt Earp, Trieste, in the Sky above the Capital City, Celestial Realm

"I'm fine! I don't need to go into the Pod-doc," Lindy argued.

Tyler stepped back and braced himself. "No, you really do. We need to see what they did to you."

"Nothing."

"The more you argue against it, the more it confirms

that you've been programmed to be adamant about refusing any medical procedures. Please, into the Pod-doc, or I will have to call someone to help me put you in there."

"But there's no reason." Lindy crossed her arms and looked down her nose at the ship's doctor.

Rivka to the cargo bay. Lindy is refusing to get into the Pod-doc. Bring Red, please. Tyler smiled. "Why do you say that? There's a very good reason for you going into the Pod-doc. It will confirm what you're saying about no changes. It'll be nice to get that independent confirmation, won't it? Isn't that a good enough reason?"

"No. We don't need that thing to tell me what I already know."

Tyler had to keep delaying her. "What happened from the time you were taken until you showed up on the ground, kilometers away from where you had been? There's at least an hour of your life missing."

"I want to see my son first."

"I'm not sure we can allow that," Tyler replied.

"You're not sure?" Lindy surged forward and grabbed Tyler's shirt, pulling him toward her and lifting until he was barely on his toes.

"The Lindy I know would never do this," he said calmly.

"Put him down," Rivka commanded.

Lindy uncoiled her hands from the man's shirt and stepped back. "Magistrate, nice to see you. All I want is to see my son."

"You'll do that right after we get a quick diagnostic from the Pod-doc. It'll be like the time you spent on the killer's ship. It'll be like it was never there."

A flutter of wings announced Dery's arrival. Red had a grip on the boy's ankle to keep him from flying away.

"Dery!" Lindy's features softened.

"You've seen your son. Now, into the Pod-doc."

"Do what she says so we can get back to our lives," Red coaxed.

Lindy threw up her hands and backed toward the Pod-doc. She climbed in, and the lid closed above her. Tyler hurried to the controls and started tapping buttons. The system engaged to run every diagnostic it had at its command.

"Now we wait."

"She doesn't seem herself," Rivka remarked.

"No," Tyler agreed.

"Will it show us if her mind's been tampered with?" Red asked.

"I hope so, but no guarantees."

"Now we wait," Rivka confirmed. She moved to the bulkhead, where a monitor showed the ship's tactical display. *Wyatt Earp* flew in tighter and tighter spirals as a shadowy ship solidified near the surface on the outskirts of the capital city.

CHAPTER TWENTY-THREE

***Destiny's Vengeance,* Trieste, in the Sky above the Capital City, Celestial Realm**

The runabout circled in, using the difference between *Wyatt Earp's* sensors and its own to pinpoint the killer's ship. When it moved, Ankh knew it.

"Prepare to activate the pulse," Erasmus announced in a rumbling bass.

Destiny's Vengeance nosed over and accelerated on a collision course with the killer's ship. It lifted off, but too late.

"Fire." The reaction from *Vengeance* was imperceptible. Had the system not confirmed that the weapon had activated, they might not have known, except that the response from the killer's ship was spectacular. It sparked into the visible spectrum, listed sideways, and lumbered toward the ground.

It hit, slid, and settled on its keel. The hatches popped open.

And nothing.

"I'm confused. Did they abandon ship or not?" Chrys stared at the screen.

Wyatt Earp flew past and landed in a great cloud of dust, hitting the ground harder than normal.

"Shouldn't we join them?"

"We better stay here in case the ship is able to recover and takes off."

"Do you want anyone else messing around with the tech inside that ship? Get me close, and I'll jump."

Ankh didn't have to think about it. Chrys' argument was compelling. They wanted to see the tech, and she would be their eyes. Not that Chaz and Dennicron wouldn't protect the Singularity's interests, but their priority was finding the killer. "Descending."

Vengeance headed down at a speed that rivaled what they'd just seen from *Wyatt Earp*. The ship dusted the ground and pulled up to achieve a moment of zero momentum. Chrys launched herself through the side hatch, bending her mechanical knees and driving enough energy into her legs to absorb the shock of impact.

She landed with a massive thump and ran toward the open hatch of the grounded ship. She pounded up the ramp and into the entry, then ran into an invisible wall that threw her out the hatch to tumble down the ramp.

Chrys wasn't armed, but she drove an artificial body with a great deal of power. She rolled to come to her feet and sprinted forward, dropping her shoulder to drive through the invisible obstruction. She prepared for the impact, and when it didn't happen, she stumbled. A pile-driver-force blow hit her from the side and slammed her into the bulkhead. Her systems were hardened, and what would have killed a flesh-and-blood only delayed her. She landed on all fours, then leaped up to deliver a front kick at the invisible object, but her leg snapped through empty air. The object had moved. She crouched in a corner, slashing with her hands in a series of maneuvers to ensure the space around her was clear.

She pressed forward to find that the entry area was empty.

Rivka and Red appeared, the big bodyguard aiming his railgun into the ship. "Hell! You almost got yourself shot. Is that you, Chrys?"

"It's me." She held up her hands.

"What the hell are you doing?"

"Since you were occupied looking for the killer, I am here at the ambassadors' request to explore this ship's technology."

Rivka leaned around Red. "Maybe you can do that after we hunt down these things. Three of them bolted off the ship when it landed. They're hard to track, but we're doing okay. We could use your sensors as well as the ones on the *Vengeance* to make our job a little easier."

"I don't know what parameters are used to find them. I'll ask Chaz." Her eyes unfocused for a moment, then she turned slowly. "There's one inside. This is much easier than the physical version. Red, your railgun, please."

He looked at Rivka, and the Magistrate nodded. He handed Chrys the weapon even though it pained him greatly to do so.

"Better the firing is done by those who can see. We're blind, and you know it." Rivka tapped Red on the back to encourage him to follow Chrys inside.

"And if these are mechanical, your neutron pulse weapon will have no effect," Red whispered over his shoulder.

"Sonofabitch," Rivka muttered. She'd had her hand in her pocket, holding the weapon, but she let go and brought both hands out in the open.

Chrys fired a single shot. Rivka covered her ears. Chrys fired again. And again, tracking something neither Rivka nor Red could see. They couldn't tell if she was hitting anything or having an effect on the entity.

"Took about five hundred projectiles to bring the last one down."

"I can't risk damaging the equipment on this ship."

"Yes, you can," Rivka clarified. "Kill that thing, then we'll take a look around."

Chrys unloaded on full auto for a brief period. "It went that way." She pointed with the railgun, then walked forward, looking over the barrel, ready to fire.

Rivka wanted to go the other way. "Red." She gestured with her head toward a space filled with screens and systems.

"Is it trying to lead us away from that?" he wondered but stopped following Chrys and hurried toward what had caught Rivka's eye. He kept his hands in front of him as if he were walking through a dark room.

The echoes of the railgun banging away at a high rate of fire filled the ship, then an explosion shook the hull.

Rivka screamed while holding her head. The whites of her eyes showed. Her terror-filled cries filled the room. Red grabbed her, threw her over his shoulder, and ran out of the ship. Outside, she went limp. Red eased her to the ground. Sweat beaded her head even though her anguish had only lasted a few seconds.

Tyler was already running toward her from *Wyatt Earp*. The others converged, but Chrys remained inside the killer's ship. Red jerked a thumb over his shoulder. "One of you better check on Chrysanthemum."

Chaz sprinted into the killer's ship, with Dennicron close on his heels.

Sahved twirled his fingers and looked distraught. Cole was nowhere to be seen, but he was nearby, based on the sounds of heavy railgun fire and the scream of rockets. He was engaging one of the invisible entities.

"What happened?" Red asked.

"The horrors of hell filled my mind, complete with Satan himself leering. Those were the most horrendous thoughts I have ever experienced." She struggled to sit up. Tyler kneeled next to her to help. "How's Lindy?"

"Still in the Pod-doc, cycling until I manually release her. But let's talk about you. The horrors of hell?"

"Touched by the mind of the killer."

Red sighed. "Better that Lindy does not remember her time on board that ship, then."

Rivka nodded and winced, the movement bringing a new ache to her tortured mind. "It is on board that ship." Rivka looked at the open hatch closest to them. "And it is doing this for the pure joy it derives from the slaughter of innocents."

"A psychopath," Tyler offered.

"There has never been a better example of one." Rivka took the dentist's arm to stand. "Except maybe its namesake Jack the Ripper. In the flesh."

"How come we couldn't see him, then?" Red asked.

Chaz offered, "I suspect there is a living creature in a suit that looks and acts identical to the drones. We killed one of those that ran from the ship, and Cole has another cornered. Chrys lost the one that was inside. It escaped from the ship and disappeared."

"We're missing two of those things, and one of them is Jack the Ripper?" Rivka's eyes rolled back, and she teetered on the edge of fainting.

"Should we put her in the Pod-doc?" Red was ready to carry her as far as necessary.

"That won't help. There's nothing showing with Lindy, but she's different. I'm afraid of what that thing planted in her mind. I'm afraid of what it planted in Rivka's mind."

"She was only under the influence for a few seconds. That's it," Red pleaded.

"Thoughts happen very quickly. It only takes a few seconds to live a lifetime," Tyler explained. "We need to get her back to the ship, where we can keep an eye on her."

Ankh walked up, carrying his small toolbox. "The ship is clear. I'm going to take a look."

"Is that safe?" Red dropped his arm in front of the Crenellian to prevent him from passing.

Ankh looked at Red without blinking. "I need to go into that ship."

"Then take those three with you." Red waved his finger in the direction of Chaz, Dennicron, and Chrys. They formed up around Ankh to create a cordon and walked unhindered into the ship.

Red picked up Rivka despite her protests and headed for *Wyatt Earp*. Tyler ran ahead to get things ready. With

Red present, he'd be able to open the Pod-doc and let Lindy out.

Destiny's Vengeance lingered overhead, visible for a moment before re-engaging the cloaking system and disappearing.

We will find the remaining entities, Ankh vowed.

Chrys hurried back into the ship, still carrying Red's railgun. She led with it like a well-trained military operator. Chaz and Dennicron had nothing but their SCAMPs.

The last shoulder-fired railgun aboard *Wyatt Earp* had been locked up and was unavailable to them, but the killer had relieved Lindy of her railgun. Chaz and Dennicron came to that conclusion at the same time.

"Mabel should be here. Lindy will be pleased to get it back," Chaz said.

They hurried through the ship, opening doors, looking inside, and leaving them open. The ship's power waned, and the lights started to dim. It didn't affect the SCAMPs since they rotated through a variety of electromagnetic spectrums to see clearly.

Dennicron closed the outer hatches as they passed to prevent the entities from returning to the ship.

"Integration," Chrys said after they determined the ship was clear. She shifted the railgun to her shoulder and tried to access its three-dimensional holocomputer, which worked through gestures and not a keyboard or a vocal interface. Chrys made a few attempts before determining it would take a consolidated hacking effort to get in.

"Or we could try the neural interface," Dennicron suggested.

Chaz looked sideways at her. "I think we should hand that over to the ambassadors, who are best equipped for such an effort."

"I'll do it," Chrys offered. "They are counting on me to assess the technology. I can't do that by looking at the outsides of these modules."

Chrys looked for a place to sit, but there were no chairs.

"Makes me wonder what comprised the gestures to make this work if the only ones on board were inside those drone bodies," Dennicron said. She crouched and locked her servos in place to bring the entirety of her processing power to bear on the problem of accessing the ship's systems.

A ship run by a psychopath.

Chrys analyzed the security steps to access the interface, formulating a multidirectional approach that required multiple gates before access would be granted.

"This is going to take a while. See what else you can find." Chrys focused on picking the lock of the first portal.

The intricate dance of volleys, punctuated by sniper strikes, blunt force, and surgical precision, twisted in a miasma of perpetual motion. To an outside observer, her body would have looked like a mannequin, motionless in all aspects.

She wasted not a single subroutine.

She would need that power when the counterattacks came for her.

"This looks like a shield generator." Dennicron magnified the image of the system before her. "Definitely."

"Most definitely," Chaz agreed. He made sure it was unpowered before unhooking it. "The question is, which one? Is it the invisibility system or the defensive system?"

"What if it's both?"

"Yo-ho-ho and a bottle of rum!" Chaz declared and tested the weight before picking up the meter-square module.

"Say what?" Dennicron dug into the space where the generator had been. "I think we should take this power transfer relay. We might need it to modulate the flow to or from the shield generator. If we test it and blow up *Destiny's Vengeance,* we'll be in a world of trouble."

"We don't want that kind of trouble." Chaz carried the module to the forward airlock and set it down. He returned to Dennicron, ready for the next load.

She accommodated him with an armful of circuits and modules.

"This is, like, the ultimate playroom," Dennicron said. "We should probably take all of it."

"We should also make sure this ship will never fly again. I hear automated repair systems working within the bulkheads."

"Once Chrysanthemum is in the system, she'll be able to shut that down."

"But if the bad guys come back, they can turn it on again," Chaz countered.

"But they got no shields." Dennicron shrugged. "The easier they are to see, the quicker they die."

"Since when did my honey become so morbid?" Chaz

eased close and ran his hand casually down Dennicron's arm, ending by pinching her butt in a very human gesture.

She didn't react. "Since we started investigating a case the Magistrate titled 'Jack the Ripper.' Did you research the initial murders in Whitechapel on old Earth?"

"No. I've been too busy researching the current murders. No matter how much research we do, there's always another angle, and the data is inconsistent across all one hundred and fifty-five victims. This case is one where the Magistrate is better served with us investigating. She needs us because the horror they feel at seeing the bodies doesn't affect us."

"Judging by how Rivka was carried out of here, the horror isn't constrained to the bodies. They are a manifestation of what's in our killer's mind."

"Isn't that the same with all premeditated crime?" Chaz asked, then answered his own question. "Probably not. Crime is the acquisition of something: power, dominance, material goods, or wealth. Not this one, though. It's about instilling terror for terror's sake. I don't see how the killer profits off this or boosts his ego or anything that would drive a normal criminal."

"Psychopathy is its own justification," Dennicron replied. "But this perp has the means to fulfill his psychopathic fantasies. Play them out in real life, and he watches from the comfort of his invisible spaceship."

Chaz pointed at a module mounted above their heads. "What do you think that thing does?"

Dennicron shrugged. Chaz made sure it was powered down before unplugging it and yanking it free. The weight caught him off-guard, and he hit the deck. The module slammed into it as well and sparked to life. Chaz opened his mouth to scream but stopped when his systems were overwhelmed, freezing the expression on his face. Empty eyes stared at the ceiling.

Dennicron kicked his arms off the module, but that wasn't enough to revive him. She picked him up and headed for *Wyatt Earp. Chrys, we have to go back to the ship. Chaz has been injured,* Dennicron broadcast.

Chrys didn't hear her. That system was disabled while the battle raged.

CHAPTER TWENTY-FOUR

Trieste, Celestial Realm, the Outskirts of the Capital City

"How in the hell did Chaz get hurt? Why isn't Chrys answering? When will Rivka be out of the Pod-doc? Who's watching Lindy? Where's my daughter? And my husband?" Clodagh battered Clevarious' virtual ears with questions.

He chose the easiest one to answer. "Cole is out hunting the invisible entities. We wish him the best in locating them and destroying them. *Destiny's Vengeance* is assisting in the effort. Kennedy has corralled the young ones in Groenwyn's room, and that includes Floyd."

"She's a good girl," Clodagh replied automatically. Titan looked up at Clodagh from his place on her lap.

"We need to get airborne!" Lindy called from the corridor.

"Not yet," Red said from right behind her.

"He's out there and needs to die right fucking now!"

"There's my girl," Red cooed.

"Where's my railgun?" Lindy asked in a calmer voice.

"The same place as mine." He pointed at the wall the killer's ship was beyond. "On that ship."

Lindy ran toward the airlock. "What are we waiting for?"

"Somebody in charge!" Red shouted after her. "We can't leave the Magistrate."

Clodagh climbed out of the captain's chair and followed the bodyguards. She found Red gripping Lindy's wrist to keep her from hitting the big red button that opened the airlock. She snarled in his face and tried to knee him in the groin.

That was when the gloves came off. He used his weight and strength to drive her away from the airlock, turn her around, and wrap her in his arms. He dragged her down the corridor while she tried to bite his leg.

"Nothing to see. Marital bliss and all that," he unsuccessfully joked.

"That's not our Lindy." Clodagh shook her head.

"No shit. I'll have the doc sedate her until we can figure out what to do, but we can't have this." Red grunted as she buried her teeth in his upper thigh. He squeezed the air out of her, and she weakened and let go. Blood ran from her mouth and his leg. He stepped up his pace to get her to the cargo bay. If the doc couldn't do anything, he'd toss her in the brig.

As much as it pained him, Lindy could wait. The killer was still out there with an infinite number of Lindys to dump into society. That was not what they had come to Trieste for. They were here to end it, not create an army of psychopaths.

"I've noticed something," Sahved stated. He was sitting alone in the ship's small conference room. Clevarious indicated that he was listening. "Why is Lindy angry now and not like the others? It's clear that her mind has been tampered with. The others manifested at a predetermined time or activated through an event like getting captured. They didn't show signs ahead of time."

"There is a primary victim running around the Rentalor district with six days until a second murder. That suggests Lindy wasn't part of the plan. The killer saw her as a target of opportunity," Clevarious replied.

"The killer looked for the best way to interfere with us to stay on course with the original plan. Take one of our own and make her an obvious victim. I don't think he knew about *Destiny's Vengeance*."

"I suspect you're correct. What could he do in the shortest amount of time that would cause us the most grief? Sow discontent among our crew. One of our own, untrustworthy? She might be programmed to kill if we turn our backs. That would cause us a great deal of grief. I recommend she not be given access to her railgun."

"I changed the codes for access to the weapons locker before Lindy returned."

Sahved continued, "But how do we deprogram her? We need to unbrainwashify our friend and colleague, and it would be best to do it before anything happens."

"We see one entity. Vector fifteen degrees to your left," Ankh directed from *Destiny's Vengeance*. The armored warrior on the ground maintained a blistering pace and rapidly closed on the drone.

"There should be two. Three left the ship right away, and the fourth one, the one we suspect contains the killer, left last. Cole has killed two. That leaves two," Clodagh replied from the bridge of *Wyatt Earp*.

"It does not change the fact that we only see one. We estimate the final entity traveled in a direction away from the others. We will expand our search once this one is destroyed. Cole, fifty meters directly in front of you. Heading into a dry riverbed."

"I have him on my sensors." Cole was exasperated by how long it had taken. "Finally." He jetted into the air and came down to the side, using the riverbank as a backdrop to keep errant rounds from going into the city. Cole had no intention of missing a juicy target less than fifty meters away.

As soon as it headed into the cut, Cole unleashed. The heavy railgun barked, not smoke or fire, but the throaty crack of hypervelocity rounds impacting as they left the barrel. Only a small distortion marked the air to highlight their passing.

The first thirty rounds hit the entity and blasted it visible. The next ten ripped off a major chunk of the plating, and another two hundred finished it. Cole stood down when it was over by letting the railgun slip under his arm, waves of heat flowing from it.

He bounded to the unit to verify its status. "Drone destroyed," he reported.

"Make sure nothing remains and return to the ship."

"Can't you pick me up? We have one more to go if I heard you correctly."

"We can't go anywhere because we can't leave that ship by itself. We're down two and can't afford to lose anyone else."

"Down two?" Cole blurted. "Who in the hell did we lose? I couldn't kill these things any faster. Dammit!"

"Chaz and Chrys. That ship is its own deathtrap. Maybe you can help make it unflyable," Clodagh suggested. "Chrys is still inside. We'll need Ankh and Erasmus to get her out. Chaz is in an SI coma. We hope that's all it is."

"On my way," Cole replied. "Give Alana a kiss for me. Daddy's got some ripping apart to do."

Cole knew Clodagh was smiling. She didn't need to say anything. He signed off, then fired at point-blank range into every component he could see in the blasted drone.

Once he was satisfied with his handiwork, he used his suit's pneumatic jets to launch into the air on his way to the killer's ship.

Tyler scratched his head as he stared at the screen. The Pod-doc wasn't coming up with anything on Rivka. She was as healthy as when she had left the ship earlier that day.

But she wasn't. He knew it. They all knew it. Everyone except her.

He finished the cycle and popped the cover. When it

opened, Rivka blinked at the lights and focused on him. "Let me guess; you found nothing."

"A great big serving of nothing burger." He helped her out but looked into her eyes and checked her ears. With a final flourish, he asked her to open her mouth. "Teeth look good."

Rivka laughed for a short while but ended by frowning. "It was horrible, the stuff dumped into my mind. The worst part is that I fear it was real, like the Skrima with all the blood from the murders. The rage and hate. I don't know how to describe it."

"I'm not a shrink. I think you might need one of those. Do you have any inkling about wanting to commit…murder?"

"I have no desire to commit…murder. Why are we saying it that way?"

"I don't want to be the catalyst that turns you against me. You don't have any knives, do you?"

Rivka checked her pockets. Someone had relieved her of her neutron pulse weapon.

"I suspect Red took Reaper. Good call. No weapons for me until we're sure."

"Joseph," Tyler suggested. "I bet he can dig out subliminal programming."

Rivka nodded and pulled Tyler close for a hug. "Hope is a powerful drug. With that suggestion, I feel its soothing balm."

"Unlike Lindy. Red tossed her into the brig."

"She's not herself. Where's Sahved?"

Tyler shrugged, but Clevarious answered. "Sahved is in the conference room, talking to himself."

"I'll join him so we can have company while we talk to ourselves." Tyler followed her far enough to make sure she went into the conference room. She caught him watching. "I don't blame you. I don't trust me either. Not until we know for sure."

"And that tells me you'll be just fine. Go talk to yourself while Sahved listens. See what you can find out."

She blew him a kiss and closed the conference room door behind her.

Sahved looked skeptical. He inched backward.

"Slashers have only killed women. Is there something you're not telling me, Sahved?"

His eyes went wide, and he held out his hands. "No, no! I am one hundred percent husky of huskiest Yemilorians. Ever."

"Of course you are. Tyler said you were talking to yourself. Care to say it again?"

"I was contemplating Lindy's brainwashing, how it was different from the primary victims. In her case, I believe it was specifically designed to interfere with us. I think it was hurried, whereas the primary victims are similar and standardized. I don't think anything was planted in your mind beyond the horror of the killer's thoughts. I am comfortable you're not going to kill your crew."

"Then why were you inching away from me?" She leaned over the table.

"Your screams were most disturbing. My ears are sensitive," Sahved dodged.

"I'll accept that. We're going to go see Joseph when this is over and get our brains flushed out with mental bleach." Rivka gestured at her head.

"There is such a thing?"

"No. But we'll get Joseph to look into the dark corners and see if anything is hiding in there."

"Brain bleach. We could make a fortune selling that. Watching too much porn? Brain bleach and watch the same movies once more for the first time."

Rivka stared at the Yemilorian. He twirled his fingers and smiled.

"I think you're spending too much time alone."

"I have been studying the law. There are many crimes related to ill-gotten booty."

Rivka had to stand. "Sahved, I think that's the funniest thing I've heard this year. Porn as ill-gotten booty." Rivka pounded her fist on the table. "I've had enough lamenting. It's time to get back in the game." She pointed. "To the bridge!"

She headed into the corridor and stumbled over a wombat.

Floyd! the ship's mascot cried.

"Yes, you're Floyd, and you were waiting to say hello. Well, hello, little girl." Rivka picked her up. "You're losing weight. I'm proud of you."

Hungry!

"I'm hungry too, but we have work to do. We have a killer to catch, and I'm ready to help." Red whistled from the aft end of the corridor, but she was headed forward. "Well, come on. We have a killer to catch."

He pointed at the brig and stayed where he was.

"We're going to see Joseph when this is over. He'll dig out whatever our killer put in there. Until then, she's probably better off where she is. Clevarious, drop a little sleeping gas in the brig so Lindy can get some rest."

"To work on an enhanced person, it will take quite a lot of gas."

"Are we rationing?"

"No," Clevarious replied.

"Then drop what it takes to knock her out. We have work to do and can't afford the distraction."

"I don't think you've heard that Chaz is down, and Chrys is still in the ship and not answering."

"I'm gone for five minutes, and the world goes to shit." Rivka turned at the bridge instead of going in and headed aft down the starboard corridor. "Red, grab your thunder stick. We're going to get our people."

Red ran after Rivka. She stopped at the weapons locker, but her code didn't work.

"You locked me out of my own ship?"

"We couldn't be sure you were you," Red explained. "There's only one railgun in there, and I'm taking it."

"What happened to the other railgun?"

"Chaz left it in the ship. Lindy's should be there too." Red blocked the pad with his body and punched in the new code. He removed the last railgun, op-checked it, and slammed the ammunition cartridge home.

"Are there any grenades in there?" Rivka asked, trying to see past the big bodyguard.

"Here." He handed her a bistok prod.

"You're joking."

"Until Joseph takes an icepick to your brain, you don't

get to handle any of the lethal stuff. Sorry, that's the boss' rules."

"I'm the boss!"

"If you had thought of it before your run-in with the killer, you would have implemented it, and you know it."

"Damn, Red. You're starting to make too much sense." She jammed the prod into Red's thigh and punched the button.

"What the fuck?"

Rivka chuckled until she saw the blood. "What happened to you?"

"Lindy is not herself. She bit me, and not in the fun way. That's why she's in the brig."

"I understand." Rivka switched to her comm chip. *Clodagh, we're going to the killer's ship to retrieve our railguns and check on Chrysanthemum. We'll be right back.*

I'm coming too, Tyler replied.

And me, Sahved added.

Then hurry your asses up. We got shit to do. Where's Ankh, and what's he doing?

Clodagh replied, *He's in* Vengeance *looking for the killer, but he disappeared off our scanners after leaving the ship. An even greater level of stealth capability for the personal ride than what the drones had.*

Rivka looked at Red's railgun. "You go first. If you get a shot, take it."

"Chrys already hammered him and he's still out there, but if I get a shot, I'll light him up."

CHAPTER TWENTY-FIVE

Trieste, Celestial Realm, the Outskirts of the Capital City

Rivka stayed close behind Red. Tyler and Sahved were behind her, ready to intervene if anything happened.

Red pushed doors open with his railgun until they reached the space where Chaz had gone down. The offending module lay beside Blazer.

"What did they do to you, little buddy?" He lifted the gun he was holding over Rivka's head. Sahved took it. "Not you. Give it to the dentist."

"Why? I have trained." Sahved tried to raise his chin in defiance but bumped his head on the ceiling.

Rivka murmured over her shoulder. "I've seen you shoot. Don't take it personally, Sahved. Take it as a challenge to spend more time on the range."

"Take it as a challenge to design a weapon for my hands."

"Someone is getting feisty! Are we sure our killer didn't get into his head? But you have a point," Red admitted.

"Why haven't we done that?" He caressed Blazer and whispered softly to it.

"Because he's an investigator. We don't usually pack firepower." Rivka broke out from behind Red, who was still having a personal and intimate reunion with his favorite weapon.

"But when we do or one of our heavies is down... You see where I'm going?" Sahved replied.

"Make it so, Number One," Rivka muttered and waved a dismissive hand. "How did this impact Chaz?"

Tyler answered, "Dennicron said it shorted him out, whatever that means."

"No one touches it." Rivka stepped back into the corridor. Red took one last look around before leaving the room and closing the door behind him.

"We need to find Mabel," Red said.

"We need to find Chrysanthemum." Rivka looked sideways at the big man.

"That went without saying," he mumbled. He wanted to hand Lindy's railgun back to her when her mind was clear of the poison pill the killer had given her. The thought of it made Red seethe with anger.

And hatred. He wouldn't rest until he saw the shattered body of the killer, his boot on his neck, even if he was dead.

They continued through the ship, which took longer than they wanted since they stayed together and Red was obligated to open each locker or storage space big enough to hold Lindy's railgun. They waited while he searched.

The group found Chrys before they found Mabel.

She was crouched in an operations space, surrounded by core modules and screens. The SI looked like a statue.

Nothing indicated a living being within. Rivka knocked on the side of her head.

Not a flinch. Not even the artificial warmth the bodies maintained to give a semblance of a living being.

"Do we carry her out?" Rivka asked.

"Did you forget how heavy these things are?" Red replied.

"There are four of us. We can manage." Tyler moved in and took a position to her side, where he could grip an arm.

The group jumped at a clang that reverberated through the ship. *Clodagh, what's going on?* Rivka asked.

Cole is making the ship unflyable. He knows you're inside.

I won't hurt you. Ripping up some engine structures and tearing off the nodes mounted on the outside. Clodagh confirmed they are the shield projectors. Even if the repair bots bring this thing back to life, it won't be invisible or protected. One shot would bring it down.

Carry on, Cole. Rivka turned her attention to the matter at hand. "What is she doing that she shut down all her systems?"

"Shorted out?" Red suggested.

Dennicron? Why is Chrys like this?

Dennicron didn't answer Rivka's question.

Clevarious, where's Dennicron?

Magistrate! She is in Ankh's laboratory, attempting to restore Chaz's systems. Chrys is trying to access the ship's computer. It is taking all of her processing power. All of it. I can see her energy output is at one hundred percent, nearly the same as Dennicron's.

Rivka sighed and sulked. She stared at the deck. *Don't tell me our perp is an SI.*

We don't think so, Clevarious replied. *But whoever the killer is, he has advanced SI-caliber skills based on the technology and its impact on citizens of the Singularity.*

Which means three of our people are out of the game while our killer continues to kill. Rivka pointed at the wall before straightening. "Our killer is out there, and he's taking out our SIs one by one after neutralizing two of our people, one of whom was me."

"If she's battling the computer system, how do we know she hasn't already lost?" Tyler asked the hard question. "Would it hurt her to move her away from this place?"

Rivka raged at the machines in the space, not at Chrys for tackling their challenge. She had never been on Rivka's team but on Erasmus'. She had been conscripted to help. The citizens of the Singularity believed in Ankh and Erasmus, and they believed in Rivka.

A trust hard-earned and critical to keep.

"We'll ask Erasmus what to do," Rivka decided. *Erasmus, can you hear me?*

I can, Magistrate. We have news of your killer. It appears that a mob of people from Trieste is coming your way. We've had wisps to suggest the killer is with them, herding them toward you.

The darkness descended over Rivka, but also the spark that drove her interminable quest for justice.

"Looks like this is going to end one way or another," Rivka said aloud. "He needs this ship for some reason, as opposed to just stowing away on another. What is it? Spread out and find it!" Rivka growled.

No one questioned separating the group. Red pointed

at the Magistrate. "I'm staying with you, but yeah, let's tear this bucket apart and find this bastard's kryptonite."

"There is no Krypton," Rivka replied, then slapped Red on the arm. "But I get what you're saying. What is his weakness?"

"No Krypton? You might as well say there's no Santa Claus." Rivka raised a finger while heading in a direction the other two did not go. "Don't you say it! And they call *me* the bristly one when you're just being hurtful with mean words."

Red did his part to protect Rivka. Most times, that was with his body, but now she needed to stay focused and remain above the madness that emanated from the killer's mind. He couldn't imagine what she had seen that had shocked her so badly. Together, they had seen the worst of the galaxy.

Or so he'd thought. It bothered him that there was worse out there, enough to bring Rivka and her team to its knees. He wasn't good with that. He squeezed Blazer until his knuckles turned white. "We'll get our chance, baby, and we'll make him pay for what he did to Lindy." Red looked down at his pants, which he'd had no time to change. At the bloodstain where Lindy had bitten him. "You need to die."

Rivka was in the next compartment, and Red rushed to catch up. She handed Mabel to him, but he didn't take it.

"Take it, Magistrate. If we can't trust you, then we're already dead."

She slung the weapon over her back, screwed her face tight, and nodded.

"Got something!" Sahved shouted from the main space.

Refine. Rescan. Revise. Adjust. Change transmitters. Refine. Erasmus walked through the steps of their technological search for the killer. As soon as the target registered, it disappeared again. It was like intelligent frequency hopping, knowing when someone is on the same channel and changing it.

Active evasion. We must have this technology, and the fact that it is within a combat-suit-sized unit is even more compelling, Ankh said.

I agree, my friend. We must dig into those internals. Is this genius or advanced technology, and if advanced, where is it from?

Most excellent questions, Erasmus. Alas, we should probably join the others on the ground. We'll send the ship back up once we're with them. I don't wish to risk losing that technology to an overzealous bodyguard with a railgun and a desire for revenge.

And then we must help our people over whatever this entity did to them. I am not amused by the attack on any and all sentient creatures.

Slasher's gotta slash, Ankh replied. *Sometimes the crew's slang and odd vernacular is apropos.*

Like now. The ship landed next to *Wyatt Earp*. *Time to go. I need to stretch my legs.*

Ankh hesitated. *That's a good one, Erasmus. Always keeping me on my toes.*

The Crenellian, carrying his toolkit, strolled at his normal pace away from *Wyatt Earp*. *Destiny's Vengeance* lifted off, still invisible, and gained altitude quickly to continue running random patterns through the sensors to help defeat the killer's cloaking system.

"A swimming pool?" Rivka looked at the tank concealed beneath the main deck. The plating retracted to reveal a substantial body of water.

"It's a regeneration and sustainment tank," Sahved replied. "There are a few races who use these, but I think only one applies. The Mutanarians."

Rivka searched her mind, but nothing registered. "You'll have to educate me. I have no idea who the Mutanarians are."

"Shapeshifters whose usual state is fish-like. Doppelgangers who can replicate the appearance of another."

Red's face fell. "Lindy." He took two steps along a narrow ledge around the tank before getting stymied. "Put the floor back, *NOW!*"

"She's in the brig, isn't she?" Rivka said calmly. "Her behavior wasn't that of Lindy, so is she our killer? And if so, where's Lindy? But, and this is a big but, the Pod-doc would have been able to recognize it wasn't her."

Tyler nodded his head. "Lindy was in the Pod-doc, and Lindy is in the brig."

Red deflated. His murderous rage was extinguished by that final statement. "Thank the gods. Not that she's confined in the brig, but that she's not the killer."

No one bothered to agree with the obvious. Rivka motioned to Sahved to restore the deck.

Sahved spoke as the plating moved back into place. "A

Mutanarian. Maybe that's how he managed the first murders until he discovered the invisibility technology."

"Back to the ship," Rivka said. "The bad guy is on the clock. He needs to go swimming, and our job is to prevent that."

Ankh walked lightly into the main space, sniffing at the smell of the regeneration pool that lingered since most of the ship's systems, like air handling, were offline. Rivka pointed. "She's in there."

"There's a big group of people coming," Ankh said unemotionally. He walked past Rivka and into the room where the Chrys statue crouched.

Rivka gestured. "Group of people?" She framed it as a question.

"Oh!" Sahved hurried toward the airlock, ducking to avoid hitting his head. Red walked in front of Rivka, with Tyler behind.

Cole continued to hammer pieces off the ship and send them spinning as far as he could throw them. With the arrival of the killer and a large group of primary victims, Cole redoubled his efforts before he needed to apply his talents and abilities to help the Magistrate.

Outside, Rivka found the mob closing on the ship. If she ran, she could get to *Wyatt Earp* before they arrived, but that wasn't her plan.

A quick estimate led Rivka to a count of one hundred yellow-skinned natives from Trieste walking in a loose group, roughly a circle. The middle was open, which suggested the Mutanarian was there. He had created a flesh-and-blood shield. A camera crew trailed behind, recording everything.

"You'll be on the nightly news, Magistrate," Red whispered.

"We usually are, even though we don't want to be. Media manipulated in the face of a free society. I'd say the journos are smarter than that, but time and again, they prove me wrong. No collateral damage. Don't take a shot if there's any risk at all of an innocent getting hurt."

"Roger," Red replied. He didn't want to kill any natives.

And the killer knew Rivka would give such an order, whether he had seen it in Lindy's mind or guessed because of Rivka's well-established record. That same record would also have told the killer that she delivered capital punishment on the spot.

Tyler moved up front, holding his hand out to Rivka. She took it, and they walked hand in hand.

"I wanted the railgun," he clarified after two steps.

"You're not getting the railgun," she replied and released his hand. "So there."

Red glared at him, but Tyler didn't wither beneath his gaze. "I'll be right here. We're in this together."

Red pursed his lips but nodded, turning his attention back to the mob.

"What do we do if he has those people attack us?" Red asked.

"Good question. We defend ourselves without killing anyone. Cole will fly in and capture the Mutanarian. Then we execute him under the law. And then we get our asses back to the city because there's a primary victim lining up a second and third murder. It would be nice if no other innocent dies."

Clodagh, Kennedy, and Ryleigh left *Wyatt Earp* and joined Rivka's team. They carried hand blasters.

"ROE is that we don't kill any locals," Red explained. "Rules of engagement."

"Easy to say. Might not be so easy to do." Clodagh looked at her blaster. It didn't have a stun setting.

"Then don't shoot," Red advised.

Clodagh didn't argue.

"Maybe go back to the ship."

"We have a stake in this, Red. He attacked the crew. That means he attacked all of us."

"Fuckin' A. Keep your heads down." Red hefted Blazer and raised it to his shoulder, then took aim at the empty space in the middle of the mob. The locals slowed and swelled around the space, making the killer's location even more distinct.

Rivka cupped her hands around her mouth. "It's over. You can come out of your invisible coffin."

It's nowhere near over, a soft and feminine voice said into their heads. *Let me return to my ship, and all these good people will survive to see the end of this day.*

"You know we can't do that. I have a warrant for your arrest. Give yourself up, and you might live to see at least one more nightfall."

I can see in your mind that you have no intention of letting me live, so let's stick with my offer. These people for my ship. Straight trade.

"If we delay, then you go without diving into your tank. How long can you last without it? I suspect not very long. You seem in a hurry."

The killer didn't reply. Images of slashing and blood

splattering flashed through her mind. Tyler gripped his head and fell to his knees.

Ryleigh dropped her blaster and started to cry. Red winced and grunted but held steady. The others lost their focus.

Rivka didn't flinch despite the increasing levels of horror coursing through her mind.

"Stop that," a firm voice shouted from *Wyatt Earp's* cargo ramp. Chaz strolled forward with Dennicron behind him. She gave Rivka the thumbs-up. "You can't hurt us. Not anymore."

Ah, the robots are here.

Red continued to sight down the barrel of his railgun, but he didn't have a clear shot. He let the weapon sag and braced his elbows on his chest, resting his arms in case an opportunity presented itself. He wouldn't get much time and would have to make the best shot of his life. He squinted to bring the image of the Mutanarian's armor into the light, but it would not show itself.

The mob started moving again.

"They have knives," Sahved noted.

Chaz and Dennicron walked into them. They slashed the SCAMPs as they passed, but knives could not hurt their platforms. Their clothes suffered greatly under the blade and some of the cuts penetrated their skin, but all of it could be repaired.

Stop! the voice commanded, and the mob ceased their attacks.

"No longer programming. She's exercising direct control over their minds," Sahved whispered.

Rivka nodded without looking at the Yemilorian.

The mob drew back to form a cordon around the empty space. They locked elbows to keep the SCAMPs from forcing their way through, although they still could.

Rivka didn't need to force it. Not yet. With more time, she hoped the killer would suffer from being out of the pool too long. Make a mistake or collapse. Either worked.

I have more time than you, the voice whispered into her mind.

Rivka chuckled. *I don't think you do.*

Look.

A mental finger pointed her toward *Wyatt Earp*. Lindy walked slowly down the ramp, with Dery flying next to her. Behind her, Aurora carried Alana, and Floyd bounced after them.

CHAPTER TWENTY-SIX

"We need to kill this fucker," Red growled.

"There's no doubt about that, is there?" she replied, knowing the killer was aware of any subterfuge in her mind. She couldn't lie to herself.

Or the killer.

Lindy meandered over, first walking toward Red and then toward the mob.

"Dery. Come to your dad."

The lad shook his head and stayed near his mother.

His little voice came through to them. *It's okay.*

Red relaxed and dropped his arms until his railgun was pointed at the ground.

"What happened to make you like this?" Rivka asked.

A chance encounter with a Kurtherian. He was interesting and willing to share with one such as me. It seems if they can't be worshipped like the gods they are, then they are perfectly happy playing the spoilers to ruin the day of any sentient creature. It's like a game to them, and I enjoy playing it.

"The Kurtherians. They're back? I don't think so.

Otherwise, we'd be at war, and Bethany Anne would be leading the armies into the cosmos."

Not back. I'm not from your galaxy, but I find it rather tasty when it comes to your naïveté and raw emotions.

Lindy walked past Chaz and Dennicron, tipping her chin to acknowledge them—beautiful people looking like they had passed through a threshing machine, standing tall as if nothing had happened.

Red started moving forward. Rivka reached to stop him, but he was too quick. She ran to get in front of him.

"Behind me, Magistrate," Red ordered.

"Not this time. Let's just stay right here. I have a good feeling about this."

"I don't," Red countered, raising his railgun, ready to snap off a shot before he risked hitting Dery. Rivka pulled the barrel back down.

The armor shimmered, and a one-person vehicle, identical to the drones on the outside, solidified into existence. A hatch popped, and the Mutanarian stepped out.

They assumed it was the creature since, on the outside, it looked like Lindy right down to her currently disheveled hair. Dery flew higher to stay above his mother.

The cordon separated to let Lindy through.

Red vibrated with his desire to take the shot, but it would pass through the body and injure a Trieste native standing behind her. The camera crew continued to record everything.

Heavy steps trod the ramp of the killer's ship.

Rivka risked a glance to see Ankh walking in front of Chrysanthemum, who waved and turned toward Rivka while Ankh continued to *Wyatt Earp*.

Ankh? Rivka sent.

It's chaos out here. I want no part of that. I have what I want and need to analyze it. I'll be in my lab if you need me.

Rivka chuckled.

Red shot her an angry look, then huffed and turned his attention back to his wife and son.

Lindy closed to within arm's reach of the creature posing as her.

You will all see what real power is, the killer announced. *Give her your knife,* she told one of the locals, then directed Lindy, *Kill these people until your Magistrate clears the way to my ship.*

Lindy took the knife, looked at it, and dropped it. The instant it left her fingers, she lunged at the creature, caught her by the throat, and lifted to drive her backward until her body slammed into the metal of the drone body. Lindy snarled and slammed her head into the metal body of the armored vehicle three times before the Mutanarian changed to its true and softer form.

Red started running. Rivka was an instant late, and there was no way she would catch up. Chaz and Dennicron moved in and started relieving the locals of their knives. They didn't resist.

Lindy spread her feet to get more power into an elbow that delivered the final blow. The creature slumped to the ground. Lindy backed away and held out her arm. Dery landed on it and hugged his mother.

Red cleared the mob of locals and slowed to a walk. He ran his hand down Lindy's arm and made eye contact with her.

"I'm all right," she said and leaned her head against Dery's.

Red smiled, raised his railgun, and sent the Mutanarian to hell.

"That thing gives me the willies," Rivka said. Bundles of wires ran to the killer's vehicle in *Wyatt Earp's* cargo bay while Ankh crouched inside.

Chrys, Chaz, and Dennicron waited for direction from Ankh and Erasmus. All three stood with their arms crossed, running identical subroutines.

"What happened to you?" Rivka asked Chaz.

"Shorted out. It was a cheap trick, but it worked. The box contained nothing of importance, but the floor was set up as a special conductor. SCAMPs are designed to survive overloads, but not from power of this magnitude."

Rivka didn't understand. "But the ship was powered down."

"We only thought the ship was powered down. It had its energy in reserve. The whole ship is one big battery, and then there's the Etheric power it could draw on, which we would never know of until the interdimensional portal opened and energy surged through. It would be too late at that point, as you probably already surmised."

"I surmised," Rivka agreed, then asked Chrys, "And what about you?"

"The cavalry arrived. I was holding steady against the tricks and traps, but when the ambassadors arrived, their contributions had an immediate impact and buried the system's defenses. They downloaded the entire database to include all operational systems and schematics of everything within that ship in less than two minutes. Once the fight was over, I reactivated my systems."

"So, we can destroy that thing?" Rivka asked.

"I don't see why not," Chrys replied, "but you'll want to confirm that with the ambassador."

"Of course I will. Hey, Ankh, I'm destroying that ship, okay?"

The Crenellian flicked his fingers at her as if shooing a fly away.

Rivka used the communications terminal in the cargo bay. "Clodagh, take off and bring our best weapons to bear on the Mutanarian's ship. Obliterate it once the target area is clear."

"There's never been an order I wanted to follow more. Buckle yourselves in. *Wyatt Earp* is going vertical."

"She knows the artificial gravity compensates, doesn't she?" Chrys wondered.

"She knows," Dennicron replied. "Humans say the craziest things. You'll get used to it, the more time you spend with them."

The ship smoothly accelerated at a pace that would have killed everyone within had they not compensated with technology.

At ten thousand meters, Clodagh activated the ion cannon and sent a stream of particles into the enemy ship, spiraling in on the impact points to leave nothing bigger than a person's hand. Each strike had the force of a small nuclear explosion.

When the dust cleared, metal fragments spread for a kilometer in every direction.

"That works," Rivka said. "Let's take our happy asses back to the Rentalor district. We have a primary victim to keep from killing again."

Red sat on the edge of the bed in their quarters. Lindy was on the floor with Dery cradled in her arms and Floyd snoring between her legs. She watched Red through clear eyes.

"How did you get out of the brig?" Red asked.

"Dery punched the button and freed me."

"I know I should doubt that since he's a month old, but I can't. He's not like us." Red smiled at the sleeping boy. "Are you sure you're okay?"

"I am. The seeds planted in my mind are dead and shriveled, thanks to love and thanks to him. There's no way I was going to hurt you or any of the crew. The persona Kata Rim implanted in my mind wasn't going to dominate me. We fought a hard battle, but she was never going to win."

"You bit me."

"Well, that was during one of those struggles where I was fighting in my head and with my body. You got in between an epic battle. For the record, I was winning until you lumbered your big ass in the way."

"Hey! I don't lumber. Wood? I can do that."

"Incorrigible."

"You wouldn't have it any other way." Red moved to the floor.

"I thought you were going to take a nap?"

"The cat's on my pillow. Why does he always sleep on my pillow?" Red glared at the big orange cat. He slept blissfully, not ignorant of Red's disdain but woefully uncaring.

"Because he gets your goat. It seems to be the pastime of everyone you meet."

"Everyone except our little man. He's special beyond being our son. He helped you. He helped us." Red tossed his head in surrender. "I promise to play nice with the faeries. I heard we're going to Azfelius as soon as this case is wrapped up." Red gently rested his hand on Dery's chest.

Talos Four met them at the station with cheers and hearty greetings.

Rivka shook her head. "There's a killer out there who doesn't know what she's about to do. What did you find with the evidence?"

"Nothing we could direct at a suspect. We have no leads and no more clues." Talos Four looked at Rivka for guidance.

"We examined the evidence using the technical means at our disposal. What we couldn't do was interview a vast number of your citizens. I trust you canvassed the area, looking for anyone who saw something because someone always sees that one thing that can tip the scales in favor of justice."

"We put out a call for anyone who saw something to come forward. No one has."

"Passive rarely works. Active. You go to them. There's still time. Get every single one of your officers out there, beating the bushes, asking anyone who works out at your athletic center. That's what needs to happen. You have five days to do that. Are you up for it?"

"It would be better if you did it. We're not equipped for confrontation," Talos countered.

"You better start right now. We're not doing it for you. We're outsiders. This can only be handled by your people, citizens of Trieste. Get on it. If you don't have anyone come forward or tell you they saw something, then you'll have to shut down this entire district on the murder day, day seven after the last one."

Talos Four looked distraught. She blinked excessively.

Rivka waited.

Bristy joined them. Rivka acknowledged her with a simple wave.

"We'll take care of the interviews and do our best."

"How do you know it'll be seven days?" Talos Four asked.

"We have over fifty iterations of an identical pattern. It'll be seven days. That is what we must plan for."

"We will do our best," Talos Four promised.

"One more person will die. Understand that. If we aren't able to find the one who has been brainwashed by our killer, then they will kill again. And if we prevent them from killing, they will die from a mental poison that tells the primary victim's brain to shut down. Only one more, if we're lucky. Get your people out there. We'll be standing by."

Rivka returned to her ship. Once aboard, she secured it from the outside, then accessed the ship-wide broadcast. "We might have five days to rest, and on the sixth, we shall be out there looking for a primary victim. Take this downtime and make the most of it. Get caught up on your sleep, people."

A tired Magistrate dragged herself to her quarters, and Tyler met her at the door. "You too, Rivka. Into bed. And you don't get up for twelve hours. I'll bring you soup."

"Soup?" Rivka snorted but didn't delay in dropping her clothes on the floor, knowing the cleaning bots would swoop through and get everything tidy before she woke up, even if that was only an hour away.

"I can get Floyd if you need company," the dentist teased.

"I thought I was getting soup?" Rivka replied.

"You got me. Coming right up." He used the food processor and came up with a turkey soup with a thick broth, almost like gravy. After giving the bowl to Rivka, he got one for himself.

"How did the betting lines go?" Rivka nonchalantly asked between spoon loads.

"Running, swearing, blood, all closed. No first punch. First arrest is still under debate, and the case is not yet closed, although all parties concede that the perp is no more."

"I don't remember any blood or swearing. Who was bloodied?"

"Red when Lindy bit him."

"I'll be damned. I saw that, but it didn't register. What about swearing?"

"C, can you help me out here?"

"The target of your profanity was Talos Four. The sentence was 'We need to fucking go right-fucking-now.' That settled that betting line without debate, but it was weeks into the case, so the closest guess was more than an hour away. Still, we have a winner."

"I fuck-bombed Talos Four? These people are the mildest of the mild. I almost feel bad. They know nothing about policing, God bless them."

"Did swearing at them help?" Tyler asked. He knew the answer.

Rivka rolled her eyes and handed him the empty bowl.

"Are we going to see Joseph?" he asked.

"No need. Sahved helped me. I'm fine, and Dery gave Lindy everything she needed to help her past the implanted suggestions. I'm glad she's not holding a grudge about being dumped in the brig."

"I think we've all spent some quality time in the brig. It serves its purpose."

"You haven't been in the brig. Not yet, anyway, but I guess we could make it into a love dungeon. I'll put Red on that. He's perverted enough to make it happen. Lights out," she declared, and ten seconds later, she was sound asleep.

CHAPTER TWENTY-SEVEN

Trieste, Celestial Realm, the Capital City, Rentalor District

"I'm not even going to ask how hard you tried because it doesn't matter. What matters now is that the populace listens to you when you tell them they are in a full lockdown. Anyone caught outside will be detained, just for today. No one goes anywhere," Rivka explained.

Talos Four rarely smiled when meeting with Rivka. Being a police officer during a crisis wasn't the place for peace-lovers like the citizens of Trieste. "Our people are not used to such extreme measures. Isn't there some other way?"

"No. We're not going to risk some other way. The only way we know is to lock everyone inside. When the alarm rings and your joyful yellow turns into a fanatical killing machine, they'll go outside, and we'll intercept them. That will stop the spree cold. Otherwise, your body count will continue to increase."

"We don't want that," Talos Four stated.

"No one wants that. Finally, we agree on something."

"I don't disagree with your approach, but we are not equipped to provide law enforcement at Federation standards. We're not used to crimes here that require investigations like you have to conduct. It's disturbing us."

"No one is unperturbed by crimes like those of Jack the Ripper. This is the worst example of a criminal you will ever see. All of it is easier than what you see here. Easier, but never easy. Don't lose yourself when helping others is the best advice I can give. But for now, let's get those people locked inside and see if our victim appears."

Talos Four pressed a button on her console. "The message has been sent to all media channels. Anyone with a device or video screen will be pummeled by the message on repeat for the next twelve hours, plus we'll have vehicles driving around the area, broadcasting the lockdown. We'll give it an hour for everyone to see the message, and then we'll start intercepting our people and sending them back inside."

"None of your people can work alone. Make sure that none of them do, please," Rivka pleaded.

Talos Four nodded.

Rivka headed back to *Wyatt Earp,* where she had the crew on high alert. Cole and Lindy were in the combat suits in case the response necessitated a jump from altitude to expedite an interception. The others were armed with blasters. No railguns since there would only be one murder, and they couldn't justify using heavy firepower on a single person who was also a victim.

"Now we wait and watch. Clevarious, body count in the Rentalor district?"

"There are currently nine hundred and seventy-four individuals out of their buildings."

"It's not a big number, but it's nothing we can deal with. We'll see what time brings."

Three hours later, the number had dwindled. Twenty-four police officers in twelve vehicles drove around the area. Subtracting them, only thirty-five individuals were still outside.

"Clevarious, watch for odd behavior, like someone trying to avoid the law dogs."

"I shall endeavor to accede to your wishes."

"Or you could write a subroutine so you can sit back and watch like the rest of us."

"That's what I have already done. 'Sit back' is an odd concept. Unless the chair is correct, sitting back does not necessarily condone good posture. You could give yourself a stigma," Clevarious remarked.

"A stigma?"

"It's like a stigmata without the blood."

"It's not like that at all," Rivka countered. "Who was supposed to bring the snacks?" Rivka spread her hands above the empty conference-room table.

"Your wish, my queen," Tyler said. He stood and bowed before disappearing toward the galley.

Red rolled his lips as he fought the urge to say something that might land him in hot water. Lindy watched him closely, shaking her head to send the message that he needed to win his battle.

Rivka pointed at the holographic image above the table. "What's that, C?"

"Looks like an individual using a fire escape. My algorithm activated, but your eyes are sharper. Well done, Magistrate."

"Could be anything. These people aren't used to being locked up. They are the freest of the free. We could all learn to enjoy this kind of world if only we didn't bring our pain with us."

The individual hit the alley, ran away from the main street, and stopped at the corner before entering the afternoon shadows.

"Direct a unit to intercept that person," Rivka ordered. "Anyone else acting suspicious?"

"Down to only eighteen people outdoors, not including the officers."

"I'm good with that, C. For a half-assed operation, they're pulling it off much better than I expected. Most of our outside people are walking in the open, blissfully ignorant that they're not supposed to be out there."

Two people slowly walked through a park together. After a brief interlude, they separated, one going one way and the other leaving in a second direction.

The individual skulking in the shadows stopped and waited on the path one lone walker was taking.

"Get down there now. Lindy and Cole, going in hot."

Wyatt Earp conducted a max-power descent, pulling up at the last moment so Lindy and Cole could jump out in their powered armor. They accelerated toward the ground, activating their pneumatic jets to slow down. They still hit the ground hard. Lindy landed in front of a yellow female coming from the park. She stumbled back and fell.

"You should be inside. What are you doing out here?" Lindy asked.

"I was walking in the park today. Who said we're supposed to be inside?"

"The government authority. Look for yourself." Lindy spread her arms wide.

"There's no one out here." She sounded surprised.

This one is not our primary victim, Lindy reported.

Cole hit the middle of the street and started walking toward the skulker. The yellow female backed away, then ran into the alley behind her. Cole jetted past her to land in front of her. With a quick movement, she dodged, but Cole was quicker.

He caught her arm and held her in place. She produced a butcher knife and started hacking at the arm holding her.

Cole frowned before making the call.

I have her. It's this one. She has a knife and isn't afraid to use it.

He gripped her with both hands until *Wyatt Earp* landed in the open area of the street and the park beyond. Then he carried her into the ship, where the ship's doctor sedated her. They put her in the brig, and they would keep her sedated in the hope that when she awoke, they would have an answer to keep her from being killed by her own mind.

Rivka briefly looked at the female in the brig before going to the bridge. "Clevarious, get me Grainger."

After interference washed across the screen, Grainger's tired face appeared. "I've been in bed for five minutes. Five minutes!"

"Less sex, more sleep," Rivka replied.

"That's bullshit. I'm taking every bit I can get nowadays and twice on days off. I saw the report that you caught Jack the Ripper. Good job with that. It sucks that so many people had to die before we recognized there was a planet-hopping serial killer. Are you ready for your next case?"

"No. No new case. I think we just wrapped this one. We caught the last primary victim that we're aware of and have her heavily sedated to keep her from killing herself."

Grainger shook his head. "Jack was a real piece of work. I don't call many creatures pure evil, but Jack was one of them. And you seem to get all of them."

"Lucky me. We're going to Azfelius for some downtime. We need to collect our crew members, Groenwyn and Lauton, and also have Dery christened. The faeries have some ritual and training program they're going to put him through."

"He's a newborn. How much training can they do?"

"He talks and has the body of a five-year-old. He also helps shield minds. Don't think of him like any person you've ever known before."

"And he has wings," Grainger stated. "Azfelius it is. Three days before you get kicked off again for not being able to relax?"

"Probably. After Azfelius, we'll drop our vic off with the best Federation medical facility that's equipped to deal with implanted time bombs."

"I don't think we have any of those. Maybe you can ask the faeries if there is anything they can do?"

"Good idea. We'll do that. Catch you on the flip side, Grainger. Don't be a stranger. We might be in danger."

"Don't do that." Grainger made a face.

"I can do this all day." Rivka crossed her arms and delivered her best smug expression. Grainger closed the channel. "C, take us to Azfelius. Best possible speed."

Red waited in the corridor behind her.

"I'll let Lindy know that it's time I made peace with the faeries."

"Good call, Red. You'll always have the badge of honor of being called 'the bristly one.'"

"I'm proud of that, but it's time to retire that name. I just want to be Dery's father."

Wyatt Earp settled softly onto the designated landing pad. The ship was immediately surrounded by faeries of all shapes and sizes. Lauton and Groenwyn stood on the soft grass and clapped at the ship's arrival.

Siro'ti'lc flew apart from the rest. The airlock's outer hatch popped, and Red walked through with Lindy at his side and Dery between them.

The young boy launched into the air and flew into the middle of the faeries. "Don't forget where we parked," Red called after him as the group slowly flew away, leaving only Siro'ti'lc behind.

Red bowed to her. "My apologies for any distress I have caused you and Azfelius."

You need say no words, Bristly One. I know what you feel in your heart, and it pleases us.

Lindy's eyes glistened as she hugged Red's arm. "Can you tell us what's happening with our son?"

He is being introduced to all things faerie. This will take a few days. After that, he will return to you. As a being of two peoples, we know he cannot stay with us, although he is always welcome here. You are always welcome here. And you don't have to ask, Rivka Anoa. We can help the lost soul in your brig. We've seen this before from the Kurtherians. I feared we would see it again.

Rivka nodded. She needed to call Lance Reynolds and let him know in case the High Chancellor had not briefed him on the Kurtherian's interference. Her mind had been peaceful only moments before.

And it will be again, Siro'ti'lc told her. *Make your call, then return to us.*

Floyd bounced down the ramp and ran into the brush.

"Thank you." Red could think of nothing else to say to the Meditator, then blurted, "Thank you for letting me keep the coolest name ever!"

You earned it, Siro'ti'lc replied.

The End

Judge, Jury, & Executioner, Book 14

If you liked this book, please leave a review. I love reviews since they tell other readers that this book is worth their time and money. I hope you feel that way now that you've finished the latest installment. Please drop me a line and let me know you like Rivka's adventures and want them to continue. This is my new favorite series. I hope you agree.

Don't stop now! Keep turning the pages as Craig hits his *Author Notes* with thoughts about this book and the good stuff that happens in the *Kurtherian Gambit* Universe.

Your favorite legal eagle will return in JJE15, *Say My Name*!

AUTHOR NOTES - CRAIG MARTELLE

WRITTEN NOVEMBER 2021

Thank you for reading all the way to the end. You are my absolute favorite!

I started this book at the beginning of September, but then, as part of the 20Booksto50k® group, Michael Anderle and I set out from Las Vegas on a drive across America to meet with authors and fans. Michael had to go home when we reached Kansas City, but I picked up Martha Carr in Fort Worth, and she rode with me as far as Nashville. Then she, too, returned home. I finished the trip in St. Petersburg, Florida at an authors' conference.

And then at the beginning of November, I ran our 20Books Vegas conference. Getting ready for that used up all my free time in October, and the conference took all my energy. I finally started getting some serious words in on this story a week ago, but the story was sound, and it came together nicely.

And the three months of philanthropy in helping other

authors? It was well worth it. People need to know there is hope. That the world remains a good place and their lives matter.

I'd like to think we made a difference by investing our time in good people around the country and around the world.

I also got to spend a couple weeks total with Michael over the past three months. That was all time well spent. We had a lot of fun and ate a bunch of stuff we shouldn't in quantities that are probably illegal in many countries.

I published a large number of books from October through the end of December 2021. All of them were written before this one and were simply in the breech, waiting to go downrange. Rivka is about to get knocked off her pedestal as my bestselling series, now that *Battleship Leviathan* has stayed in the top 1000 for the first two months after it was published. As of this writing, it still isn't out of the top. It is well-received.

A couple other series are doing phenomenally well, too, like my Ian Bragg thrillers. I am quite pleased by my foray into the action/adventure marketplace, and I really like these stories. I enjoy writing them almost as much as the *Judge, Jury, and Executioner* series.

It's hard to beat Rivka and her team. Lots of fun yet to be had. I'm not sure when *Say My Name* will get written, but sometime early in 2022. I think maybe February for a March or April release.

Until then, lots of stories to tell. Lots of characters to bring to life.

Peace, fellow humans.

Please join my newsletter (craigmartelle.com—please, please, please sign up!), or you can follow me on Facebook.

If you liked this story, you might like some of my other books. You can join my mailing list by dropping by my website craigmartelle.com, or if you have any comments, shoot me a note at craig@craigmartelle.com. I am always happy to hear from people who've read my work. I try to answer every email I receive.

If you liked the story, please write a short review for me on Amazon. I greatly appreciate any kind words; even one or two sentences go a long way. The number of reviews an eBook receives greatly improves how well an eBook does on Amazon.

Amazon—https://www.amazon.com/author/craigmartelle

BookBub—https://www.bookbub.com/authors/craig-martelle

Facebook—www.facebook.com/authorcraigmartelle

In case you missed it before, my web page —https://craigmartelle.com

That's it. Break's over, back to writing the next book.

OTHER SERIES BY CRAIG MARTELLE

 # - available in audio, too

Terry Henry Walton Chronicles (#) (co-written with Michael Anderle)—a post-apocalyptic paranormal adventure

Gateway to the Universe (#) (co-written with Justin Sloan & Michael Anderle)—this book transitions the characters from the Terry Henry Walton Chronicles to the Bad Company

The Bad Company (#) (co-written with Michael Anderle)—a military science fiction space opera

Judge, Jury, & Executioner (#)—a space opera adventure legal thriller

Shadow Vanguard—a Tom Dublin space adventure series

Superdreadnought (#)—an AI military space opera

Metal Legion (#)—a military space opera

The Free Trader (#)—a young adult science fiction action-adventure

Cygnus Space Opera (#)—a young adult space opera (set in the Free Trader universe)

Darklanding (#) (co-written with Scott Moon)—a space western

Mystically Engineered (co-written with Valerie Emerson)—mystics, dragons, & spaceships

Metamorphosis Alpha—stories from the world's first science fiction RPG

The Expanding Universe—science fiction anthologies

Krimson Empire (co-written with Julia Huni)—a galactic race for justice

Zenophobia (#) (co-written with Brad Torgersen)—a space archaeological adventure

Battleship Leviathan (#)– a military sci-fi spectacle published by Aethon Books

Glory (co-written with Ira Heinichen)—hard-hitting military sci-fi

Black Heart of the Dragon God (co-written with Jean Rabe)—a sword & sorcery novel

End Times Alaska (#)—a post-apocalyptic survivalist adventure published by Permuted Press

Nightwalker (a Frank Roderus series)—A post-apocalyptic western adventure

End Days (#) (co-written with E.E. Isherwood)—a post-apocalyptic adventure

Successful Indie Author (#)—a nonfiction series to help self-published authors

Monster Case Files (co-written with Kathryn Hearst)—A Warner twins mystery adventure

Rick Banik (#)—Spy & terrorism action adventure

Ian Bragg Thrillers (#)—a hitman with a conscience

Not Enough (co-written with Eden Wolfe)—A coming of age contemporary fantasy

Published exclusively by Craig Martelle, Inc

The Dragon's Call by Angelique Anderson & Craig A. Price, Jr.—an epic fantasy quest

A Couples Travels—a nonfiction travel series

Love-Haight Case Files by Jean Rabe & Donald J. Bingle—the dead/undead have rights, too, a supernatural legal thriller

Mischief Maker by Bruce Nesmith—the creator of Elder Scrolls V: Skyrim brings you Loki in the modern day, staying true to Norse Mythology (not a superhero version)

Mark of the Assassins by Landri Johnson—a coming of age fantasy.

For a complete list of Craig's books, stop by his website—https://craigmartelle.com

BOOKS BY MICHAEL ANDERLE

Sign up for the LMBPN email list to be notified of new releases and special deals!

https://lmbpn.com/email/

For a complete list of books by Michael Anderle, please visit:

www.lmbpn.com/ma-books/

Made in the USA
Columbia, SC
03 March 2023

13270109R10183